# Collapse and Delusion

# Book Four
# of the Jack Commer Series

## Michael D. Smith

For my wife Nancy

# CHAPTER ONE
## A Mix-Up of Many Emotions
### *September 17, 2038*

Thirty people were setting up tables for the reception when Amav heard gasps and found herself stepping back on a man's toes.

"Oh! Joe! It's *you!*"

Her brother-in-law blinked. "Wow! Amav!"

"You're really here! You made it! God, are we happy to see you!"

An older woman with russet hair clasped Joe.

"You must be Ranna!" Dar's astrology certainly hadn't mentioned how lovely Ranna Kikken was. "I'm Amav Commer, Jack's wife. We were all just waiting for you. This is all so strange, even though we knew it would happen!"

Joe shook his head. "Wow, can't believe we really made it!"

"Me either!" Ranna laughed, extending a hand which Amav took in both of hers. It was a firm grip from someone who'd just gone through a sickening, miles-long drop of a passenger shell snapping off an accelerating spaceship. Amav had never done a Heuristic Time Transition, but from what she'd heard it seemed to wipe out whatever previous mood you were in, fully resetting you for your next moment of timespace. Many people said they entered the new time in a state of extreme calm.

Of course, that theory was shot when Amav saw the man in the white tux with long white hair grappling with Alycia Klave in her transparent light blue wedding dress.

"Oh my *God!*" Urside Charmouth groaned. "The damn rocket was just about to *blow!*"

"You're here! I knew you'd be here!" Alycia cried.

"*Alycia!* You *waited* for me!"

"Of course! Of course!"

Amav supposed everyone expected this slurping and fondling, but there was nervous tittering from four hundred guests as Alycia pulled Urside into a utility closet, babbling:

1

"We need to *talk!* Oh, Urside, we need to *talk!*" She slammed the door behind them.

The noises that followed suggested that very little talking was taking place in this closet. The guests took it all in bemused silence.

"I thought the human groom wasn't supposed to even *see* the bride before the ceremony, much less ..." joked Dar, Emperor of the Martians, in a baby-blue tuxedo with his pink fin protruding from a slit in the back.

"Well, she hasn't seen him since February '36," Amav offered.

Joe laughed, squeezing Ranna. "Hey, we're next!"

"Joe! Damn, it *is* you!" Jack Commer said, tall and tanned, striding up in his navy-blue Supreme Commander uniform.

"Jack! God, it's good to see you!"

"Two years, Joe! Two and a half damn years!"

Joe fell into a hug with his older brother. "Wow! Of course, it's been about fifteen minutes for me, more or less. How the hell are you, Jack?" He turned. "Sperry! Dude! Hey, man, did you get Gooney elected mayor?"

Amav was taken aback at the sight of Phil Sperry in civilian clothes. She hadn't seen him in ages. "Oh, that's right," said the gaunt, graying Phil Sperry, taking Joe's hand. "You HTT'd out before the election. Yeah, we got him in. It was a damn landslide. Greeney's right over there. Up for reelection next year. We're already working on it."

Amav saw Jack's cheek tighten in disapproval. Well, there hadn't been much he could do about it once Phil had resigned from the USSF. And of course there was no controlling Greeney.

"Churchill's here too," Joe said, pointing. "All four of us made it."

Amav saw USSF officer Will Connors pulling a big Russian Blue cat off one of the buffet tables. There were so many Martians in the room that their combined telepathic outradiance merged into a roar of static, but she still picked up a cat protest, not terribly angry, followed by the sensation of something fishy thoroughly savored.

"I'm going to pretend I didn't see that," Amav said. "I only spent six months planning this wedding, and I wasn't about to allow *cats* on the tables."

"So this is *your* doing. And you got the whole Command Suite," Joe said, indicating the vast space on the 130th floor decked out in balloons and bunting, all bathed in pink-yellow evening Martian light.

"Yeah, Jack let me clear away all the cubicles." Floor-to-ceiling windows showed the slender spires of Marsport and the desert stretching beyond, with dark wispy clouds on the horizon. "Except for the outer hall, that is. That's got to stay out of sight."

At Joe and Ranna's puzzled looks, Amav went on: "It's one of those time-travel things. There's another HTT event tied to this wedding besides the four of you guys. The Alycia of February '36 will time-travel to this event. Actually, she's due in a few minutes, I guess, but anyway she goes to the outer hall where the wedding photos are on display. Which still need to be taken, by the way. So Alycia grabs the display tablet, goes back to 2036, then she shows it to Urside, but when he HTT's back to 2028, the thing follows him. So it proves to everybody that he *will* show up with you guys today for his wedding."

"Huh," Joe said.

"Anyway, we've told everyone to stay away from the outer hall and to port their photos of the wedding and the reception over to the comm we have on a table out there. We don't want anyone seeing 2036 Alycia in the hall. She's apparently out there for just a minute. I had to threaten to strangle *our* Alycia for wanting to keep an eye peeled for her past self. Dar says that would be a disaster."

"He also says that after Urside saw it, the display was pulled back to the present," Phil put in. "It probably arrived way before today, because obviously a lot of us have seen it."

"I just *bought* it the day before yesterday," Amav said.

"Yeah, Dar said nobody would see it wink back into existence or whatever it does," Jack said. "Something about conservation of time. I don't have the slightest idea what he's talking about. I've just about given up trying to follow all this

Time Transition crap. Thank God it ends in 2075."

"Well, everything's okay now. We've got everyone here who's supposed to be here," Amav said. Ranna, Joe, Urside and Churchill were all safely back from November 2033. Amav hoped Ranna was up for all this time-travel madness. Dar's astrology had Ranna Kikken fully explained, didn't it? Did Ranna have the slightest clue she was about to be appointed Chronology Coordinator on Dar's Time Committee?

Amav had been determined not only to celebrate her friend Alycia's wedding with Urside, but also to welcome home her brother-in-law. The USSF Command Floor was the perfect space for the event. She'd assumed Alycia would be lined up at the end of the chairs on the far side of the hall, waiting to be given away by none other than Jack Commer himself, then Urside would materialize in a flash of light and they'd walk down the aisle together. Instead the four newcomers had just wandered in from the ozone while Amav's workers were still setting up for the reception to follow the ceremony.

"Joe! Forgot to tell you," Jack said. "We're going ahead with the *III* Project. We got the funding to build a pair of 'em. *Typhoon III* and *Typhoon IV*. I'm holding the *III* for you, just as soon as we reactivate your commission and promote you to captain. And you'll direct the whole damn project."

"Really? Really?" Joe babbled. "Damn, Jack, how's the war going anyway?"

Jack frowned. "Nothing as big as DamnStar. Dar's still saying that's the worst we'll get, but a couple months ago we had some bad skirmishes near Drultar. Nothing we couldn't handle once we got Gooney in there, but we need you, Joe."

"And Ranna Kikken. We need Ranna," Dar said, coming up to extend a long pink claw to her. "There are so many HTT messes we still need to undo. The one in 2049 is still completely impenetrable to us, and may well remain so."

Ranna blinked at the high-pitched singsong English coming in above a hundred layers of telepathic radiance surging with images and mathematical equations, emotions and philosophy. Amav could sense her confusion at picking up the thoughts of dozens of Martian wedding guests, if her first sight of five-foot pink fish-creatures with giant fins wasn't the main problem.

But she knew Ranna was probably staggering more because Dar, in his enthusiasm, had just downloaded the entire vexing problem of chronicling and understanding the interrelationships between 8,178 Heuristic Time Transitions, more than a fifth performed as acts of warfare by the Alpha Centaurians, most of the rest being the reckless experimentations of human thrill-seekers who'd used HTT like a recreational drug over the past few decades. Dar went on to radiate that the Time Transitions, though confined between 2013 and 2075, had nevertheless caused endless timeline screwups that apparently Dar, Ranna, the cat Churchill, and a few others were destined to repair as best they could, with the understanding that there would always be some ragged edges taking the form of suffering and tragedy.

"Well, glad to be of service then," Ranna said gingerly.

"Of course, one theory is that '49 can, by definition, *never* be investigated," put in Star General Gooney, striding over with his cocksure walk so foreign to most Martians. He bowed to Ranna, and went on in scarcely intelligible English: "That was, or will be, the node that allowed the Centaurians to flow 2049 technology backward and surprise us at DamnStar in '36."

"Star General Gooney," Amav said quickly. "Also Mayor of Marsport. Greeney, this is Ranna Kikken."

Ranna took his claw. "How do you do? But you--"

"He doesn't radiate," Amav explained, seeing that Ranna had already soaked up several terabytes of data concerning Martian one-way telepathy from the numerous Martians in this room.

"He's developed an Amplified Thought routine that can turn it off," Phil said. "Nobody knows how he maintains it. Dar and some others can do temporary shields, but they don't last very long. Greeney here can turn it off and on at will."

Star General Gooney produced his most charming Martian smile and said: "It's always very comforting to shield myself. I can see how much psychic energy you humans save by retaining what we call your *darkened house*."

Ranna frowned, then finally nodded. "I can see it might be exhausting to just hang all your thoughts out there, but never receive ours."

Gooney shrugged. Once again Amav marveled at how he'd appropriated that human gesture and used it so eloquently. Meanwhile she picked up Churchill as he weaved in and out of Ranna's legs: *Not an insoluble problem,* the Russian Blue radiated. *Dar had the basic shielding down long ago. The subroutine Closed Dissemination will work if combined with Survival Mode.*

"No, that was just a temporary fix," Gooney said. "Closed Dissemination only works if Survival Mode is greater than the limit of Mass Reality Index."

*Forget it! We can amplify Survival Mode to include the entire Tao if need be!*

"Still won't work. Individuation Mode would *cancel* Tao and then where would you be? No, I don't think I'll be letting out the code any time soon. I even keep it locked up when I do radiate."

*I will get it from you!* Churchill laughed, trotting away.

"Nice to meet you, too!" Gooney called after him.

Amav caught Jack's narrowed eyes. She knew Jack hated Gooney going dark. What might Star General Greeney Gooney be *plotting?*

"By the way, sorry I didn't introduce myself properly," Phil said to Ranna. "I'm Phil Sperry. I worked with Joe on both *Typhoons,* then retired to become Gooney's campaign manager."

"Nice to meet you, Phil. Do you know if my sister's here? Jackie Vespertine?"

"Should be. I know she's on the invitation list. We'll circulate you around, don't worry."

"What about Huey?" Joe said.

"Well, he's going exclusively by Polot now. It's weird. He still *looks* human, but he's getting more and more *Jujl* every day, if that makes any sense. He had to decline, though. He wants to keep away from Jackie, mostly for her sake, I guess. They got divorced a couple years ago, as you can imagine. But also, he's working on the HTT stuff twenty hours a day now, so he's pretty exhausted most of the time."

"*Jackie!* There you are!" Ranna said, moving off.

"Wow, I can't believe any of this," Joe said. "We really made it! And I have *Ranna* now."

Amav saw that Urside and Alycia, finally out of their closet, were lining up for photographs both professional and amateur. "Look, Joe, you can meet your nephew, too," she said, pointing to a floating crib bathed in white light and surrounded by cooing women.

"My nephew?"

"Yes. Jonathan James Commer. He's eleven months now."

"You mean, named after John and Jim?" Joe choked. "Wow …"

"Come over and introduce yourself. Wait'll you see how much he looks like you!"

Joe moved to the crib where crew-cut General Scott poked at the dark-haired child. Scott was looking good these days. Amav was already helping plan his sixty-second birthday party next month and everyone remarked how well he'd recovered from a couple years of illnesses following his retirement as SCUSSF in early '35. His back injury had improved considerably and he shot his small powerful torso across the room with a lurching grace, his laugh booming through his old office suite. It was a sound people hadn't heard much since before the Evacuation. Almost everyone had thought that being Supreme Commander during the Evacuation had been a death sentence for Scott, and they'd secretly expected those mysterious illnesses to do him in. Amav was delighted at his continued recovery.

"Jonathan … James?" Joe said in wonder, leaning over the crib. "I can't believe it!"

"Listen, we know he's not *your* son," joked tiny Hedrona Bhlon in an extremely low-cut gold dress, "since you've been gone the past couple years."

"Oh, can it," Amav said. "We've heard that enough the past

year." Then, in falsetto: "Joe and I are *friends.* Nothing more!"

"Hey, that's my sister-in-law you're maligning," Joe said. "Hey, Johnnie James, hey Johnnie."

"Well, really, we just call him JJC," Amav said. "But seriously, he does look just like you. Must be some terrible Commer gene mutation."

# CHAPTER TWO
## Why Aren't You in Uniform?

Phil had to admit it. Amav's deep voice, and that crimson dress hugging her thighs, had him wanting her again. That luscious round ass, those delightful full breasts, could still *unhinge* him. What kind of an idiot was he? Hadn't he said he'd never feel this way again? Three years ago. Now they couldn't even be friends anymore. Phil was cut off from her, cut off from everyone. Why would he feel this way? Was he really so lonely?

He had to chill out. It was just a wedding. So he'd had a few drinks and Amav was turning his head. But there had to be twenty or thirty women here who were also turning his head, including Alycia the bride if the truth be known. So what? He couldn't get all worked up about it. It was just sex energy. No big deal. Everybody was looking beautiful for the wedding, honoring Urside and Alycia, after all. He just had to accept it.

What a leap of faith it had been on Amav's part to invite four hundred guests and spend a fortune decorating the Command Suite, all on the bet that Dar's astrology was correct. It was as if Joe, Ranna, Urside, and Churchill arriving on the dot meant that this night was truly destined to be a celebration of male/female union. And the women were definitely stunning. Phil was surprised that even tiny Hedrona Bhlon would dare wear something so low-cut. She was so uptight and snippy at Earth Animal Rescue that he'd never really registered that she had quite a decent body. Especially for such an older woman. That gold dress really did something for her.

Phil had never had much to do with Hedrona. He did recall looking down her blouse at a meeting last month between the mayor's office and the EAR Program and thinking, wow, who'd have thought such a tense, irritable woman had such shapely boobs? Phil remembered being surprised that she'd dyed her hair brown and that it looked good on her. Then later someone had told him brown was her natural color and that she'd been coloring it blond since she was a teenager. Probably more of her tight-assed neurosis. Maybe, in all her nonprofit machinations back on Earth, she'd felt a need to be what people called "the little blond bitch." She certainly knew how to intimidate you at a meeting.

In any case it was probably best to just think of all these women as being pretty things and surf over the top of it all. Maintain his balance. Appreciate beauty and all that. Just not let it get to him. Maybe someday he'd have somebody. He couldn't get carried away by this sex business. Ever again.

"You look a little bummed, man. Can I get you a drink?" Joe Commer said, eyeing Phil's empty champagne glass.

"I should be getting *you* a drink. How the hell are you, man?"

"Listen, Phil, are you back in the USSF yet?"

"Uh, no, I retired, you know. And the political situation's such that I think I'm really needed here, with Greeney."

"Look, I may be a newbie here in '38, but from what Jack was telling me, the new *Typhoons* will need every experienced physician/engineer they can get."

"I know, I know. But, hell, Joe, I'm Greeney's chief of staff now. Everybody's pretty freaked at the whole idea of fifteen more years of war, and Gooney's been such a great force for calm here, that, well, we need to keep him going, you know. He's really got more power than the president of the United System Council, if you want to know the truth. I think it's really important for me to stick with him just now."

Joe digested this. "Yeah, but Gooney belongs out in the war zone, and so do you, Phil."

"Look, Joe, you've only been here a few minutes, and things have changed. We've got Greeney's political and military duties all laid out. We just Star Drive him wherever we need him. It all works out."

"Seems to me there's a danger of getting complacent, man. Dar's supposed to have figured out everything that's going to happen between now and '53, but then again, what if he's wrong? What if we let our guard down and get walloped by the Centaurians?"

"C'mon, man, that can't happen. You standing here in

September '38 is proof that HTT is real and that the predictions hold."

"One thing I've picked up in my couple minutes here is how stressed everyone is about the war. Even at this wedding, where everyone's supposed to be enjoying themselves."

Phil nodded. "Yeah, you got that right. Everyone here's feeling it. It's always right under the surface."

"I HTT'd out right after DamnStar," Joe said. "It's still totally fresh for me. The total shock. But it doesn't really seem to have changed much in two and a half years. Yeah, Gooney beat the goddamn ACs back, but what was the goddamn cost, Phil?"

"I know, man, but--"

"And you're going to sit here in Marsport being a politician, and *soothing* the populace or something when you could be my engineer on the *III?* When we could be out there making *sure* Dar's predictions come true?"

Phil closed his eyes. "Look, Joe, you just don't understand yet."

"I can tell that even Ranna's already picking up all the stress. Hell, any of us can read it straight out of the Martians here. They're *broadcasting* it. Ranna didn't even know this war existed a few minutes ago, but she's already involved in it. I can feel the Martians interacting with her. I can feel she's gearing up for working on the HTT problems. So what the hell are you doing counting votes for Greeney Gooney? Jack says we've got people dying in skirmishes in AC, and we still have to patrol for these damn suicide ships trying to navigate to Sol. Jack says they still haven't perfected their stupid Warp Transfer. It still kills 'em half the time! But they keep trying. They just don't know how to quit. You know we can't just lie around and wait for May '53 and say we don't have to do anything."

"Dammit, Joe! I do know it! Every single person here knows they're *called upon* somehow. There's no way we can back down or gloss this over. But, look, I've thought it over and I just think I'm where I need to be, at least for now."

"Jack was saying he thinks Gooney's brainwashed you

somehow."

Phil reeled. "Did Jack really say that?"

"Wow, take it easy, Phil. I did say the B-word, didn't I? Must still hurt, huh?"

"How can you be *saying* all this stuff? Are we drunk?"

"No, I just HTT'd and went through a couple passenger shell disasters. And I found my future wife, all in the space of a few minutes, so I guess I'm free to just pop out with whatever I need to!"

"Your wife? You mean Ranna?"

Joe grinned. "Yeah, I just proposed a minute ago. It's amazingly solid. I know I really just met her a few minutes ago, but I've never met anyone like her. And somehow it seems as if we've known each other for *centuries*. We're *perfect* for each other."

"Well, congratulations, then."

"We're thinking of waiting a few months, but you're definitely invited. But anyway, listen, Phil, I know about the B-word, believe me. I still feel guilty myself about the *Typhoon II,* but at least now I know that somehow I've got to move *past* that."

How could Joe just spout off all this honesty? He had to be drunk. Phil had to be drunk to even listen to this. That they could even *mention* that word. "Look, Joe, I'm glad for you, but I just can't talk about that. Let's just drop the subject, okay?"

*Brainwashed in Alpha Centauri.* Part of the goddamn Grid. How could anyone get over that? Wasn't that why he'd quit the USSF and gone into politics? Telling everyone he needed a new life?

DamnStar '36 still hurt so much. Had Phil somehow contributed to the disaster, even though he'd come out of the brainwashing the year before? Was there something in his mind the ACs had picked up and used for their '49 technology?

"C'mon, Phil," Joe pressed, "I'm no counselor type but I can sure as hell see you need to talk to someone about the *Typhoon II.*"

"You know, Joe, I even took a punch at Lee Borman in this

bar when he said I was *brainwashed* by Greeney. I just let him have it. He said he didn't feel a thing, but damned if he didn't need a hundred thousand AresCredits in dental work. And the bastard's still my friend somehow!"

"Whoa!" Joe laughed, setting his drink down on a small table and dancing in front of Phil, pumping his fists absurdly. "Are we gonna fight now, Phil, huh, huh? Are we gonna fight?"

Phil finally laughed too. "Oh, God, no! C'mon, Joe, you've only been back here a few minutes and already you're telling me how to run my life!" He chugged his champagne.

"Damn, Phil, all I'm saying is we *need* you!"

Phil looked away.

*

"I still don't understand why we're having the reception *before* the wedding," Joe said, picking up his champagne glass and pointing to the rows of tables stocked with cheeses and meats.

Phil shook his head. "Well, Amav told everyone to keep their paws off the food until after the ceremony. I guess Churchill thought he was exempt. But, since we weren't quite sure when the groom would arrive, well, we had four hundred guests and all that champagne, so …"

"I can see there was no stopping it once it got started. Are they still taking pictures over there?"

Phil turned. The pre-ceremony photo rituals seemed to be finishing up. The empty chairs twenty rows deep at the far end of the offices waited to be filled. Now that Joe had rammed all his damn new honesty down Phil's throat, Phil could feel the war tension in the room even more clearly. He realized how much he tried to block it out every day, to no avail. Even Martians, each with hundreds of years of accumulated wisdom and armed with the programming for Dar's future history, were reeling with anxiety. Anyone could pick it up out of their outradiance.

"So …" Joe said, taking in the same unease. "Fifteen more years of this, huh?"

Phil sighed. "You know, Huey posted something on SolNet recently that really summed it all up. Of course, he's writing as Polot, and he really *is* fully Polot now, but even from his Jujl perspective, he nailed it. Everyone's been talking about it. It's called 'The Bridge to 2053.'"

"Yeah, Jack was just telling me about that," Joe said. "I'll have to call it up on my comm in a bit."

"Yeah, somehow it perfectly sums up how pissed off we all are at having this foreknowledge. That we have to just *suffer* through the next fifteen years."

"Dar's astrology," Joe said. "Jack said that's what people call it."

Phil nodded. Polot's article had ruefully acknowledged something nobody else had put into words: that everyone's exasperated mockery of the demented Alpha Centaurians for fighting on, knowing that they'd be defeated no matter what on May 14, 2053, applied to humans and Martians as well. Neither side could give an inch, neither could relax. Though no battle would be as devastating as DamnStar, each one would offer the possibility of a serious reversal of fortune if not combated with the utmost vigor. Knowledge of the future, whether it was of victory or defeat, simply didn't matter. Both sides were fated to fight and die. The ACs were Sol's spiritual brothers in a sense. Polot had even pulled in that Nietzsche quote:

*Honor your enemy, for he makes you strong.*

And who knew how the soldiers and spacemen of the near future, in their teens today, would face the Battle of Plar in '47, knowing they were destined to suffer the one space battle the USSF would *lose?* Would they get a taste of what the so-called "insane" Alpha Centaurians had lived with since 2036 when they first discovered that their empire would end precisely on May 14, 2053? That despite every launched meson bomb, every ship they so desperately boarded, every thousand humans or Martians they blasted and hacked to pieces in hand-to-hand combat, they would *lose,* and their entire way of life would be *eradicated?*

"It's been really hard to get used to," Phil said. "About all that keeps us from really going off the deep end isn't really 2053 and the end of the war. It's 2075, when we know that this whole goddamn HTT loop finally closes. No more time-traveling. What a relief *that'll* be."

"I guess I'm kind of looking forward to that time myself. 'Course I'll be an old fart then."

"Not necessarily. There've been a lot of medical breakthroughs the last couple years. Apparently rejuvenation therapy is the next big thing. People living hundreds of years and all. Hopefully we'll all look like teenagers."

Joe grinned. "Sheesh. So Dar's figured it all out? We have a real history of the war? Do they pull off any more of this future technology crap?"

"It's not in the cards, as far as Dar knows. DamnStar was an insane shock, that the ACs could get that far into our system with 2049 tech. But apparently they aren't ever going to be able to mount that sort of attack again, and meanwhile we'll still be outpacing them in technology. Dar's still insisting that the Empire collapses on May 14, 2053."

"So what role do we play in all this? You and me and Jack and everyone?"

"Hell, Joe, I knew you'd come to that. Everyone asks Dar sooner or later if we're mentioned in any of his predictions. But the weird thing is that it's like anyone close to Dar is somehow *blocked* from his calculations. The most he might get about you or Jack or Amav might be a scrap of a mention on SolNet from '43 or '52 or whatever. And sometimes some major public figure crops up. The most explicit one we saw was when Greeney beat back the ACs at Drultar this summer. The entire thing was predicted a few months before it happened. We were all surprised by the level of detail in the prediction. And it all came exactly true."

"Wow. So what about you, man? Does Dar say if I get you back on the *Typhoon III?*"

Phil grimaced. "No. Have to admit I did ask what might be in store for me. That was sometime this spring. And Dar does this little mental calculation, and you can feel it unwinding. The only thing on me was my name coming up in some press release about a meeting between Earth Animal Rescue and the mayor's office last month. That was it."

Okay, so it had freaked Phil at the time. Everyone wanted some reassurance they'd live through the war. But Dar's astrology had only taken Phil up to August, and like an idiot he'd panicked, thinking he was going to buy the farm in August. But here he was in September and he was still standing.

"Hmm," Joe said. "So maybe you *do* become my engineer after all."

Phil shrugged. "*You* have a mention in '51, I think. All you have to do is ask Dar, and he'll calculate it and radiate it right at you."

Was he seriously worried there was nothing else on him? Even if he did serve with Joe on the *Typhoon III,* that didn't mean he'd be alive in '51, because Joe could live and Phil could die in the same space battle.

Across the way Hedrona Bhlon chatted with a USSF officer, sipping a clear tumbler of wine as she adjusted a gold shoulder strap slipping off her shoulder. The officer, twenty years younger than she, was clearly entranced. Yes, Hedrona did have a lovely pair. Now Phil realized that Dar's astrological scrap on him happened to be for the same EAR meeting where he'd been looking down her blouse. He smiled at the picture. Wasn't that an odd coincidence? Then he shivered at the thought of his own demise possibly occurring right now, September 17, 2038.

What a superstitious idiot he was. He'd never been jumpy like this before. What on earth was wrong with him?

\*

"So Greeney can be mayor here, and then just warp out to Drultar?" Joe said. "How does he stand the Star Drive?"

Phil shrugged. "It's amazing. The same way he developed his telepathic shielding, I guess. He just found a way around the Star Drive anxiety. Some Martians handle it better than others, but almost all of 'em have some sort of trouble. Greeney just breezes through it. He's been trying to teach the technique to other Martians, but they don't seem to get it."

"That is one unusual dude. Saved our asses at DamnStar, that's for sure. Rounding up the entire Fourth Fleet with Amplified Thought! Is that why he got elected mayor?"

"Probably. Of course, we ran into that little public relations problem. Did Jack tell you about it?"

"No, man, we haven't had time to catch up on everything yet."

"Well, it has to do with the origin of Greeney's name."

"Yeah, sure we had to shorten the damn thing."

Of course, nobody could pronounce it. Phil could hear *G'rea'nyaigu'nye* in the Martian outradiance right now, but simply couldn't make his mouth form the syllables.

"Well, it goes back to the two kinds of Martian families," Phil went on. "The ones with short names like Dar being the practical, no-nonsense types, and the ones with long unpronounceable ones being the ancient nobility."

"Right, so we've always got nicknames for those guys."

"But the deal was, the first person to call him Greeney Gooney was none other than Sam Hergs."

"Wow, how did *that* happen?" But all Joe had to do was concentrate. Phil watched him sort through the chaotic Martian telepathic flux in the room, then frown. "And we never *knew* that?"

Phil shrugged. "I guess nobody ever really hunted for that concept until Gooney was running for mayor. Or maybe we assumed that since all Martian warriors got amnesty when they became citizens, we just weren't about to pry too closely into any individual Martian's mind."

"He worked for *Hergs?* He ran the two twerps who killed General Douglas? He was a *terrorist?*"

"Shhh!" Phil said as heads turned. "I can tell you we had fun spinning *that* one during the campaign. 'You've changed. He's changed. The war changed us all. A leader who understands.' That sort of stuff. Damned if he still didn't win seventy-nine percent of the human vote, and all the Martian."

"Well, I guess war is war. He's on our side now, thank God."

"I think that about sums up everyone's attitude. He saved us at DamnStar and now he's our mayor. We're going to run him again next year. I know Jack's pissed at him being both a politician *and* a Star General, but there *is* that loophole for Martians in the USSF."

Joe laughed. "That bastard's going to be emperor one day!"

Phil felt a slender finger poking him. He turned. It was Alycia in her transparent blue dress. "Hey, can you guys maybe move a little? You're standing right where Urside and I are trying to get married."

"Whoa, I forgot why we were here!" Phil laughed, managing to ratchet his head back up to her eyes. "By all means, let's get the show underway!"

Yes, the bride was sexy-lovely. Urside was so lucky! Who gave a flip about all this political crap anyway?

# CHAPTER THREE
## Dar's Astrology

Night was falling. The 130th floor of the USSF building was immense, and everyone had a clear view out hundreds of feet of glass at Marsport and the vast purpling Martian desert. People drifted towards the miles of exotic meats, cheeses, and cakes arranged on five rows of buffet tables, each eighty feet long. The decibel levels grew with wine and laughter.

Amav had to get those photos out to the hall. What if she didn't send them in time? Could the past Alycia go back with a blank display tablet? That could change everything. When should she cut off the pictures?

*Damn this time-travel crap!*

The flushed Alycia and the giggling Urside were surrounded by a fresh batch of photographers documenting the newly married couple.

"Hey, guys, c'mon, wrap it up!" Amav called. "Everyone send your stuff to my comm here! I need to copy everything out to the hall! I'm cutting off *now!* Nothing after this will go!"

Drunken guests complied, shrugging at the obviously uptight wedding planner who'd been yelling this the past few minutes and who had to be too stupid to know they could all send their own photos to the hall's tablet. But they didn't know that Amav had a USSF AI program on her comm that could analyze a hundred thousand photos and videos in a couple seconds and transmit them in one superbly organized presentation to the hall tablet. She didn't know if the coming HTT required the photos to be organized or not, but she had a feeling that her own mania for organization was part of the process.

Amav had made sure to position the hall tablet in Display Mode as the only object on a long table in the outer hall. She also didn't know if the HTT required locking the hall doors but she'd done so, temporarily inconveniencing any number of folks who needed to process their excessive champagne consumption further down that hall.

Amav sent the photos. She fought the urge to peek into the hall herself. She hoped Jack remembered to turn off the security cameras out there. Would it make a difference?

She turned back to the newlyweds. It was done. Urside had shown up and he and Alycia were married. It had all happened so fast. But Amav could relax now. She wasn't even worried about the past Alycia arriving. It had to be happening about now.

The crowd congregated at the reception tables. Hedrona had pushed Jonathan James' floating crib to the far end of the hall where a dozen women hovered amid much less noise. Amav's child was in good hands. He did look like Joe. He'd been an angel tonight.

Amav saw Jack offering his congratulations to the newlyweds, then gathering a group of military personnel and other leaders including General Scott, Dar, Joe, and Greeney Gooney. Amav wanted to march over there and break it up, but she knew war talk would be inevitable anywhere USSF personnel gathered. And now that Joe was back and the *Typhoon III* project could ramp up, there'd be even more of it.

Phil Sperry hovered near, and Amav felt for him. Now an outsider from the USSF, he couldn't really enter the discussion, even though he was chief of staff to Greeney, who stood there speaking as Star General. She could feel Phil's tension as he struggled to neither go forward nor retreat.

Should she speak with him? Or would that make him more nervous? It was so frustrating and unfair that they couldn't talk anymore. Had Phil ever gotten over her? Was that the problem? All that stuff he'd written about her on the *Typhoon II?*

Jack had not forgotten. He was still furious with Phil three years later. Why couldn't he understand that Phil had been brainwashed, that he'd been lonely and afraid and would blast out all sorts of awkward feelings? Amav could never have returned what he wanted, and she'd declared that over and over to Jack, but he was still irrationally jealous. She and Phil had been good friends before the *Typhoon II,* and now there was nothing. Didn't Phil understand she'd *insisted* he be here tonight?

Amav had convinced Jack that offering the Command Suite for this wedding, and inviting many of the people he'd had run-ins with over the years, might be a way of healing rifts in the face of war needs. Still, it was obvious he and Phil weren't about to become buddies anytime soon. Jack felt that Phil had betrayed the USSF by resigning his commission and falling under the charismatic Star General Gooney's spell, slacking off a soldier's duty for civilian fun and games. Of course, the entire USSF was reeling at losing the greatest physician/engineer the USSF had ever known.

One day Jack had stormed home fuming about the *insults* Phil had just delivered. Amav hadn't believed him until she'd seen that evening's AresNet reports. There was Phil, shouting in front of USSF headquarters that Jack was a *racist* for trying to quash Greeney's mayoralty campaign on the grounds that USSF officers couldn't run for political office. Ranting that the Martian military was officially a guest of the USSF and didn't have to follow *fascist USSF rules* and that the USSF was just as much a brainwashing institution as the entire AC Grid.

That went far beyond the bounds of even an angry argument. Jack and Phil hadn't spoken for over a year, and Jack continued to blame Phil for every bureaucratic foul-up involving the brilliant Star General Gooney, accusing Phil of illegally meddling in USSF business when political and military duties overlapped, as they often did. While all Martian military forces now reported to Jack as head of the USSF, there were loopholes that, when radiated telepathically by twenty Martian officers in a meeting, were hard to untangle. In Jack's eyes, Phil was to blame for all of them.

Why couldn't Amav and Phil just talk again? Openly and deeply, as they used to? Could she resolve the conflict between him and her husband? Or would Phil again get the wrong idea? He was so terribly lonely. Why didn't he find someone? Didn't he ever really understand how much she and Jack loved each other? Why would he pursue *her?*

"So I'll be switching SCUSSF to the *III,*" Jack was saying. "Anyone can see the *II's* had its day. But it'll still serve as a training ship for new pilots. Don't worry, Joe, you'll still be the *III's* pilot and captain. I'll just have my little flagship office aboard and sure, I'll give you some trouble now and then."

Joe grinned. "I can't wait. I have so much to catch up on *Typhoon* technology."

Jack turned to Greeney Gooney. "Of course, Gooney, I want you to command the *IV*. Or else use it for *your* flagship. Or both. Whatever suits you."

Amav felt a surprising hint of Martian emotion leak from Greeney. Then the telepathic shield came down hard. But Greeney smiled that crooked Martian smile. Here was Jack Commer offering him one of the two most powerful weapons ever created, and granting him coequal status with himself.

"I would certainly be most honored," Greeney sang back. "I will naturally do my best to fulfill your gracious trust in me."

"Well, we need you for the war effort, Greeney," Jack said. "And you're the best, no doubt about it. These new *Typhoons* are the most advanced tech we have, and we need you and Joe flying 'em."

"Thank you, Admiral. I am quite pleasantly surprised!"

Amav looked over to Phil, who was grinning.

"G'rea'nyaigu'nye will make a fine commander of the *IV*," Dar announced. "This Martian youngster, all of 230 years old, has superb integrity and infinite ability. His quick reaction to the destruction of DamnStar and his routing of the AC invasion fleet are well known to all. And his two years as mayor of Marsport have been a period of unprecedented success and development. We are confident of his ability to serve the United System well in the future." Everyone could obviously read what Dar was thinking. The entire history of Greeney Gooney was already known to everyone.

Of course, this history included all Greeney's unauthorized hacks into the Amplified Thought Archives, and his uncanny ability to perform many of the highest-level AT functions by himself, rather than with assistance from a pair of other Martians. And then there was his mysterious unreadable mind, which made so many nervous, including almost all his fellow

Martians.

But it was polite not to acknowledge any of that.

*

"This is a very important day," Dar went on. "As you know, I don't normally offer speculation about the coming events between now and 2075, when the events of Heuristic Time Transition finally come to a close. But I must tell you that I've known for a long time, and recent calculations have been confirming, that this day, September 17, 2038, is a major nexus of HTT forces."

Everyone leaned to hear. Here was the HTT encyclopedist ready to spill details everyone normally had to beg him for.

"Not only has the main HTT team fully assembled on this date, that is, myself, Mandy Frederick over there, Churchill and Ranna to my right, and Polot of Zorex who unfortunately cannot be here tonight, but Alycia and Urside are now reunited, which in itself is a major contribution to our understanding of HTT, as Urside was its first practitioner and his trips to Mars to see Alycia sparked our understanding of the phenomenon. Furthermore, we have Joe Commer back with us, and this date marks the beginning of much important work he and Jack will accomplish over the next several decades. And while not all my calculations are finished yet, and the true meaning of September 17th resists rigorous analysis, I can definitely see that this date marks the beginning of even more responsibility for our young Star General G'rea'nyaigu'nye here, and even for Jack and Amav's infant son, Jonathan James Commer."

"*Oh,*" Amav gasped. She turned to the crib at the far wall. She didn't want to think about her son as being important in any way. That could only mean danger in this era of war and uncertainty.

"The actual details are still hazy," Dar went on, oblivious to Amav's distress. He may have thought he was making her and Jack proud of their son's future, but he was doing exactly the opposite. "But someday in the future young Jonathan James will work closely with G'rea'nyaigu'nye. I can definitely see a tie in their respective karmas, and there may be an HTT event coming shortly in which we can research this connection further."

As much as Amav loved Dar, she was always exasperated by his predictions. Yes, he'd mapped out some actual battles between 2036 and 2053, and he'd been right every time. He'd made some HTT trips to various points between now and 2075, hoping to clean up *time messes*. But everyone knew the total number of HTT trips was fixed, and so far Dar had cataloged over ninety-five percent of the 8,178 time-travel episodes by humans, Martians, and Alpha Centaurians between May 29, 2013 and May 29, 2075. But of the 1,755 Alpha Centaurian time intrusions--and Amav, like everyone else, had memorized all these numbers and was to some extent obsessed with them--over two hundred remained unaccounted for. Dar tended to gloss over this uncertainty, always saying that "further research is needed."

Many of his pronouncements sounded suspiciously like the "Your Lucky Stars Today!" feeds on SolNet, and Amav suspected not a few members of the wedding party thought Dar was pandering to the human custom of spreading nonsensical good cheer at the occasion.

No wonder people nervously joked about "Dar's astrology." Amav wondered if everyone wasn't waiting for the day when it all failed spectacularly. People wanted to consult this Amplified Thought-indexed, HTT-certified astrology, but deep down they worried that his suppositions would prove inexact. They'd dismiss an unsettling prediction as "not necessarily destined," or think, "If we try hard, we'll be able to prevent that." Some future histories had been retrieved by Dar and Mandy, and Amav could see that the full team would gather more, but the ones plotted so far were full of gaps, digitally ragged, and rarely mentioned individuals. Which after all was what everyone wanted to know about.

Greeney Gooney disengaged from the military personnel and walked straight for Amav. "You are uneasy?" he said.

Amav didn't know Greeney well despite dozens of meetings and social events as wife of the Supreme Commander of the USSF. But Greeney, like Dar, was determined to learn how to read human body language and facial expressions. It was ludicrous to watch Martians, helplessly radiating their innermost thoughts to all, trying to decipher what they called "the darkened human house." Now Amav realized she had the same problem with Gooney. She expected to be able to fully read a small pink creature with a back fin. But she couldn't, and now he was reading *her.*

"I guess so," she said. "I guess I was thinking about, you know, Polot's article and all these future predictions, and not being able to do anything about it."

"Yes, we all have that to deal with now. It's hard enough not being able to change your actions over the *last* fifteen years. But in the *next* fifteen as well? That's just too much!"

"That's it exactly! All this time-travel stuff, and the war, and predictions of the future, and how I have to *act* through it all. Sometimes I just want to curl up in a ball somewhere and forget all this."

To Amav's surprise Greeney dropped his AT shielding and let his radiance flow. She was shocked that he would endanger his cherished privacy in front of four hundred wedding guests, but then saw he was releasing his thoughts in a narrow beam aimed only at her.

*We Martians experienced something similar thousands of years ago. When we connected all Martians in a net of telepathic outradiance, we soon saw that concerns for the results of past actions, and concern for these actions causing suffering in the future, could spread karmic panic throughout the net much more efficiently. For a brief period, the entire planet was convulsed in a tangle of fear and anxiety.*

*I do not know exactly how we came out of that. But every Martian lives with that legacy. It even briefly appeared again when we all fell under the sway of the Emperor Hergs five human years ago. But that was a mere influenza as compared to the cancer of what had gone on before.*

"Are you saying you all *relaxed* somehow?" Amav said.

Greeney shrugged and went dark again. "I just don't know,

friend Amav. I suppose the species decided it wanted to survive. Not to be insane."

"Or maybe you *did* curl up in a ball and forget about it all."

Greeney shot her another dose of radiance.

*Well, we curled up in a ball and forgot about it all. But with our eyes open.*

# CHAPTER FOUR
## Hedrona

"C'mon, Phil," Will Connors said, waving his champagne glass, oblivious to its contents slopping across the tiled floor. "You know physician/engineer's the last command vacancy for the project. Even Scott's trying to get Jack to hire you back."

Phil stood with his old buddies from the *Typhoon II*. Patrick James, Will Connors, and Lee Borman had just turned their *II* duties over to replacements, and all three had been promoted to Lieutenant Commander and were heading new departments for the *Typhoon* project. James would spearhead Communications, Connors Navigation, and Borman Weaponry. Each had several dozen engineers and USSF crew working on both the *Typhoon III* and *Typhoon IV,* but when the time came to launch the ships at the end of 2039, each of the three would be onboard as the commanding officer of his respective department.

"C'mon, you can pick either the *III* or the *IV*. We all can, whichever we want!" Borman cackled. "C'mon, Phil, it'll be just like old times!"

"These new *Typhoons* are *fantastic,*" James said. "They're *huge*. They've got *everything.*"

"Yeah, they make the *II* look like a school bus," Connors said.

Connors wasn't thirty yet, but Phil saw his hair was already graying. Hell, Phil's own hair was going from all this stress. Of course, Will had spent a month marooned on that damn asteroid after being shot down over Altrouda. That would make anyone old.

"We need you, Phil," Borman said. "This Sortie guy is totally incompetent!"

"Well, he's not *that* bad," James said. "Just not up to speed, really."

"He *worships* you, Phil!" Connors laughed. "Says he reads your manuals every night!"

Phil managed a grin. While he was secretly irritated that anybody could be named his replacement, he'd been somewhat mollified by Physician/Engineer Draka Sortie's hero worship. The guy was certainly overeager. But he was damn sharp, and might even wind up designing the *Typhoon V.* Who knew?

Phil was flattered his former comrades wanted him back. But didn't they understand his reflexes were shot? He'd been brainwashed by the very ACs he'd be going back into combat against. Why would he put himself in a position where he'd let everyone down?

How had all these guys recovered from being part of the goddamn Grid anyway?

"Give it some thought, Phil," Borman said. "Jack would take you back, I know he would. In a damn second."

"It's just not gonna happen, Lee. I burned those damn bridges a long time ago."

He burned them back in Alpha Centauri on the *II,* when he'd *converted.* When he'd been locked in the Pod with the brainwashed refugees. *When he'd written Jack about how much he loved Amav.* He couldn't remember a word of it, just that it had been pretty gamy. Because that's what he'd felt for Amav three years ago, the worst sort of *lust.*

Sure, when they'd been rescued and deprogrammed, Phil had gone to Jack and told him that he'd been deluded. That Jack should forget all that stuff he'd said about Amav. It had just been the brainwashing, it was just that Phil needed to find a wife of his own and settle down. But Jack hadn't bought it.

Phil looked beyond Borman to Amav Frankston-Commer over by Jonathan James' crib. She was heartbreaking, with her long dark hair flowing down over that delightfully low-cut dress. Childbirth had done nothing to alter that figure. In fact, she was sexier than ever. But the *brainwashing* had killed that doomed fantasy long ago. There was no way Phil could ever again indulge in romantic fantasies about Jack Commer's beautiful wife.

There'd once been real friendship there. They really used to *talk.* They'd shared so much. But all that was dead as well. Amav probably thought they'd just drifted apart as people sometimes do.

Nobody from the *Typhoon II* was really close anymore. They drank together, they had laughs, but they were distant. Phil never saw how Borman, James, or Connors could go back and resume their duties as if nothing had happened. He sure couldn't understand how Jack Commer could make the *II* his flagship and continue to function as its captain. By July of this year, after Borman and James and Connors had moved to the *III* Project, Jack had five new crewmembers with him including Sperry worshipper Draka Sortie.

What Phil really couldn't get over was Amav as a mother. He knew she'd been pregnant and accepted that. He'd even briefly seen Jonathan James when he was two months old, but he'd never connected that with the Amav he'd been so infatuated with for so many years. Now here she was, hostess of the Urside-Alycia wedding, in full control, showing off not only her eleven-month-old child but also the sensuous perfection of her post-childbirth body.

It had always vexed him that at the exact moment the Zarj stormtroopers had captured them on the *Typhoon,* Jack and Amav had been naked on the floor of the ship. Phil had seen everything of her, but, being Grid-brainwashed and in the presence of Alpha Centaurians he was programmed to worship, it just hadn't mattered. Now he couldn't even remember what her nude body looked like.

Phil was getting more soused than he'd intended. The champagne was superb, easy to swallow, and available in immense quantities. All you had to do was raise your hand and someone passed you a fresh glass. This was probably why Phil found himself in the crowd around Jonathan James' floating crib. The infant was asleep, despite the din of a wedding reception still ramping up and heading towards eleven PM. But of course Amav's child *would* be so well-behaved.

Greeney Gooney, the only Martian who'd bothered to take more than a passing interest in the Supreme Commander's son, peered into the crib. Jonathan James did resemble Joe Commer, with his dark hair, olive skin, round face, and little arms punching out in his sleep. "And has Jonathan James learned to walk yet?" Gooney asked.

"Well, he's *tried* a couple times," Amav laughed. "So how do you know when human children are supposed to start walking?"

Greeney emitted his high Martian laugh. "Well, anyone can consult SolNet, you know. I saw several ballpark figures: one year, or nine to fourteen months, and so on. Apparently it can vary a great deal."

Joe was also at the crib and seemed to be getting even tighter than Phil. Well, Joe had just survived two passenger shell disasters within the space of a couple minutes back in 2033. Phil just hoped this Ranna woman understood Joe's need to plaster himself.

So who was going to understand *Phil's* need to plaster himself?

Phil knew he was making a fool of himself, staring down the bodices of every pretty woman who entered the loving circle round the crib. And at this wedding almost every woman *was* wearing something enticing. Phil decorously kept his eyes from Alycia. She was the damn bride, after all, but she was truly stunning tonight.

He also tried to keep his eyes off Amav, but once she caught him looking down *her* bodice across the crib, and frowned. Phil was so devastated that he decided to stalk off in a huff to show that he was above all these petty flirtations, but at that moment Hedrona Bhlon came up to coo over the sleeping Jonathan James Commer, and as she bent over the crib her golden dress fell forward and Phil saw everything.

She wasn't wearing *anything* beneath the silky gold.

Phil, the only man on this side of the crib, stared enchanted at both her naked nipples for possibly an entire minute. She was fifty, sixteen years older than he was. How could a fifty-year-old woman have such a classy set of breasts?

Her hand finally went to her chest, closing off this delight, as if she were finally aware that ex-Major Sperry was committing some deceitful intergalactic espionage and needed to be arrested immediately.

But then Phil stared at her ears, her cheeks, her lips, that new brown hair, the bronze choker collar with the matching earrings. Stared drunk and stunned, awash in revelation. He chugged his half glass of champagne and even turned to Amav for help, but she was chatting amiably with Ranna Kikken.

The floating crib was awash in white light, surrounded by wedding guests focused on this eleven-month-old kid who was oblivious to all of them. There was something timeless and holy here, magnified by the champagne and the wedding and the beautiful women and by Phil's awful desire for Hedrona Bhlon of all people. Hedrona Bhlon, who Phil regularly warned people not to trust. Hedrona, whose Texas twang *irritated* him.

*Out of drink! Damn! Maybe offer fetch more, just two us? Walk to bar, tell how appreciate Animal Rescue? Isn't winding down, what next for you, and be having boobs for myself, walking you for myself, everything in the open, everything?*

"Goddammit, get your hands *off* me!" came the cry.

# CHAPTER FIVE
## The Borman Challenge

The entire 130th floor hushed. Hedrona stared into Phil's shocked gray eyes.

"I didn't … I mean, *did* I?" Phil gasped.

"What are you *talking* about? What's going on over there?" she snapped, moving to the disturbance at the buffet tables. Too bad Mr. Phil wouldn't get in any more peeping. She'd actually been getting a little flattered.

At the tables Lee Borman, in his new Lieutenant Commander's uniform, rubbed a bright red mark across his cheek. Alycia Klave rushed away, hiking her dress to get traction, shaking her head in disgust.

"Hey, what's going on?" Urside Charmouth said, long silver hair flying as he turned.

"That bastard *groped* me!" Alycia hissed. "Goddammit, he ruined my wedding! *Our* wedding!"

Urside followed her outstretched finger. "Who's *that?*"

"I don't know! Some damn USSF slob!"

To Hedrona's astonishment Borman climbed onto a table with a full champagne glass in either hand, swaying badly amid the sausages and cheese. He kicked away a silver tray which banged hard on the tile, echoing throughout the vast space.

"Borman, you *idiot!*" Jack yelled.

"I jus' wanted ta kiss da goddamn bride!" the toothy crew-cut Borman yelled. "Why wuz dat so terrabull?"

"Dammit, Borman, are you drunk again?" Jack snarled, moving forward. "Get down from there, for God's sake!"

"He *groped* me!" Alycia repeated.

"Look, the guy's plastered on his ass," Urside said. "We don't have to worry about him."

Borman raised both stubby champagne-enhanced arms above his head and shouted: "Screw it! Got 'n 'nouncement ta make! Got 'n 'nouncement!"

"Get down from there!" Jack shouted. "Borman, that's an order!"

32

"Fergeh it! Lazies 'n gennelmen, got 'n 'nouncement!'"

"He got stinking drunk," someone muttered in disgust. To Hedrona's surprise, it was Phil Sperry at her side.

"Wow," Joe Commer said. "Did Borman fall off the wagon since I was gone or something?"

Phil shrugged. "Not that I know of. Connors says he's been super-sharp on the *Typhoon* project. He even wrote another book."

The gesticulating ape was gathering a crowd. "I'm challengin'! Yah, I'm challengin'!"

"*He* wrote another book?"

"God, this is *insane!* At Alycia's *wedding!*" Hedrona said, watching Jack assemble a squad of USSF guards.

"Yeah," Phil went on. "He wrote this thing called *Who is Lee Borman?* Some sort of autobiographical trip about his fighter pilot kills in AC. I sure haven't wanted to read it."

Hedrona made sure the six-foot-five Phil Sperry was in no position to leer down her dress again. She thought he'd been about to reach into it back there. It was just like that meeting last month where she'd kept trying to get him to talk, hit him up with personal questions, see what was there, see if he'd open up. But it was like having a conversation with a teenage boy. All he could do was look down her blouse.

So this was the super-capable Phil Sperry everyone talked about? The master politician? Okay, he was cute. Those gray eyes were wondrous. And he was so tall. But he was a child. What was she thinking? That she could impress a guy sixteen years younger than she was?

Well, at least *part* of her had impressed him.

Meanwhile Joe rolled his eyes, no doubt recalling Borman's 2035 opus, *The Sexual Conquest of Your Inner Mount Everest.* Borman's sex manual for men hadn't sold well, either electronically or in print, and had probably only gotten published because Borman was a war hero with his four thousand kills in Alpha Centauri. In fact, that was probably why he was even on the *Typhoon III* project to begin with, although Hedrona was beginning to suspect he'd be permanently off in about two minutes.

"Yah, I'm challengin' Gooney for mayuhr next year! Whaddya dinka dat? Me! Lee *Borman!* Runnin' fuh mayuhr!"

To Hedrona's dismay a coterie around him applauded this statement.

"You--you are not!" Jack sputtered. "Just get down from there! You're wrecking this wedding!"

"Am not! Am not! Jack baby, I filed yestaday! First day I could! Figger if *Gooney* kin be mayuhr, so kin *I!* And my platform is dis: da mayuhr is fuh *humans!* Marsport's a damn *human* siddee! We doan want no stinkin' Marshuns screwin' it up!"

And USSF personnel were also applauding.

"Oh my God," Phil said. "That *Who is Lee Borman* crap is probably some pre-election propaganda. Damn, why didn't I *see* that?"

"Wow, did Borman turn into a bigot too while I was gone?" Joe said.

"Well, there *has* been a lot of idiot talk about 'Mars for humans' recently. I had no idea *Borman* was into it, though. And these other jerks here." Phil yanked out his comm and whispered: "Public Records. Election Filing. Marsport Mayoralty. March 2039."

Hedrona blinked at how quickly Mr. Teenage Boy Peeper had sobered. She didn't want to think why she now glued her right breast to Phil's forearm and read the results coming up on his screen: *BORMAN, L. RANSOM, R. PETERSDORFF, W. THOMP--*

The feed cut off. The screen froze, then went white.

"Cripes, what a thing to happen," Phil said in disgust, but he kept his left arm exactly where it was. Hedrona pressed in another eighth of an inch.

"Wow, I can't remember the last time I had a comm freeze," she said.

"Damn, I need some *background.* I haven't even filed Greeney yet."

"Hah!" Borman said, picking Phil's voice out of the uproar.

"Greeney boy should stick ta bein' damn Marshun genral! Leave our damn siddee alone! *We* built it, afta all! It's *ours!*"

Fresh clapping erupted around Borman. The murmuring from the rest of the crowd turned decidedly dark.

"You *can't* run for mayor!" Jack cried. "USSF personnel *can't* hold political office!"

"If Greeney kin do it, and *he's* in da USSF, *ah* kin do it!"

"Dammit, you know there's a difference! We have Martian customs to take into consideration!"

This was a surprise to Hedrona. The story had been that Jack was trying to end the loophole that allowed a Martian Star General, nominally under USSF command, to run for office. Still pressed against Phil, looking over his frozen screen, she could hear the political gears meshing in his head as he factored Jack's statement into his coming campaign strategy. Maybe there was more to this man than she'd given him credit for. Maybe he'd talk politics, maybe that was the way to get to know him.

"Aw, crap on Marshun custums! Crap on 'em! Thass whah ah say! An when ah'm 'lected--"

Jack motioned his squad of four big USSF guards forward. "Okay, Mr. Borman, you can go ahead and run for President of the United System Council if you want, but I'm sick of all this politicking and you're out of the *III* project as of now!"

"Naw, ah'm gonna command 'er!" Borman bawled. "Da tree's mah baby, man!"

"You *can't* command her! You don't even hold a pilot's license, you fool!"

"*Joe* kin pilot my ship if he wants ta! Ah'll command da whole BS from mah goddamn *turret!* Blast 'em outa da sky! Whaddya dinka *dat?*"

The gray-clad USSF guards rushed to the tables and grappled with Borman, sending more silver dishes clanging to the tile, cheese and meats and lettuce and cucumbers whirling in the air. Borman let out a stream of truly foul curses.

Jack turned to Dar. "Dammit, Dar, is *this* your idea of a great significant event for today?"

Dar shrugged as the banging, clattering, and grunting went on from atop the buffet table. Borman slipped from his guards and ran straight down the tables, but abruptly the entire row overturned down its eighty-foot length, dumping Borman in a deafening roar of metal bowls, flower vases, china plates, and champagne bottles. Borman stood and was tackled, swinging a punch at a guard who took it personally and decked him in return, knocking him cold.

Jack turned to Phil. "Dammit, Phil, my comm froze. Can you get some help for Borman here? Anyone else hurt? *You guys okay?*"

"Wow, *my* comm froze too," Phil said.

Hedrona pressed in further.

Every light in the place went out, replaced by a bright blue flash and acrid ozone.

"*Get your hands off me!*" came the female cry from the other end of the hall.

"Not *again,*" Hedrona muttered.

A heart-freezing screech tore through the hall.

She couldn't register what she was seeing. Tall bright blue forms, undulating. Bathed in blinding blue light. Waving arms? *Tentacles?*

Those tentacles brandished sticks of some sort?

"God, those are *pulsar tubes!*" Phil cried, pointing to the apparitions gathering around Jonathan James' crib.

"*What?*" Hedrona said.

"*Alpha Centaurian pulsar tubes!*"

"No! They can't be!"

"They are! Those are Zarj from Alpha Centauri!"

*Zarj.* Four-armed monsters with their nasty purple whirlpool eyes and all their tentacles. The most merciless killers of Alpha Centauri.

Why was she running right at them? Punching wildly, she tried to block the creatures from the crib. Amav lay beneath it writhing. Hedrona looked back for help, but the four oblivious USSF guards were still handcuffing Borman.

"*You damned sons of bitches!*" yelled General Scott,

rushing up with a heat blaster and firing. Two Zarj fell flailing against the white wall, spewing blue-purple blood, arms blasted off, heads and torsos fried. Scott ducked a pulsar tube blast that took a twenty-foot-long chunk out of the ceiling.

Hedrona beat against the aliens in slow motion. The air was thick with electromagnetic sludge, but the crib was bathed in its own white light, and Greeney Gooney was atop it, drawing his Martian shattergun.

A Zarj crushed the gun and Greeney's hand into one bloody mush. Then two Zarj had him on the floor.

A Zarj trooper, seven feet tall, lifted a screaming Jonathan James Commer out of the crib as Hedrona flung herself on both of them.

The shrieking intensified. The Zarj language? But all comms were frozen and there was nothing that could be translated.

Phil wrestled a pulsar tube from a Zarj and struck the monster again and again.

The tube banged to the floor. Phil was *gone*.

The Zarj holding Jonathan James vanished. Greeney Gooney *vaporized.*

And Hedrona was flying out of herself. Amav's despairing screams faded as Hedrona felt herself being sucked--*elsewhere.*

# CHAPTER SIX
## Into the Continuum

Nothing but that *screeching*. Phil hurtled through thousands of miles of viscous fog, for thousands of years, Zarj shrieking all around him.

Greeney. And Hedrona and Jonathan James. Had the Zarj just killed them all? Was this the afterlife? Gray blur and screeching insanity?

He bashed into a white metal wall.

Jonathan James screamed. Zarj troopers, dizzily scrambling to their feet, grabbed for the pulsar tubes clattering across the hard white floor.

Hedrona and Greeney lay sprawled against the wall.

More screeching, then:

"*Idiots!*"

Phil stared at the comm on his belt rendering this word. The device showed no life beyond activation of its translator.

More screeching, overlaid with: "Blundering idiots! You put Gurar and Fivrk through the bulkhead!"

Phil heard these words in eerie stereo. Greeney had pulled out his own comm which also translated the screeches. Phil gazed up at the bloody remains of two Zarj troopers who hadn't smacked against the bulkhead like the rest, but were embedded in it. Phil gulped at the blue-purple spaghetti.

Demented *squealing,* and the two comms translated:

"Suytx, you told me this timespace adjustment would be precise! *Precise!* And it has *completely failed!*"

"But Captain Clopt, we have gained hostages!"

Captain--*Clopt?* No, it couldn't be. The translators couldn't be right. Clopt had to be some sort of common Zoraxian word. No, it couldn't be a name from Phil's past, could it?

"*Worthless* hostages! Emperor Dar was untouchable! The timespace would not allow capture as you promised! Thus you die!" rasped the tall blue trooper whose mouth folds seem most agitated. He raised his pulsar tube and fired at not just the underling who'd spoken, but swept across five of them, the narrow beam of concentrated short-lived mini-neutron stars slicing these troopers to soggy meat.

"Oh my God!" Hedrona screamed.

The leader swung his tube at her and screeched. "Silence!" came from Phil's comm and Greeney's. "Hostages will be silent or die!"

"Oh my God!" Phil gasped. "It *is* you! *Clopt!*"

Clopt, who'd captured Phil on the *Typhoon II* three years ago. Three years? His comm's calendar function chirped to life and struggled to ascertain the date, offering suggestions of September 17, 2038, September 20, 2038, March 5, 1872, March 5, 2039, April 4, 2033, and April 4, 2049.

It put a question mark after April 4, 2049 and steadied there.

A pulsar tube swiped the comm from his hand. Phil looked up to see another Zarj trooper ripping away Greeney's and stamping it with his boot.

More shrieking. Then Clopt jammed a button on the wall.

"We will use our own translation system," he announced. "Hostages will remain silent. You are all worthless. Prepare to die."

Greeney stared intently at his mangled claw, flexing it. Was he running Amplified Thought to fix it? Phil met Hedrona's crazed blue eyes. He crawled over the chilly floor to retrieve the screaming Jonathan James, whom everyone seemed to have forgotten.

Everyone but the Zarj translator, which tried its best to make sense of JJC's cries:

*"Sand dusk piece twelve limit art crack potion lift."*

Clopt whirled his pulsar tube to the infant. Phil swallowed, covering Jonathan James as best he could.

"Captain! That may be a valuable hostage after all!" a Zarj cried. "Records from the time adjustment indicate this is the son of human emperor Jack Commer!"

"The big one or the little one?" Clopt said, adjusting his aim.

"The smaller one, captain!"

Hedrona threw herself on top of both JJC and Phil.

"Fools! Can't you hold these puny vermin in one place?"

"No!" Hedrona wailed. "Don't shoot Phil! Please, God!"

Phil stared. Did Hedrona Bhlon really give a damn about his hide?

Clopt studied the three, finally using his hot pulsar tube to pry Hedrona off Phil, who found himself staring down her cleavage again, aided by the fact that it had been thoroughly ripped in all the scuffling. But he could hardly make sense of what he saw.

"Phil Sperry. The engineer."

"My God! How do you know my *name?*"

Clopt stood above him, pulsar tube aimed at his heart. "Release the small loud one to the vermin female. I sense he regards her presence as desirable. Then you shall stand."

Hedrona had a hand over her mouth, but picked JJC up and scooted back. Phil met her eyes again and stood shakily, expecting the *neutrons* any second.

Clopt's tentacles waved, his eye whirlpools squirmed, and his mouth folds quivered. "You were once one of us, Phil Sperry. Yet you reverted. You forsook the emperor and traitorously resumed worship of the Jack Commer emperor. Explain."

"How do you *know* any of this?" Phil gasped.

"We Zarj recall everything that has ever happened to us. It is a military necessity. I recall every detail of our meeting onboard your barbarian ship. You were already one of us then. I felt your kinship. Yet you betrayed us. Explain." He shifted his pulsar tube to Phil's nose.

"Well, I guess maybe it, like, *wore off?*" But to his dismay Phil found himself recalling the loveliness of the Alpha Centaurian Grid. The Head. *To know the Head.* To worship the emperor, *to be One with him.*

"We will take you back, Phil Sperry, and you will again become one of us."

"*No!*" Hedrona and Phil screamed together.

Clopt swung the pulsar tube to Hedrona's head, but his whirlpool eyes remained fixed on Phil. "You will become one of us, and you will explain your treason to the emperor in person."

"Oh my God," Phil groaned. "Please don't hurt her."

"It is obvious that our so-called engineers were unable to properly understand time transition. Our invasion failed as a result."

"Your--invasion?" Phil finally realized what Clopt was referring to, if this really was April 4, 2049.

Phil looked over to Greeney, who let off a microburst of narrowly focused thought. The others couldn't pick it up, but Phil and Greeney confirmed each other's guess.

Everyone knew that Dar had pegged the Alpha Centaurian date for their attack on DamnStar: in Sol reckoning, April 2, 2049. The Centaurians had hoped to overwhelm the 2036 DamnStar outpost using 2049 technology and so gain a foothold on the outskirts of the Sol system. Their Warp Transfer had improved a great deal since their ludicrously dangerous versions of the early '30s, but it still wasn't anywhere near 2036 Sol technology. Greeney had fought them to a standstill and then wiped out ninety-seven percent of the attackers, but everyone knew a few AC ships had made it back to wherever they'd come from.

So if DamnStar was February 9, 2036 for Sol, and April 2, 2049 for the ACs, and if today was April 4, 2049--

Then Clopt and these Zarj troopers had just escaped from the battle two days ago and were primed for revenge.

"You, Phil Sperry, will work on time transition as we mount a new invasion."

"N-no ..." But Phil already felt the melodic soprano of the Head pulsing through his blood. The emperor called to him as he'd done three years ago. He needed Phil to work on an updated Heuristic Time Transition invasion. Phil's engineer mind raced with surging Head. He knew next to nothing about HTT, but with Greeney's full grasp of Martian Amplified Thought, they could round up a new fleet and insert it at the most vulnerable timespace points for the USSF.

Yes, really a simple engineering problem. Phil knew exactly how to figure it out for the emperor.

*Philip!* Greeney hissed in another tightly controlled

telepathic beam. *Resist! If you become part of the Head, they will know everything you know!*

"*Goddammit!*" Hedrona shouted. "You monsters are going to *lose!* May 14, 2053! That's the date you're going to *lose!* Why don't you just *admit* it?"

"Silence. Or die. Your choice," Clopt said, aiming his pulsar tube at Jonathan James in her arms. "We have heard your tiresome human logic many times. Your human calendar means nothing to us. You calculate this time to be your 2049, and you believe that in four of your years the emperor will die and your evil Dar will destroy us. That is your filthy religion. *Kartuthuck* to your filthy religion!"

Hedrona shrank back, protecting JJC and gasping: "It's 2049?"

"That's what Greeney and I think," Phil muttered. "We must have Transitioned. But really, Hedrona, it's *got* to be all right. Look, we can at least *sympathize* with these guys, can't we? I mean, they love their emperor, they don't want anything to happen to him, and in a way they're just like *us*. Like *me,* I mean."

"Phil!"

"Look, I don't want anything to happen to you. So maybe we can try to *understand* them."

"Understand these *monsters?* Phil, they just *kidnapped* us! They're going to kill us all!"

Philp stared back. He was betraying everything for this Head. He was a fool. Didn't he remember how bad it was three years ago?

Oh, yes. But dammit, he was now One with these monsters. He was a monster himself.

Jonathan James screamed anew, the Zarj translators again failing to make sense of it:

"*Line tube force precarious atom push delineation craft spoke table.*"

Clopt extended two crimson tentacles and snatched JJC from Hedrona's arms.

"*No!*" she moaned.

Clopt stood to his seven-foot height with the infant. JJC smiled and stopped crying. He looked up into those messy whirlpool eyes and laughed.

"He--he *converted!* How can a baby *convert?*" Phil gasped.

"He did *what?*" Hedrona cried as Jonathan James turned to her with cold dark ancient dead eyes.

"I told you silence!" Clopt raged. "This entity is now one with the emperor. We welcome Jack Commer's son to the Head, where he will gloriously serve the Empire!"

Hedrona scrambled to her feet. "*Nooo!*" Two Zarj rushed her with pulsar tubes. Phil pushed her back as she kicked and pummeled to get at the Zarj captain.

"No! Leave her alone!" Phil said. "In the name of the emperor!"

"*What?*" Greeney and Hedrona gasped together. Phil grabbed her.

"Clopt! Listen to me! I'm One with you! Hedrona may be a bit headstrong, but she'll convert! I know she will! She can't be harmed! She's *mine!*" And Phil twisted her face and slobbered at her like a drunk teenage halfback behind the stadium at 3 AM.

"Dammit, Phil!" Hedrona jerked free. But Phil's hands were pulling at her torn gown, ripping it away, exposing everything.

She punched him hard and pulled back for a kick at his groin, but a Zarj smacked the back of her head with a pulsar tube and she went down.

Jonathan James, still in Clopt's tentacles, pointed and laughed.

Phil met Greeney's stunned eyes.

"This Bhlon beast shall remain alive," Clopt spoke. "We shall trust our new comrade Phil Sperry's word that she shall soon convert. We are in kinship with Phil Sperry. He wishes the *Jkucll-Atkat-Hfucl* with his mate Hedrona Bhlon. He shall have it."

Jonathan James gurgled with delight at the thought of Phil bedding the dementedly beautiful, lusciously sexy Hedrona Bhlon of the revealing ripped golden gown. JJC and Phil read each other perfectly. They read Clopt and the other Zarj perfectly. They were One.

Phil laughed with relief. "Oh my God! Oh my God! I'm *back!* I was so *lonely* all these years! So cut off! God bless the emperor! *Bless* him!"

And because Phil was completely One, all was indeed revealed to the Zarj.

Clopt turned to Greeney. "Interesting. So we have captured Star General G'rea'nyaigu'nye. This is pleasing news. Fate has grinned gloriously on our time raid after all. We failed to capture Dar. We wished him to protect and extend the Grid he claims he is fated to ruin. but fate has instead led us to the creature who thwarted our assault on DamnStar."

"Sire!" Phil cried in ecstasy, unsure of how to address Captain Clopt but not caring. "Greeney Gooney will assist us in our next invasion!"

"Yes. This curious technique these Martians call Amplified Thought. From your mind I see that he is a master. But I cannot read his mind as I do with other Martians. When shall he convert?"

"I don't know, Sire! Lord! Last time the other Martians converted faster than anyone! Even Dar did for a while! I'm sure Greeney will too!"

And then Phil felt the blast of Greeney's mind. The Martian leapt to his feet, loosened all restrictions and let his telepathic outradiance flood the room.

*Killers all! I defeated you at DamnStar and I will defeat you again! My mental silence will protect me from any conversion!*

To Phil's astonishment all the Zarj troopers knelt before Greeney. Even Clopt. Even Jonathan James bowed his head.

Hedrona came to on the floor. "What? What?"

But Phil understood. "We honor you, Star General! All Alpha Centauri honors you! The victor of DamnStar!"

"G'rea'nyaigu'nye, we shall follow you to victory!" Clopt shouted. "Lead us, with your marvelous Amplified Thought, to final victory for the emperor!"

Greeney laughed. *I will not convert to your Grid insanity! We have lost Phil Sperry, we have lost Jonathan James, but*

*Hedrona and I are strong! You will never use my Amplified Thought! I invoke the* Kuth'rr'kq!

"No!" Phil turned to Clopt. "That's the Four-Hundred-Year Martian Hibernation!"

*In this case I only need make it four years, to May 14, 2053! Bye for now!*

And Greeney toppled unconscious.

"He's dead!" Hedrona cried.

"N-no, he's just *sort* of dead." Phil whirled to Clopt. "If we can't revive him, we can't get any Amplified Thought out of him!"

"Damn you, Phil!" Hedrona hissed from the floor. "I can't believe you!"

Phil stared entranced at her ripped dress. Everything was on display for him. So it was true. Women really were beautiful when they were angry.

"Hedrona, you're everything to me!" he cried. "You're as good as the emperor! Don't you know what that means? It means *I love you forever!*"

# CHAPTER SEVEN
## The Games at the Collapse of Empire
*May 14, 2053*

Phil sighed as the *Brooding Eagle* came out of Warp Transfer.

"Stable orbit around Cssarr," the nav system announced.

"Got it," Phil said, wondering why he bothered to talk back to the computer. Some pilots trusted the entire sequence to the autopilot, coming out of Warp to immediate autolanding, but Phil wanted to make sure he was in one piece before entering the atmosphere, and he liked to take his ship down manually. He'd improved Centaurian Warp Transfer tech over the past four years, but it was still guesswork, even though he'd boosted the success rate from fifty to eighty-five percent.

Not bad. But not desirable either. Phil was sure he'd wind up in *Garr/thahg* one of these days. Of course, Clopt maintained that *Garr/thahg* was an honor for any warrior, but Phil wasn't a damn warrior. Not anymore.

He cruised in above the Territory of the Games, over hundreds of multicolored sleds scattered on the tarmac thousands of feet below, and glided down to Facility A.

Why was he so edgy today? He didn't buy all this superstitious crap, did he? But he could feel the anxiety spreading throughout the Empire. He upped his Soothing as high as it would go, and as a Citizen of the Head, in total communion with the emperor, he felt twenty trillion Alpha Centaurians upping their own Soothing to the max.

*The Brooding Eagle* settled near a clutter of sleds, blasting up dust and forcing dozens of gladiators back. Hedrona Bhlon stepped out of Facility A. The harsh Cssarr sun glistened on her heartbreakingly tight black flight suit.

She was still alive. God, she was beautiful. Of course, everyone knew that. Twenty trillion Alpha Centaurians shared this moment, shared Phil's relief that she hadn't been killed. Then again, Phil would've known if she'd bought the farm. He was One with the Head, after all. He also knew that if Clopt ordered her death, Phil would dispatch her himself. And dammit, she had to know that.

But Clopt was a Zarj of his word. If it took Hedrona fifty years to finally convert, Phil was fine with that. Because she was his *Jkucll-Atkat-Hfucl*.

But until then, of course, as an Animal, Hedrona was sent to the Games.

*

Phil was so Soothed that he was surprised to find the emperor himself was only giving Partial Head that morning. Apparently he was indisposed, according to a Head Alert sent from the Grand Council, and in fact wouldn't be attending the event at all. Of course, the Crab Emperor hadn't visited Cssarr to see the Games in two years, so nobody was expecting a physical visit from the Imperial Flagship. But everyone thought he'd be in his usual Head Attendance.

Phil shook his head. It was just superstition to think anything could happen to their immortal emperor. Those prophecies were just wrong. They were all started by the traitor Polot. *He* was the one who invented Heuristic Time Travel and started the Empire on the path to destruction.

*No! Forget it! There's no destruction! There can't be!*

Phil couldn't get Polot out of his head. Polot, the first Alpha Centaurian to ever break free of the Grid. How was that even possible? Maybe inventing HTT had done that. Phil knew the human vessel that Polot had warped into and taken over, the obese Huey Vespertine, whose already shaky human personality had crumbled under the influence of the Jujl Polot's brilliance. And once the former AresNet commentator had fully become Polot back in '36, the Huey part had finally evaporated, as far as anyone could tell.

But somehow Polot's evasion of the Grid had caused a tiny but growing number of Alpha Centaurians scattered throughout the seventeen-sun AC Empire to likewise cease to be part of the Head.

All Alpha Centauri was shocked at each treasonous abandonment of the Sacred Head. It was easy enough for every AC, from the emperor on down, to instantly know who'd just dropped out. The offender was usually so terrified by his sudden total loss of Head that he was easily located and given ten seconds to kill himself. Which almost every Animal--for that's what they were called--instantly did, essentially by dying of shame on the spot.

A few resisted the order, but these Animals were usually so psychotic that they put up no serious resistance when AC troopers arrived brandishing pulsar tubes within minutes to *decontaminate* the entire area.

But unbelievably, a tiny percentage could *fake the Grid*. Like Polot in 2035, these newly created *individuals* somehow managed to transmit a fake "I'm here, I'm One with You" signal throughout the Grid even as they eagerly explored their blasphemous new freedom. Many went undetected for years until stronger Emperor Queries were developed and sent throughout the Grid to test and expose the false signals. Thousands of these Animals were discovered and executed until it was realized they could be put to a more intriguing use.

So starting in 2046, the Games took hold of the Centaurian imagination. Not only did they serve as punishment for the transgressor who'd committed the ultimate political, social, and religious apostasy, but they served to take the collective mind of all Alpha Centaurians off the looming date of May 14, 2053.

Damn, that was *today*. May 14th. What was so special about *today?* The Games, ending today? That was silly. They *needed* the Games. The whole Empire did. In fact, they needed more of these damn Animals going off the Grid so they could have even more Gladiators.

It was true they were getting more and more Gladiators all the time. What was happening to the Empire? Was it really breaking down? Were they really ripe for destruction? Had they been playing the Games too damn long? Were the energies of the Head too wrapped up in the Games to hold the Empire together and win any sort of war? Especially one everyone knew they were going to lose *today,* May 14, 2053?

*Oh my God! Twenty trillion of us didn't just think that, did we?*

\*

Hedrona gripped her gun mount, hovered her sled up a few feet and twirled it around. Spectators backed off as twelve thrusters blasted bright blue ion streams and Hedrona shot the sled up a sharp angle to five thousand feet. She hadn't even let Phil do the pre-flight. She hadn't even said hello.

Was he superstitious because of Hedrona? Was he jumpy because it was her last day? She'd survived all these years, but what if something happened on her last day?

But why should it be her last day? There was no last day for a Gladiator. Not until the day of death. The Games themselves would go on forever.

The crowd cheered. *Score! Score for Hedrona Bhlon!* twenty trillion Alpha Centaurians roared in Phil's mind.

Phil blinked. He'd entirely missed it. Two thousand feet up FalconBark-33334-881 was an expanding cloud of dark yellow blood and guts amid a careening sled.

This FalconBark-33334-881 had been a major Games contender the past few months, a Tarl who'd defected from the emperor's personal retinue and shown an amazing capacity for deception and cunning, along with impressive flying and shooting skills. Phil went into the Centaurian Archives for an instant replay. The son of a bitch had pounced on Hedrona before she'd hit six thousand feet, not exactly a rules violation but considered bad form for the opening match of a Game, especially combined with diving out of the sun.

All Alpha Centauri wanted to experience the replay along with Phil. Hedrona's spiraling twist from FalconBark-33334-881's cannon shells was magnificent to behold in slow motion. The Head swooned as she spun in a hundred directions at once, and all Alpha Centauri gasped in delight to see Hedrona wind up six feet behind FalconBark-33334-881's shoulder blades and pump in a hellish burst of cannon fire. Those two-inch wide explosive projectiles would bounce off the sleds themselves, but if they hit an organic object ... *yuck.*

FalconBark-33334-881's bloody sled fell, flipping end over end, then finally struck the ground and exploded, taking out several hundred Fkuuh spectators in the grandstands. Well, they were low-class barbarians. They wouldn't be missed. They always wanted the cheap tickets right below the action, thinking it was such a great view.

Hedrona glided in for a landing as two more Animals went up to duel, sleds thundering down the runway, blue ions blasting side by side. The Head confirmed that Hedrona would have fifteen more sorties today. Seventy-three Animals on the field today. By law they had to be whittled down to at most four before sunset. If there were more than four, as often happened, since not every duel resulted in a kill, the lowest scorers would just be tied to a post and shot to pieces by the highest scorer from a grounded sled. The ultimate disgrace.

Hedrona was always one of the survivors. How had she made it through four years of this insanity? How could she make it through this last day? *What* last day? What was this superstition about a last day?

In any case, sunset was a long way off. Since Cssarr had a seventy-four-hour day, each hour of a standard Earth day was over three hours here. Phil always set his watch to a standard twenty-four units, and just slowed them to match the 74:31:22 rotational period of this planet. So he could call a time in the morning "9 AM," and then, three hours later, it would finally be "10 AM."

But a morning's sledding was way more than a standard workday on Earth.

Hedrona sauntered over, pulling off her black gloves and flight cap, shaking free her long dark hair. "Well, look who showed on the last day," she mocked. "I'm surprised you're not on the *GnlSaljPraraq* saying bye-bye to Mr. Crab Guts."

Phil winced. "What are you *talking* about?"

She shrugged. "From what I hear, Crabby-poo is fatally

*indisposed* at the moment. That's what all the Gladiators are gabbling about."

Phil pulled in extra Soothing from the Grid, but there wasn't much of it for some reason. There was something *wobbly* he couldn't place.

Could it have to do with the fact that the emperor would *die* in a few minutes, at which time total chaos would permanently disrupt the Empire?

"N-no, I'm sure he's all right. I mean, really, the reason I'm here is that I was *concerned* for you." Phil tried to avoid staring at that glossy black flight suit. None of his lust for her had ever been slaked. He simply couldn't function around her. She refused to be part of the Head, scorning him for being One with the greatest bliss any sentient being could ever know. She was an Animal. And he loved her.

Hedrona shrugged. "I'm all right. I'm always all right."

Phil struggled to steady his mind, already overrevving from the ragged extra doses of Soothing and the disturbing sense that something was definitely out of kilter today if the emperor himself wasn't fully participating in the Games.

"Dammit, Hedrona, sooner or later your number's gonna be up, you do realize that, don't you?"

"Hell with it. I've made it this far. After today I'm home free."

"Home ... free? What do you mean?"

"What do you think I mean? Mr. Crab Guts buys the farm today, and the whole insanity *collapses!*"

"Col-lapses? I don't understand."

"Sheesh, Mr. Sperry. I forgot how brainwashed your little mind is."

"Well, it's not, not really. C'mon, Hedrona, this is hard for me. Today's really hard. I don't really know why. And I *do* worry about you, you know."

"Well, if you want to worry about anything, check the thruster matrix on my damn sled. I've only been hitting eighty-nine percent the past couple days."

"Eighty-nine?" Phil frowned. "Hedrona, you should have

called me the instant that started! God knows what could've happened with anything below ninety-seven!" He headed to the sled. Hedrona followed, which surprised him, since she usually just wanted to hit the john or grab something to drink before her next duel.

Phil opened his toolkit and unsnapped Service Compartment 1 on the sled's port side. Gladiators of the Sled were normally required to fly and self-service whatever machine was assigned to them on a given day, but as the highest scorer in Game history, Hedrona was allowed to have a personal sled, and so Phil always had the same machine to work on, to upgrade, and to trust. It was no longer just an anonymous piece of equipment strewn around the Territory of the Games, but, given Hedrona's exalted status, a Holy Artifact of the Empire. Hedrona's rank entitled her to choose her own mechanic, and so Clopt let Phil visit Cssarr once a week.

Which was another good reason to improve Warp Transfer survival past eighty-five percent. Phil sure couldn't do anything for Hedrona if he wound up in *Garr/thahg*. Didn't she know he put his life on the line every time he came here?

Then again, she put her life in *his* hands every time she flew. He wondered if she ever thought about that.

## CHAPTER EIGHT
### Hedrona's Sled

The *Seven of Cups* looked like any sled other except for the bright color scheme: the royal blue HEDRONA BHLON painted along the stern, and her personal blue, yellow, and red Tarot card across the top surface of the sled. The sled was a flat slab of metal seven feet wide, eleven feet long, but just six inches thick. The twelve thrusters, each a four-inch circle, were recessed into the aft panel. Likewise the two-inch maneuvering thrusters along the sides and top and bottom corners of the craft were flush with the surface to keep the aesthetic impression of a cold hard rectangle.

The interior of the slab consisted entirely of a HtkARR 658 Prime Antimatter engine, except for the volume required for a thousand rounds of two-inch explosive shells and a feeding mechanism up to the gun mount.

Phil looked away from the creepy image on the surface. She'd deliberately chosen that damn Tarot card to gall him. He should never have admitted it scared him. Did she really want to take advantage of any weakness she could find? The card was *human pollution,* just one more infiltration of the Centaurian system. It was killing them.

He had to calm down. Nothing was killing them, nothing was killing their dear emperor, all was well, didn't they all know that down deep?

No, *that* was the illusion. They were *dying.* The Tarot card was real and they knew it.

Phil couldn't stop the accelerating anxiety. Since all events throughout Alpha Centauri were instantly known by all citizens, as mediated by the wisdom of the emperor, the Alpha Centaurians had never worried or speculated about the future. But ever since the Martian Emperor Dar had broadcast relevant portions of his Amplified Thought proofs that the Empire would cease to exist on May 14, 2053, something evil had found its way into the Grid.

They'd never needed fortune-telling, but now it was

everywhere, imported from Sol. Tarot and I Ching and Ouija boards and God knew what else had all leaked in. Everyone was using it. They knew it was blasphemous, but they had to have *something* to combat Dar's goddamn astrology, didn't they? To combat *today,* May 14, 2053?

Phil was ashamed that each time he came to Cssarr he made Hedrona sit with him over his own Tarot deck. On every reading she insisted that the cards spelled doom on May 14, 2053, and Phil heatedly offered a counter-interpretation based on the same cards. But even as the *Alpha Centaurian citizen* knew perfectly well he was right, the human being still within him knew he was blowing smoke.

It was the Seven of Cups that came up, every time, whether Phil asked the Tarot about himself or the Empire. It was the Waite deck image, the man shocked to confront seven cups floating in the clouds, each holding a promise: love, sex, fame, riches, power, even mystical revelation. They were all so obviously *illusions.* And they annihilated Phil even as he wanted them so badly.

And Hedrona would laugh. As he shivered and babbled all his fears about the Seven of Cups, she'd cackle with delight. She'd painted the card on her sled to tell the entire Empire that Phil's whole life was an illusion. He was deluded, the Empire was deluded, and everything was *collapsing.*

Phil tore his gaze from the surface of the sled and probed inside Service Compartment 1 with his diagnostic monitor. "Look, the Postulation Matrix needs alignment. I can fix it. Shouldn't take long."

"Good, because I'm up in twenty minutes," Hedrona said, kneeling by him. Phil shivered at her proximity. "Thanks for checking, Phil."

"No problem," he said, moving for Service Compartment 2 on the starboard side. "Once I have Postulation aligned, I'll rebalance the Thruster Interface and then we'll check Hover Implementation. It's pretty close but not quite where we want it."

Unbelievably, she followed him to the starboard side and

again knelt. "Phil, seriously now, you *do* know what today means, don't you?"

"N-no … need to set this relay here." Phil focused on the oscillating Parameter Index. "Okay, 209 … 210 … 211. Okay, set."

She touched his arm. "*Phil.*"

"I'm okay, I'm okay. Really."

"Phil, the emperor's *dying* right now."

Phil jerked. "No, that's impossible! He's *immortal!* We've heard those rumors for years. Clopt says it's *human frailty* being imported here that's screwing everything up."

"Aw, screw Clopt! He's brainwashed, but *you* don't have to be! Not anymore!"

Phil looked away. Free Time had begun. Some young bulls who couldn't wait for their next Gladiation were taking their sleds up to gambol and target practice on their fellows. Between sets they were allowed to fly and maraud at will, and sometimes twenty would be up there at once. Usually three of four would be shot down and killed, but Free Time was considered a test of whatever passed for manliness in Alpha Centauri.

"Listen, how's your cannon?" Phil said. "Got a good feed? Because, well, since this *is* the last day and all, I don't want you taking any chances."

"See? So you *know* it's the last day. And you don't see what that *means* for you."

Phil shrugged. What was with her today? He climbed onto the sled and stuck his feet into the magno-stirrups so he could get a good feel for the mount as he swung it back and forth. Good play. He looked at the screen: 455 shells. "Dammit, Hedrona, were you gonna take this damn thing up with only 455 shells?"

"Relax, Phil, the armorer's on his way now." She pointed to a seven-foot Jujl driving a tractor full of cannon shells on long belts. Phil was relieved to see it was the humanoid kAqNNOTk. Despite being fully part of the Head, Phil still retained an aversion to non-humanoid species, and the Jujl, who most closely resembled humans, were easy to be around. And kAqNNOTk was a reliable weapons expert. He and Phil had often spoken via translator of their puzzlement that Animals could even exist and whether they enjoyed Gladiation.

"Greetings in the name of the Head," Phil said as kAqNNOTk began loading Hedrona's fresh batch of shells.

"Greetings in the name of our Immortal Emperor," kAqNNOTk replied. They shared an uneasy Head Communion that the dismembered Crab Emperor was currently writhing in his little glass box after he'd accidentally used an extensible waldo to open a portable nuclear reactor.

*Never assume a reactor is off and flushed clean,* Phil transmitted, bypassing the translator.

*Indeed,* kAqNNOTk transmitted back as he finished the last belt. *Surely he will recover. The rumors must be false.*

Phil just nodded as kAqNNOTk drove off in his tractor, waving goodbye. He'd picked up that human gesture from Phil.

Phil felt sick and dizzy. He pulled up the English language interface on the gun panel and ran a fast diagnostic to confirm that one thousand shells were slotted into position. He revved the hover thrusters and tried to decide if the balance was right. The readout said it was, but there was a certain feel to a sled that had to be experienced. His gut told him something was wrong.

Phil looked up at the Animals dive-bombing each other and firing wild bursts. He goosed the hovers and the sled rose several feet as he stood at the gun mount.

"Gonna test the Interface Alignment!" Phil called down.

"Are you sure?" Hedrona said. "My set's in fifteen minutes!"

"I only need a couple minutes to see." Phil initiated the magno stirrups and felt his feet sucked in. He grabbed the gun grips. The sled was level, the hover thrusters compensating for wind currents and whatever weight shifts Phil made. He spun the sled in a circle. Perfect. He'd often maligned Alpha Centaurian engineers and spaceship designers for the ugly, unstable, malfunctioning stuff they came up with, but the Gladiator Sled was a true work of art. All that marred its clean slab aesthetics were the gun mount four feet back from the front of the slab, and the magno stirrups designed in this case for human feet.

It was always a rush to fly one of these things. They could do a thousand miles per hour, but a rider simply couldn't hang on at that speed, so most contests involved speeds of between a hundred and two hundred miles per hour, with the wind flow usually incapacitating you anyway. A few of the Centaurian species could withstand higher speeds, and the opposing pilot had to compensate by being especially maneuverable, as Hedrona was.

"Wait! Phil!" Hedrona cried.

"What?" he called back.

"Be *careful,* Phil!"

Phil shrugged. What was she talking about? Those crazed Animals up there? They wouldn't dare mess with the Head. None of those young bucks, so eager to blast each other down in Free Time, would ever challenge a Head, and if one did, he'd know he was committing suicide. The sleds were so programmed that if a Gladiator ever decided to draw a bead on a Head, say a visiting dignitary watching the Games, the cannon shells simply wouldn't fire. And while Animal fire was a game of skill and marksmanship, Head fire was computer-assisted. Certain royal personages often used sleds to hunt the AC equivalent of foxes or boars. Some even participated in the Games themselves, though the shooting matches were so fast and uneven that everyone got bored, including the flying royalty themselves.

"No! You *can't* go!" Hedrona cried. "You fool! It's the *last day!*"

Phil gripped the gun mount and throttle assembly. He hovered the nose of the *Seven of Cups* higher, then cut in all twelve rear thrusters. In seconds he was several thousand feet up, straining to hold onto the grips, his feet securely sucked into the magno stirrups.

Yeah, this baby *was* in great shape after all. The readout confirmed one hundred percent on all thrusters. The alignment was perfect. What had he been so worried about?

Phil rolled and dived and climbed, exuberantly testing every capability of the *Seven of Cups*. Nothing was going to mess up her last day.

Her last day? Last day of what? Of being a Gladiator of the Sled? What did *that* mean? Was she somehow *not* going to be a Gladiator after today? Why? How?

Phil was up among the swashbucklers now. One had a mirror-finish job and was pouncing on another sled, blasting off a hundred shells in wild shots from too far away, clanging them off the older corrugated sled desperately whirling to shield its rider.

But this poor rider now experienced the unfortunate software glitch known as *magno clamp failure.* His five feet swirled free as his sled flew upside down, his four arms frantically clinging to his own gun mount. The sled slowed and twirled, exposing its flailing rider, one of the Cjathpur species with the buried head and pulsating exoskeleton that always made Phil want to vomit, to the shells of Mr. Mirror, who quickly closed the gap, firing another fifty cannon shells right into the small of the Cjathpur's back, blue-green pus bursting everywhere.

Phil watched the guts-filthy sled whip into the crowd below. Thank God not near Hedrona.

Now Mr. Mirror swung around and made directly for him. Phil wondered what passed for testosterone among these damn Animals.

Phil was up to 155 and his radar said Mr. Mirror, a former Zarj trooper who should know better, was moving at 356 miles per hour, thus giving a combined closing speed of 511. Did the idiot really not know he was challenging the Head? Phil could fire way off to his right, and his gun would auto-correct and send just one cannon shell straight into the broad stupid forehead of Mr. Mirror, who up to that point would undoubtedly have been pondering why his own firing mechanism seemed "stuck."

Too bad. You really couldn't feel anything for an Animal, of course. Phil had shot down his share of them during various test runs. Sure, it was unfair, but the sleds needed to be tested, and he was an Engineer of the Head, after all. He'd practiced every maneuver just to be sure he knew the sled's capabilities.

He'd even fancied he could've been a real Gladiator with no safeguards, but as an Engineer of the Head, he didn't have that choice.

So why was he feeling sick about having to take a life for no reason? He was just doing his duty to the emperor, after all.

Except that there was no emperor. The emperor had just died of radiation poisoning. A freak accident. He should have lived another thousand years.

The Empire was in chaos.

The New Emperor shone forth.

*Dar.* Of course. The Martian had come to be their New Emperor. Thank God.

EMPEROR DAR OF ALPHA CENTAURI ISSUES HIS FIRST COMMAND TO THE SUBJECTS OF THE ALPHA CENTAURIAN RACES VIA THE HEAD. LISTEN WELL. THE HEAD IS DEAD. I, EMPEROR DAR, OFFICIALLY DISMANTLE THE GRID FOR ALL TIME. THE SOFTWARE IS PERMANENTLY DESTROYED. ALL AC SUBJECTS ARE HEREBY DECLARED TO BE INDIVIDUALS. THE GRID IS GONE, REPEAT THE GRID IS GONE.

AND NOW I, DAR, EMPEROR OF ALPHA CENTAURI, USING THE LAST WANING ENERGY OF THE HEAD, DO OFFICIALLY ABDICATE MY THRONE AND RETURN TO MY OWN TIME. THERE IS NO EMPEROR. THERE IS NO GRID. THERE IS NO EMPIRE.

Phil grabbed his gun grips in shock. His stomach felt ripped out of him. His heart went to ten thousand beats per minute.

And in front of him orange lights were winking, winking, winking.

Shells all around, tunnels of *force* carving through the sky and banging into his sled. One hit the gun mount and blew orange in his face.

The mirrored Zarj closed at 511 miles per hour and shot right over him, Phil's readout helpfully adding that it missed the top of his head by 4.56 inches.

He hadn't even had time to fire back.

The least of his worries was that the gun mount blast had

burned off his left sleeve and the frigid wind was ripping away the rest of his tunic. Idiot that he was, he hadn't worn a standard gladiator suit, just his work clothes.

Phil jerked the sled around and saw Mr. Mirror coming in for another pass.

And he could hear the shrieks of despair from the spectators below, from everywhere, from his own mouth as well, as the Grid collapsed and they were all alone forever.

# CHAPTER NINE
## But What Does That Mean to Animals?

More orange winked from another sled closing in head-on. Phil wrenched around the stiff, creaking gun mount and pressed the trigger. Two shells shot out. WHUMFF … WHUMFF

Then: *cruk cruk cruk cruk*

"Son of a bitch!" That first hit had bent something in the mount. He slid the clearing bolt back and forth and jerked the trigger.

Nothing.

He racked it furiously. Fired.

WHUMFF … WHUMFF … WHUMFF WHUMFF WHUMFF WHUMFF

*Cruk cruk cruk cruk*

"Dammit to hell!" Phil slammed the clearing bolt. But the sled ahead was tumbling end over end as its helmeted Zarj rider slid off in a cloud of blue-purple plasma.

Phil had hit the mother, but now the Zarj's sled was going to do the same to him. He pushed down hard and to port on the mount. Somehow the whirling mass whistled past, with Phil's readout inexplicably going to voice mode to add: "CLEARANCE 4 FEET, 2.56 INCHES."

A shell clanged off the sled a few inches from his right foot. Phil hurled the *Seven of Cups* to the right and circled, catching sight of a Culstati wearing the bright chartreuse Priesthood Order of Culst and sending shells his way.

A Zarj got behind the Culstati and fired, but the Culstati twisted free. Several more sleds zoomed in on both Phil and the Culstati. Before long ten sleds were whirling around him.

*C'mon, man, get steady! What the hell's going on?*

There was no answer. There was no Head. Phil struggled to connect, but there was nothing to connect to. He was *cut off*. Because he was a traitor? Was that why everyone was shooting at him? Did that mean the emperor was really still alive and all that stuff about Dar was just Phil hallucinating *treason*?

But he became aware of wispy aspects of Head evaporating

around him, thin cirrus Head clouds drying out to leave the sky a cold merciless blue. These fragmentary strands of information transmitted unbelievable, obscene tales to the entire Empire. Something about the emperor, even knowing his doom was foreordained, opening a portable nuclear reactor that was making an irritating whine. And surviving for twenty minutes, during which time he refused to appoint a successor, and had anyone executed who thought to grab his throne. *He'd* caused all this chaos.

*That damn stubborn fool! That nasty box of crab guts!*

Damn, Phil had just thought that about the *emperor*. And somehow hadn't been killed for it.

Five shells struck the rear of his sled, and one exploded instead of spanging off into the void. Phil looked at his readout. Thruster nine on the starboard side had taken a shell right up its ass. He marveled that the whole sled didn't blow right there, but it was entirely possible for the wild antimatter energy of the thruster to absorb the explosion and just punch it back out as further thrust. Nine had done so in this case, although it was now shutting down along with Thrusters Ten through Twelve, and the *Seven of Cups* was dangerously unbalanced.

The sleds were designed so that unless a shell managed to hit at almost a perfect ninety degrees, it would just strike the metal with a tremendous boom and skip off the surface, which was so slick that stepping on it was like sliding across an inch-thick expanse of ice. This was so spectators wouldn't see easy victories of exploding sleds, but more marksmanship-focused displays of sending cannon fire into the victim's body, where the shell *would* explode.

However, at least once a day a lucky shell would hit just right. It might just destabilize the sled, gyrating it into a crazy downward spiral, its rider helpless to do anything but hold the handgrips and watch the ground coming for him. Or, more commonly, it would blow the antimatter unit in a five-hundred-foot fireball.

Phil tugged the sled into the whirling circle of Animals, all of whom seemed absolutely delighted that the Grid was gone.

They were blasting each other down, blazing away at him, wild with life force and freedom and bloodlust.

And if he wanted to live, Phil was going to have to shoot down every one of those sons of bitches. He took aim at the brown-scaled pterodactyl head of a Tarl.

*Cruk cruk cruk cruk*

He slammed the clearing bolt.

WHUMFF WHUMFF WHUMFF *cruk cruk cruk cruk*

*Got him anyway!*

The Tarl's body pieces filled the air, a few clunking into the sled as Phil shot through his victim's ochre gore mist.

He was freezing. He was five thousand feet up and his tunic was gone. He registered the blood streaming along his left arm and realized he'd been grazed by that first shot on the gun mount.

SPANG SPANG SPANG! came the shells behind him. He twisted the throttle grip, much like one on an ancient motorcycle he'd rebuilt back in the twenties in Baltimore, and shot up to 250, 275, but he was veering to starboard, the unbalanced sled was sluggish, and his readout was signaling antimatter contamination.

Not good at all. Phil had anywhere from a couple seconds to ten minutes before the sled blew. The *Seven of Cups* dropped like a brick.

"TOP POSSIBLE SPEED 176 MILES PER HOUR," his readout croaked. "153 … 144."

The sled behind caught up to him and this time the shells hissed past his shoulders. He twisted to port but this just put the *Seven of Cups* into a fast plummeting spin.

Phil looked back at the madly revolving sky. Some damn Jujl was following him in a power dive, sending shell after shell. From Phil's perspective the Jujl was whirling crazily around the periphery of his vision, his orange blasts circling round and round.

A black thing twirled behind the Jujl. At first Phil thought the Jujl's helmet had fallen off, but it was another sled behind them both, ripping out a wide spread of shells.

Phil returned his attention to fighting his spin, hitting the throttle to take advantage of the fact that his unbalanced engines would now naturally spin him to starboard. Somehow he straightened out, but was he just presenting a more stable target?

*Yeah, but somebody just nailed the son of a bitch for me!*

The Jujl's sled blew magnificently. Phil felt the heat on his back, welcoming it, since his hands were nearly done in with frostbite and he'd been shivering uncontrollably all this time.

Phil managed to pull from the dive. He was two thousand feet up, amid a dense swarm of homicidal riders.

"MAXIMUM POSSIBLE SPEED 89.2 MPH," proclaimed his readout, then: "WARNING: ANTIMATTER DRIVE UNSTABLE. PRESSURE OVERRIDE RELIEF FAIL. ABORT."

"Abort *where,* you idiot?" Phil twisted to see the means of his death, the other sled behind that had killed his pursuer. It was some tiny black hunched spider creature behind a gun mount only a foot and a half high.

The sled sailed up next to him and Hedrona Bhlon, squatting cross-legged behind a mount designed for an eight-legged Gjuulkw, called over: "I'm magnetizing with you! Get ready to jump over!"

"What? Are you *crazy?*"

"You're trailing all sorts of radwaste! You're about to blow!"

"That's--that's--" he sputtered, cocking his ear at a mounting whine from the rear of the sled.

"ANTIMATTER EXPLOSION IMMINENT."

"Okay!" Phil cried as she maneuvered her sled to his, aligned her port side atop his starboard, then clanged the two together in a fierce magnetic union. Magnetizing was rarely employed, usually in the case of a hunter having run out of shells and desiring to cement his heroic exploits by surprising his opponent with an unexpected magnetization from the rear, knifing his victim to death, jumping back on his own sled and unlatching. A successful Knife Victory meant unsurpassed glory and status.

The only Gladiator of the Sled he'd ever seen pull this off

was Hedrona Bhlon, against a Zarj three times her size. And she'd still had four hundred shells on board the *Seven of Cups.*

Of course, he'd seen several knifings fail on that ice-slick surface. One hapless Fkuuh had jumped a Tarl sled only to slide right off, flailing spastically all six thousand feet down while ten thousand spectators *laughed.*

Hedrona held out her gloved hand, still several feet away. Phil glanced at his own readout showing fifty-three miles per hour. He looked back at ten machines zooming up behind the slow mated sleds. Phil knew each desired the honor of blasting two humans at once. Yes, they all hated human beings, even as they revered Top Gladiator Hedrona Bhlon.

Phil scrambled across his sled and went skidding, banged into the six-inch side of her sled, scrabbled up, slipped more, felt her hands on his back, and slid to the stern where he felt a shell bounce off the sled four inches from his thigh. He finally grabbed one of the Gjuulkw magno stirrups. Hedrona hauled him up beside her.

"Sit cross-legged, like me!" she yelled. "Behind me! Get your feet in those two there. Now get your hands in *those* two, and lean forward!"

"Why?" he gasped as he followed her orders, wrapped around her back and feeling all four appendages firmly sucked into the sled stirrups, knowing what she was about to do.

She jettisoned the ailing *Seven of Cups* and Phil felt the Gjuulkw sled kick in. He glanced over Hedrona's shoulder to the readout: 350 miles per hour. The wind tore at them. Phil could barely drag his mouth back closed.

Hedrona swung the sled around and he saw the group behind them encounter the whirling *Seven of Cups* as it blew into its own fireball.

Only three sleds remained. One, piloted by yet another green Culstati priest, accelerated so fast to keep up that its rider lost hold of his grips and spun out of control, the Culstati hanging with his three feet in his stirrups.

Hedrona put him out of his misery with four shots, then, still crouched behind the eighteen-inch-high gun mount with Phil crammed behind her, she dueled briefly with a Zarj before splitting him apart in a power dive straight into his gunfire. Then she blasted the final Scihk with a merciless volley that dismounted the crab and blew up his sled.

Phil stared. That had been a crab, a Scihk just like their beloved emperor, so easily detonated into raw gore. "Dammit!" he grunted, dizzy with G-forces he hadn't undergone since USSF training centrifuges. "How do you *do* that?"

Hedrona laughed. "Just practice, Mr. Phil. It does help if you're fighting for your life instead of just *testing* the damn sled."

Was she snuggling her back into him? What for?

"How did you get this sled?"

She shrugged. She *was* undulating into his bare chest. She was *warm*. "Had a talk with a Gjuulkw, told him I needed it to save you. He said something like 'Human go *plukkzm!*' Which pissed me off, so I strangled the twit, and here I am."

"God!" Phil stared at the deep pthalo-green stains of Gjuulkw blood along her forearms. Gjuulkw were small, but their eight legs each had claws up and down their lengths. How had she maneuvered between them?

"Aren't you even going to thank me?" Hedrona said as she swung the Gjuulkw sled to circle above thousands of Alpha Centaurians staring at the lone survivor of the aerial combat.

"Well, yes! Thanks! But what about *them?*" Phil pointed.

Hedrona brought the craft down into their midst and shut down the magno clamps. "Are you so scared of a crowd of deconverted AC?" Phil scooted off the craft and warily stood up, surrounded by *the enemy*. He was human, no longer part of the Grid. They'd kill him as well as Hedrona.

But the ACs weren't part of the Grid either.

Thousands of them. They had no idea what to do. They'd watched the combat above simply because they literally had nothing better to do.

Hedrona threw her arms around him. "You're quite sexy today without your shirt! Even if you are all covered with nasty Tarl." She flicked off some gory chunks and squeezed his pecs.

"Oh, God, Hedrona, I don't know what's going on!" Phil scanned the ocean of Alpha Centaurians staring at him and Hedrona as if they could provide a clue about *what to do next,* in the absence of Grid, of Soul, of Mind. They were all Animals now.

"You know I love you, Phil!" Hedrona cried, tiptoeing to kiss him. "I'm so happy you're back! And safe with me!"

"I--I'm *back?*"

"Yes, you're back! Everything's all right now!"

"R-really?"

"Really! I love you, Phil! I really love you!"

He knew he should say the same thing back, but he couldn't. She *loved* him. But what did that mean to Animals?

# CHAPTER TEN
## Information Wisps

Hedrona strode through the spaceport as if she owned the entire hundred-mile-long Imperial battle cruiser. Phil kept pace as best he could. He could barely remember piloting the *Brooding Eagle* through a hairy Warp Transfer to the *N8J'rallifh-hhu42jdnh,* Clopt's near-infinite flagship.

What in God's name had Phil been doing here for four years? Heading Clopt's team? Getting ready for their HTT invasion of Sol? An invasion they were supposed to win?

Now Phil knew why nothing ever seemed to come of their plans. Why he'd spent four years studying the incomprehensible manuals, straining to integrate a billion disparate strands of AC engineering through the Head, but had never felt an impulse to action. Because deep down he'd known it had been doomed to fail.

The spaceport at the bow of the *N8J'rallifh-hhu42jdnh* was five miles long, four miles wide and four high, with hundreds of levels of ship runways and service facilities. Ships were coming in, passengers both civilian and military debarking, and there was still immense activity all around them.

But it was all performed in despair. Everyone was mechanical, deflated, cut off from the Source. The only thing keeping them going was the preposterous hope that the news wasn't true, that this was all some temporary systemwide Head Software Glitch and that access would soon be restored. Phil could sense tantalizing wisps of Post-Head information in the air, a million times less intense than the former Head: fantastic, fading afterimages of the defunct Empire-wide Union.

Many of these information wisps seemed to concern the fact that Hedrona Bhlon, Foremost Gladiator of the Sled, had come to the *N8J'rallifh-hhu42jdnh* to claim the Infant Hostage Jonathan James Commer.

Phil felt the blunted and damaged survivors of the Head sharing a new wisp: that while Polot of Zorex had traitorously laid the groundwork for the Rise of the Animals, it was Hedrona

Bhlon, the Foremost Animal Gladiator, who'd nurtured the rising zeal for Separation. Her sensational exploits had inspired a growing number of Alpha Centaurian citizens to consider the possibility of Separation from the Emperor and the Grid, thus making possible the Martian Dar's underhanded ploy in destroying it today.

Hedrona ignored the corpses sprawled across the floor or slumped over railings, blood streaming in dozens of colors everywhere. Suicides by knife and laser gun, or bodies hurled from the levels above, cries of anguish cut short by the bursting of viscera on metal runways. Sometimes a few moments of life left, dying Centaurians sighing with relief at reaching the end of unbearable Separation.

Phil hardly dared look at Hedrona for fear she'd understand how badly he wanted to join these defeated souls. Why had she ordered that Gladiator doctor to attend to his bleeding arm? Why had she insisted he exchange his ripped pants for a warm black Gladiator suit? So that the Phil creature might survive? Why would it want to? Why would she want that? Anyone could see he was useless without the Head.

His torn arm seethed. But what was that compared with Separation?

Hedrona halted in front of an information kiosk. "What the hell does this stuff mean, Phil? Where's the damn nursery?"

Phil gazed at the shifting swarms of symbols on the five-by-ten-foot display. Four years of immersion in the Head had taught him little Standard Centaurian. Mostly he navigated via the ubiquitous translators and, of course, the Head. The translators still worked but they were notoriously bad at visual symbols. "Well, maybe we could ask someone?"

Hedrona snapped her fingers at a hulking Zarj trooper trying to sneak past them. "Hey! You! Where's the Commer Nursery?"

Earlier this morning that same Zarj would have calmly pulled his pulsar tube and blazed them to mini-neutron stars. Now he dropped his head and turned his whirlpool eyes away.

"Dammit! I asked you a question!"

"Madame … Your Highness … Grace … Excellency, uh,

most excellent, that is, Supreme Goddess, ma'am ..." the trooper stammered. Some of that was the translator trying to figure out what subservient flatterings a Gridless Warrior should employ when dealing with the Foremost Gladiator of the Sled. But most was terror in the face of anyone exhibiting the slightest sense of purpose.

"Jeez ..." Hedrona muttered. She probably wasn't fully aware of just how famous she was. Phil had known it all along through the Head, but somehow that was just another piece of information. Now he saw it from the standpoint of a truly lost Centaurian. He could barely stand on his own now. And like these helpless Centaurians, he needed a heroine. Someone to look up to. Someone to worship. *Hedrona Bhlon.*

But that was nothing new. He'd always worshipped her.

Hedrona tapped the information display. "Okay, Mr. Trooper. Where's Jonathan James Commer?"

"Madame ... Goddess Excellency! Please do not harm me!"

"I'm *not* going to harm you, idiot! Where the hell's the nursery?"

"It ... most Excellent ... the display will not tell you, uh, of secret ... state secret. I once knew exactly, but ... the Grid! The emperor! Oh, *plellsukkcj!* I am *cut off!*"

And he raised his pulsar tube and blasted off his head.

"Sheesh," Hedrona spat, marching past the body noisily spewing purple gore across the metal floor. "So he's saying it wouldn't be on the display. Well, that makes sense. How about you, Phil? Did you once know, and you've forgotten it too?"

"Y-yes ... but I think it's midship, somewhere."

"Try to think, Phil! We need to find him before something happens to him."

"I--I'm trying to gather some of these *scraps.*"

"Scraps? What are you talking about?"

"Scraps of *information.* Some of the Grid. Little bit of it left, you know."

"Oh, those. I can feel them too. What a bunch of crap!"

"You? You can *feel* them?"

"Sure. I've always felt this Head stuff prowling around. I

just never succumbed to it, that's all." She thought a second. "He's safe. I know it. What about the top levels, midship?"

"I … I'm getting that, too, I think." Phil looked away in shame. So she did know about the Head. She could've fully participated in it any time these past four years. But she was strong and resisted it, no matter how often he'd tried to seduce her.

Whereas Phil had succumbed one hundred percent within seconds of being exposed to Clopt and the Head four years ago. And what about Jonathan James? Phil had been allowed to see him a few times the first couple years after conversion. He remembered communing with JJC's toddler mind via the Head, and though the deep human part of Phil knew that such captivity in alien hands would've driven a normal baby insane, JJC had seemed to be coming through it all nicely, since, like Phil, he was fully converted. His bodily needs were taken care of, and as for his soul, well, it was safely in the hands of the emperor.

Phil hadn't seen the child in two years. He'd never protested because he hadn't even been able to think about JJC again until now. It had to be some sort of software prohibition. He hadn't thought the Grid capable of that, but evidently Clopt knew how to cut JJC out of Phil's memory. No wonder he couldn't remember the way.

If Phil was inwardly screaming at the loss of all Connection throughout the Empire, what was Jonathan James feeling right now? Like Hedrona, Phil knew from the information wisps that JJC was safe, somewhere midship and on one of the top levels, and he vaguely recalled the corridors where he'd last seen him. But "midship, top levels" meant two thousand cubic miles to search.

"You there! Whereabouts of Jonathan James Commer, the human hostage!" Hedrona barked at every AC she saw. The Zarj and Tarl guards, the most military of all ACs, by now fully cemented into their despair, let them roam as they pleased. Several killed themselves upon seeing Hedrona, the most vicious Animal Alpha Centauri had ever known. Others fawned over the Gladiator and offered what little they knew, and

Hedrona and Phil continued to use these hints along with the ever-fading wisps to navigate towards the nursery.

Hedrona marched, her Gladiator boots clomping on the multicolored plastimetal tiles of the infinite corridors, while Phil drifted across them like a cloud of buzzing, disconnected anxieties, hardly aware he had legs. He was disembodied. He was nothing.

Yet behind the *nothing* Phil knew there were mountains upon mountains of impassible shame cutting him off from the human race. He couldn't even let himself know these mountains were there, but he felt their cruel heights and their mocking masses. And he was beginning to suspect that loss of the Emperor's Grid was nowhere as bad as being cut off from the human race he'd so thoroughly betrayed.

Why did she let him walk next to her? He was just a ghost.

These shuffling AC creatures were just like him, pathetic remnants of their former selves. *Soldier wisps.* They were like billionaires and royalty reduced to street urchins. But unlike street urchins, they were incapable of functioning on their own. Only a handful seemed to be able to do so, and an information wisp confirmed Phil's suspicion that these were either liberated Animals from the Games or, much more numerous, a growing number of AC citizens who'd been on the verge of Disconnecting anyway.

Phil could sense these Animals. They walked straighter, and, not that Phil had ever seen any AC species smile, they did seem to wink knowingly at Hedrona.

They didn't wink at him. He was too crippled. Of course they knew him from the Grid. After all, he'd been Hedrona Bhlon's lover. It was he who fondled that Animal body and drew her nude torso atop his, entranced by those pear-shaped breasts and stiff brown nipples dangling before his lips as she lowered herself onto him, it was he who thrust into her and brought her to orgasm again and again and again, hundreds of times over the past four years.

And to no avail. Never any success. Phil was never able to convert her. Not even at the moment of her orgasm. Certainly not at the moment of his own.

He hazarded his life in his weekly Warp Transfer to Cssarr, but was it really to service her sled? No, that was just an excuse. He'd watch her soar and shoot and kill and win, then he'd drag her to her dim apartment for his rightful *Jkucll-Atkat-Hfucl,* banging her for hours, his sexuality mindlessly enhanced by the Head, ramming her into a stupor, every time knowing he was taking Hedrona Bhlon as high as she could go, making her *explode,* and *now* she would convert, *now* she would join them all, all twenty trillion Alpha Centaurians of the Head merged in glorious, intimate lovemaking, all anticipating the surging transcendence of Hedrona's Inclusion.

And then, *nothing.* Each time it would *not happen.* Hedrona would emerge from combat panting and sweating, dreamily nuzzling against his thigh, but still herself. Never becoming One.

And all Alpha Centauri, everyone from the emperor on down, knew the Animal had won again. They knew that the Foremost Gladiator of the Sled could never be defeated even as she lost herself in writhing ecstasy. Phil's failure was all Alpha Centauri's.

What could he do but soldier on, as both Engineer to Clopt and Mate to Hedrona Bhlon? After each disappointment he'd implore her for more sex, but she'd laugh, say she needed rest, and remind him that Clopt needed him back on the *N8J'rallifh-hhu42jdnh* for what she called *his nasty duties to the Empire.*

And here they were on the afternoon of May 14, 2053. Somehow they'd escaped Cssarr, journeyed to the *N8J'rallifh-hhu42jdnh,* and were working their way through its bright corridors like some old married couple on their way to sign real estate papers. What was she doing with him now? Why did she stick with him?

When they finally came to the Commer Nursery, Level 89, Sector 29 Starboard, the Zarj guards immediately let them in. Even these sullen, warped troopers knew that Phil Sperry had failed to bring Hedrona Bhlon to the ultimate climax. Along with twenty trillion other Alpha Centaurians they knew it was Phil Sperry who'd paved the way for the dissolution of the Empire.

# CHAPTER ELEVEN
## The Stellar Nursery

Hedrona's eyes adjusted to a dim room with a window to a sunny playground filled with jungle gyms, teeter-totters, and swings. And trees from Earth. How could this be? Phil had told her they'd built a special section for JJC, but this was astounding.

More information scraps presented themselves to her.

*Oh right, because I'm the damn Gladiator! Even the scraps have to bow to me!*

The wisps coalesced into the concept that a network of fifty chambers was devoted to the upbringing of Jack Commer's son. In order to keep the infant Jonathan James as a hostage, Clopt had ordered hundreds of Jujl bureaucrats to create as nurturing an environment as possible. HTT spy missions were sent to different time periods in Sol, and even though ninety-five percent of the attempts killed the spy, the successful ones brought back enough information to create this bizarre caricature of a human nursery.

"Hello, Ms. Hedrona Bhlon! Hello, Mr. Phil Sperry!" came a tiny child voice. "I see the emperor is dead and we have him no more!"

Hedrona stared at the boy. The eleven-month infant she remembered was barely discernible in this buoyant five-year-old. Jonathan James had dark, long black hair parted on the left and neatly combed over. He looked compact and muscular like his uncle Joe Commer, and wore a bright blue jumpsuit.

"You can *talk?*" Phil said. "You remember us?"

"Of course I remember you! I remember everything!"

"Of course he can talk, silly," Hedrona said. "He's five now."

"Yes. but I mean, so *well!*"

"Well, apparently he's had the equivalent of twenty trillion teachers. I bet you know everything, Jonathan."

JJC nodded. "But I *don't* know what we're going to do next. Do you? Are we going to leave this place now?"

"Yes, I think we should leave now!" came a high male voice from the shadows. "We definitely need to be away from the Centaurian military forces. God knows what they might try at this point! Hello, Mr. Phil Sperry and Ms. Hedrona Bhlon! We can use your ship, I presume?"

"Oh my God!" Phil cried as the figure, also clad in a blue jumpsuit, emerged from the darkness. "This can't be!" He staggered and Hedrona caught him.

"Who--" she began.

"*John Commer!* It *can't* be him!"

Hedrona stared. She knew about the two Commer brothers, Jim and John, who'd died on Mercury. What was Phil thinking?

"There's no problem, Mr. Phil Sperry and Ms. Hedrona Bhlon," JJC said. "This is my friend John Root."

"Allow me to introduce myself!" the man said, striding forward.

"No, *please* ..." Phil gasped, ducking behind Hedrona.

"Goddammit, Phil, stop whimpering like a goddamn cringing Zarj!" Hedrona snapped, yanking him upright.

John Root extended a hand to Hedrona. She took it. His fingers were frigid. "Pleased to meet you!" he said. "Pleased to meet *everyone!*"

"Oh, God, it's *him!*" Phil moaned. "John Commer! But he's *dead!*"

"Yes, I imagine it's quite a shock, Mr. Phil Sperry," John Root went on. "Since you managed to skip over the years 2038 to 2049, you never experienced the bestselling robotic series, *Heroes and Villains of the Thirties.*"

"You're some goddamn *clone?* This is some crazy *joke?*"

"No, I'm no clone! Clones are so biologically *messy! Nasty* things! I'm a *robot!* Can you believe it? Because sometimes even *I* can't believe it! But everything anybody ever possibly knew about Lieutenant John Commer has been downloaded into *me!* What do you think of *that?*"

"Oh my God," Hedrona whispered, beginning to understand why Phil was so dismayed by the short, cute robot.

"Ms. Hedrona Bhlon and Mr. Phil Sperry don't know about

*John Root!*" JJC exclaimed. "That's why they're panicking, John Root, Mr. Phil in particular."

"*I'm not panicking!*" Phil screamed.

"It's all right, Phil," Hedrona said. "He obviously *is* a robot, and we just need to *see* that."

Phil shook his head. "John *Root?*"

"That's my name, all right. *Heroes and Villains of the Thirties* was really quite successful. I'm a '43 model myself. Over sixty million robots were sold between '42 and the time I was taken in '46. Of course Jack Commer was the biggest seller, but his brothers did well, quite well!"

"No! You destroyed the *Typhoon I!* You *suicided* it on Mercury! You disobeyed Jack's orders! How can you be *here?*"

JJC poked Phil's forearm. "Surely you understand that John Root is a robot? Surely that information has been available to you through the Grid?"

"Well, *no!* It was *kept* from me! Just like thinking about *you!* There's been some sort of *software block!* How can that be? Am I crazy? I was fully part of the Grid and never knew *any* of this?"

"Calm down, Mr. Phil," JJC said. "Surely there's a rational explanation."

"A *robot* ..."

"Well, I have to say I've never seen one as good as this," Hedrona said.

"Yessiree bob!" John Root chortled. "There were some amazingly lifelike ones in your time in Sol, I suppose, but there were some real breakthroughs after '38. And before you knew it the price came down and there were all sorts of collector's series. Like *Starlets of the 1970s* and *Viking Berserkers in Olde England.* But RoboticsMindPump was very proud of *Heroes and Villains of the Thirties.* The John Robot sold reasonably well, as I understand it. Women were quite fond of him!"

"Clopt got him for me!" JJC said.

"Yes, Clopt thought young Jonathan required some human assistance. And he didn't quite think you were up to the task, Mr. Phil Sperry."

"And he never *told* me?" Phil said.

John Root shrugged. "Apparently not, I see!"

"He put some software block on the Grid! Aimed at *me!* That son of a bitch!"

"I'm named for John Root!" JJC said. "For Uncle John! And for Uncle Jim too! They both died on Mercury!"

"I am called the John Robot," John Root said, "but JJC had trouble pronouncing *robot* at first and so I became *root,* or John Root!"

Phil found a chair and sank into it, dazed. "Why the hell would he choose a robot based on John Commer's *stupid personality?*" He turned to Hedrona. "Look, I know the guy's dead, but that bastard always irritated all of us 24/7, just nattering on about anything that came into his idiot head! And that stupid laugh! No wonder Clopt didn't want me to know! He couldn't get a *sane* Commer!"

"So there were really others?" Hedrona said. "Jack and Joe and all the rest?"

"And General Scott, and Dar, and Churchill! The whole crew!" said John Root. "We were really quite affordable by the mid-forties. Some people would buy ten or more and enact great scenes of the war. There was even a Phil Sperry model, but it didn't sell *at all* and was discontinued!"

"A Phil Sperry robot!" Hedrona laughed. "I'd like one!"

"Oh, God," Phil muttered. "I think I *am* one."

Hedrona whirled. "Dammit, will you straighten up! I can't believe you! You have your freedom, and you're acting like-- like I don't know what!"

"I'm *not* free! I'm dead! *Dead!*"

"Sheesh." Hedrona turned to John Root. "Well, I suppose he'll snap out of it soon enough."

The robot examined Phil with eerie mechanical detachment. "Possibly. Or then again, possibly not."

"Are we ready to leave now?" JJC said, gathering up a Beagle puppy that had just wandered in.

"We got him a puppy as well, just last week. It was the last successful HTT invasion that ever will be."

"Great, a *puppy*," Phil moaned. "Clopt got him a robot and a *puppy!*"

"Well, Jonathan likes it."

"His name is Trotter!" JJC said.

"We'll leave now," said John Root. "I've already figured out an agricultural world where we won't be found. Where's your ship, Mr. Phil Sperry?"

"I don't know. I don't care."

"Dammit, Phil, straighten up!" Hedrona snapped. She pulled an oval disk from her Gladiator suit and turned to the robot. "The ship's on Level 23 of the main port. I have the access pod here."

"Hey, that's *mine!* That's for *my* ship! You can't take my ship!"

"Are you out of your mind? Of course we're taking the ship!"

"A *puppy!* For its last military mission the Empire kidnapped a *puppy!*" Phil groaned, sliding out of his chair onto the floor.

"Mr. Phil has passed out!" JJC laughed. "It's all too much for him!"

# CHAPTER TWELVE
## John Root Chats with an Individualized Zarj

Hedrona nodded approval as John Root poured a huge ceramic vessel of water and flowers across Phil's face. He came to, sputtering and coughing.

"They also stole flower seeds from Sol," Root said, pointing to the daisies strewn across Phil's gladiator-suited chest. "In fact, the world we're going to has been almost completely terraformed. It started as a USSF colonization project years ago, but of course it was abandoned when the war got out of hand."

"God, who cares?" Phil said. "Without the emperor, we're lost!"

Hedrona restrained herself from slapping his face. "Screw Mr. Crab Guts! Come *on,* Phil! You'll be okay in no time. All this Empire stuff is *gone.* You can *relax,* be *yourself.*"

"Be ... myself ...?"

"Of course! I always *knew* you'd deconvert today. That you'd come *back* to yourself. C'mon, it's *May 14, 2053.* Now let's sit up, dear."

"I'm *soaked!*"

"The suit's *waterproof,* for God's sake!"

"It got into my collar! I'm *wet!*"

"Phil, what is *wrong* with you? Now, look, John Root's right, we need to get out of here fast."

"I guess I *have* deconverted, but God, it's so awful! I feel *sick.*"

Hedrona pulled a blanket off a couch and dried Phil's face, then worked under his collar. "Don't be silly. You'll be fine in a while. Don't you understand this date has been what's kept me going all these years? Knowing you'd finally snap out of it?"

"*No* ... really?"

"I *love* you, Phil, don't you know that by now? Now let's stand up and see about getting back to the *Eagle.*"

The door pounded furiously and everyone flinched except John Root, who calmly picked a Zoraxian pulsar tube from its mount on the wall and strode over to investigate. When the door blew inwards with a deafening bang Hedrona found herself with Phil and JJC behind the couch. She peered up to see Root aiming the tube at the seven-foot-tall, four-armed Clopt, Captain of the Imperial Guard.

"You can't leave without me!" came Clopt's screech through dozens of translator speakers throughout the nursery. His body quivered and his huge whirlpool eyes throbbed.

"Well, Cap'n Clopt!" John Root cackled. "Why'd you blow the door down? Forget your access Code to the nursery?"

Clopt stared at the pulsar tube five inches from his chest. "Kill me now! Kill me now!"

"Oh, dear! I suppose you're upset about the death of Mr. Crab Guts like everyone else today?"

"You *foul robot!*" Clopt snarled, snatching the pulsar tube. "You blaspheme the Source of all! You *plissing schluckbleel!*" He whipped the tube to his own head.

"Oh, come *on,* Cap'n. There *is* no more Source. The Empire's *gone.* Killing yourself won't change that."

"*Murgsniss scuck slucks!* Don't you think I know that? But in any case, I can remove myself from this *Kashpisz slotterblaggen!*"

"Oh, really, let's all just tone down the psychodrama and relax."

"Yap yap yap!" cried Trotter, bounding to Clopt.

"*Karnblurf flazzsz!*" Clopt spat. "It's that damned creature Yor'guuyk brought back from Sol!" He grasped the pulsar tube trigger.

"No, Clopt! No!" Jonathan James shouted, rushing from behind the couch.

"*You!*" Clopt shifted his aim. "I came to kill *you* before your father comes!"

"Oh, come *on,*" John Root sighed, ripping the weapon from Clopt. "Are we just going to play musical pulsar tubes all afternoon?"

"Give that back! I swore to *eliminate* that damn aberration! That *Golld-karpathugiss!*"

"I think we're done with this toy for today," John said,

bending the four-foot metal tube like rubber.

Clopt's eyes quivered. "You--you must kill--" He lunged for JJC but John put a hand on his chest, then raised the giant trooper until his tentacled head banged on the high ceiling.

Hedrona took in a helpful information wisp: *Clopt weighs five hundred pounds in human reckoning.*

"Yap! Yap yap!" barked Trotter, whirling under the Zarj captain's flailing blue-uniformed legs. "Yap yap yap!"

"No violence today, I'm afraid," John said, reaching into Clopt's side holster and removing the ceremonial death ray. "We must be leaving shortly. I must say, I don't understand all this emperor and Grid business. Everyone's freaking! But we can't let that stop us, can we? Come on, ladies and gentlemen, we must be going."

"Let me down! Damn you! *Claz! Slif-cuck!*" Then Clopt caught sight of the others behind the couch. "Damn, Sperry, it's *you!* I've been looking all over for you!" He batted ineffectually at John Root. "Will you let me down, *snuxfarp?*"

"If you'll behave like a gentleman!" John laughed. He turned to Hedrona. "Which Zarj soldiers *do* know how to do, believe it or not. In their own way of course."

Now Clopt registered Hedrona. "Madame *Gladiator!* I did not *see* you! Forgive me!" Then to John Root: "Let me down, quickly! For I must offer obeisance to the Most High!"

John shrugged and let Clopt fall. The Zarj immediately knelt. "Madame--Goddess! Most High, of the Sled! I beseech thee!"

"Dammit, everyone's *flaking,*" Hedrona said. "For God's sake, get up! I can't stand this!"

Clopt slowly rose. "Forgive me! For I am insane! Without the emperor, I am *nothing!*"

"Sheesh, Phil, he talks just like you."

"He--he does *not!*" Phil protested. "Does he? I mean, do I?"

"You!" Clopt shouted. "Engineer of the Head! Why aren't you helping me restore the Grid? I've been looking for you everywhere!"

"Oh, he thinks it's a *software* problem!" John Root cried.

"That's great!"

"We must restore the Grid, Sperry! What the *schlarshz* do I pay you for anyway?"

"*No!*" Phil moaned. "It's impossible! There are *scraps* everywhere, but they don't *add up.* You know that! Look at the memory modules. They're totally *corrupted.* Nonexistent!"

"*Slursing son of a pliss,*" Clopt sighed, eyeing the death ray in John's hand with longing.

"Well, you just need to accept this event as a transformative node of conscious *reappraisal,*" John said. "Integrating the life lessons of this day into a broader understanding of the *karmic possibilities* inherent in the configuration of any single sentient being, no matter as what species or in which star system their initial evolutionary matrix originated."

"*What?*" Hedrona laughed.

"I'm moving into Counseling Mode," John announced. "At least two sentient beings here are unable to make the fundamental shift in their Values Alignment Postulation. I evoke Counseling Mode not only to alleviate suffering, but also to efficiently move Jonathan James Commer off this planet and to our new home, the name of which will not be revealed to Cap'n Clopt lest he take it into his black heart to pursue us there."

"You'd *leave* me here?" Clopt screamed. "With all these *Animals?*"

"Why, yes. The violent substrate of your Id is fundamentally misaligned with our deepest values, namely, the security of Jonathan James Commer."

"No! Idiot robot! I mean, *Sire!* Don't leave me here! Don't you see I *share* your concern for Jonathan James? Don't you see it was *I* who kept him alive all along? That *I* built the nursery and brought the Earth plants? And I brought *you,* you damned robot! I mean, *Sire!* I even allowed this *gnassid pleewagger puppy!*" Clopt finished, aiming an ineffectual kick at the Beagle sniffing his legs.

"Clopt loves me!" JJC burst out. "He loves me even without the Head!"

"Are you kidding?" Hedrona said. "He just got through

saying he came here to *kill* you!"

"No, Madame Gladiator!" Clopt rasped. "Heroine of the Empire! I really didn't want to hurt him! But I must be crazy! Absolutely crazy! Kill me! Kill me now!"

"This is *insane!*" Hedrona said. "Dammit, let's get out of here!"

"No! For I have sinned! Against the emperor! Oh, *cuckj!*"

"What's he talking about?" But Hedrona reeled as more information wisps coalesced. She turned to Phil. "I can't *believe* it! Clopt only *thought* he needed to kill JJC! But that was just the *surface.* Because *beneath* that--"

Clopt banged his head on the tile. "Forgive me!" He jerked several tentacles at JJC. "You see, his mind is that of a *warrior!* It fit so well into the Grid! But he was also beyond the Grid! In such a special way! And--oh, *ruddzza-scuck!* I began *training* him!"

# CHAPTER THIRTEEN
Clopt the Animal

The wisp struck home like a pulsar blast to the lungs. "To be a *Zarj warrior!*" Phil cried.

"I knew I and I alone could train him *properly!*" Clopt said.

"You bound yourself to him! But that's from *before* the Empire!"

Phil could feel Hedrona picking up the same wisp, though John Root seemed unable to download it himself. On ancient Zorax, long before it was assimilated into the Empire, a Zarj warrior entering the long Death Phase of his life picked a promising youngster and trained him in the ancient warrior ways. This practice had been outlawed for twenty centuries, since the conquering of Zarj and its assimilation into the Empire.

"My God! *You* of all people!" Phil gasped. "All along you weren't really of the Head yourself! And you *programmed* this corner of your mind where no one could see! And you've been training Jonathan James to be a Zarj *killer!*"

"I wasn't aware of it myself! I don't think!" Clopt whirled to JJC. "You! Are you my *Garthah-/yuu* or not?"

There was an extremely long silence.

"Yes!" Jonathan James shouted. "I am your *Garthah-/yuu!*"

"Oh my God …" Hedrona moaned.

"Very interesting," John Root said. "Mr. Clopt, I daresay your deception hints of a deeply buried psychiatric disorder, a personality irredeemably split and alien to itself."

"Shut up!" Phil said. "Dammit, this means we have to take Clopt with us!"

"No! He just tried to kill Jonathan James!" Hedrona shouted.

"But only because he didn't remember he was *training* JJC all along, in defiance of the Head!"

"Yes, I see that now," said John Root. "When his addiction to the Grid collapsed and his buried treason and anger began to manifest themselves, his original reaction was to transfer this aggression into a desire to obliterate the persona of Jonathan

84

James."

"No! Clopt is one of the *Animals!* Just like me! Except I was more into the Head than *he* was! I didn't have a secret corner where I could hide from the Grid!"

"No! You had *me!*" Hedrona cried. "All along, whenever we made love!"

Phil stared at her. "Did you ever really *feel* anything?"

"Of *course,* you idiot!"

"I can see that Mr. Phil Sperry could definitely benefit from the Advanced Preventative Counseling Module," John Root said. "It's not very expensive, I assure you. There's a deep discount, considering that this is the *second* time you've been assimilated into the Grid."

"*How the hell do you know that?*" Phil choked.

"It's in the Archives, Mr. Phil Sperry. The entire Grid knew it. Now, as I was saying, in order to fully integrate your human karmic parameters--"

"Silence!" Clopt roared. "Do I have asylum among you or not?"

"Yes!" Phil said.

"No!" Hedrona shouted.

"No, he *has* to come!" JJC said.

"Please take me!" Clopt cried. "When the Grid went down, I didn't know at first the emperor had died. I assumed I just fell out, like all those other Animals, I thought I'd be sent to the Games. I cursed myself! But then I realized there I must've had some sort of Seed of Disunion all along. Oh, *scuck!* I hated the emperor! I always have! Living like a coward, cut up into those disgusting guts inside that *flidpzxbck* glass box! He was no warrior!"

"Now, Cap'n Clopt, I'm sure we'll be able to upgrade you to the Advanced Module in order to calibrate your obvious Centaurian psychosis into the proper Orientation Understanding Confluence," John Root said. "After all, the basic Psychic Transliteration Performance Axis *must* be the same between human and Centaurian psyches, else how would they ever have found common ground enough to go to war with each other?

Perhaps I shouldn't invoke Philosophy Mode in this discussion, but it does seem germane!"

Clopt pummeled four claw-fists on the tile. "I would *think* these treasonous thoughts about the emperor, but somehow *suppress* them at the same time, so the Grid never picked it up!"

"I see we'll need to do something about all these tormented AC souls," John Root said. "I wonder if Dar ever really thought that one through. Imagine *trillions* of anguished souls, all cut off from their darling Grid! Are they all going to commit suicide? Let's hope not! That's a waste disposal job in itself! No, we'll have to upgrade *all* our Orientation Understanding Confluences!"

"But I *fell out!* I thought I'd be sent to the Games, and have to fight Madame Gladiator! But then I realized it's an *honor* to be this Animal! This individual! And when Madame Gladiator finally killed me, it would even *more* of an honor! An honor to die *separate!*"

The word "separate" panged in Phil's heart. *Separate.* Separate from the Source. But Clopt *exulted* in it. How could that be?

"Yap yap yap!"

"Why's everyone so sad?" JJC said, gathering up Trotter and then patting Clopt's prostrate head. "There's no problem. We all just go to Andertwin together."

"I told you not to name the planet, young man!" John said.

"We *can't* have some berserk Zarj along with us," Hedrona said.

"No, we *need* him. He's bound to JJC now," Phil said. "We can't separate them without killing them both."

"Are you kidding?" Hedrona said. "I don't believe that!" But Phil saw her frown as another information wisp confirmed what he was saying. "Oh, *man* ..."

"And another thing about our dear Cap'n Clopt," John said. "While a robot cannot be a psychological part of the Grid, I *have* been fully tied into the computer programming of this ship and, by extension, the various other ships of this zone."

"Oh, screw the computers," Phil said. "I don't care how

complex they are, they can't even begin to approach the magnificence of the Grid!"

"That's not what I'm talking about. I'm talking about the fact that Cap'n Clopt here, in all his juvenile despair, has allowed Core 1's Black Hole Timing Interface to concatenate in a four-dimensional irrational sequence."

"Oooh, that *is* subtle," Phil said. "There really might only be five engineers on this ship who'd know what an Irrational Concatenation would lead to." Clopt's computer programming skills were light-years beyond Phil's own, and that was saying a lot, for Phil knew the computers and technology of this ship inside out in spite of having avoided learning AC languages.

"So what does *that* mean?" Hedrona said.

"It means this ship is about to explode."

"I--I set it for thirty cycles," Clopt blurted, as Phil translated that to about eighteen human minutes. "My plan was to have the satisfaction of personally killing young Commer here and then blow my entire command along with me. I--I'm *sorry*."

"We're going to have to hurry to make it to the *Eagle*," said John Root, scooping up JJC in one hand and Trotter in the other. "Let's get moving."

"No! I shall die here! I have failed!" Clopt moaned.

Phil wanted to get right down on the floor and wait for the end with him, but Hedrona yanked him out of the room and he found himself running next to her down the bright, multi-colored hall.

Then Clopt charged after them, all arms waving, voice doppppering through hundreds of translators mounted along the ceiling or floating in little silver balls everywhere, handing off the translations to each other in sync with his movements. "Wait! I *have* to come! It's true that if I die here, my *Garthah-/yuu* dies too!"

"That's right!" Phil said. "Besides, he knows everything about all the other ships in this sector."

"And how to get us to Andertwin without some trigger-happy ACs blasting us to oblivion, isn't that right, Cap'n Clopt?" John turned to shout behind him.

"Yes! That's right! I *protect* you now! All of you! I protect the friends of my *Garthah-/yuu!* I have all the codes!"

"All right, dammit!" Hedrona said. "Get your damn Centaurian ass in gear, then!" She glared at Phil. "You too, mister! I'm sick of all your complaining today! You're free and you might as well act it!"

"I--I'm *trying,*" Phil gasped as he struggled to keep up with her and the tireless mechanical John Root.

"Move left at Corridor J29!" Clopt called from behind. "Then down Auxiliary Tube G77!"

"Can we trust him?" Hedrona grunted.

"Yes, he's right. It's a variable gravity shortcut. We need it. We need to be a hundred thousand miles minimum off this thing when it blows. This'll give us enough time."

They took Clopt's shortcut and were free-falling down Tube G77.

"Dammit, where are Jack and Amav?" Hedrona said. "And the USSF? Surely *they* know to come today, don't they?"

"I was wondering that, too. But I just remembered something Dar said about Grid Fade. That we'd have a wait a few days for it to go away before we could send our troops in. Grid Fade must be these *information scraps* we're getting."

"So we're on our own for a while?"

"Yeah, I guess so." Phil tapped his comm to float them to a stop at Spaceport Level 23. He signaled the *Brooding Eagle* to unlock, and they scrambled on board as Clopt took a pulsar tube from a Tarl staggering in front of the ship. Clopt blasted him and five other loitering AC soldiers into groaning, burning chunks.

"Dammit, what did you do *that* for?" Hedrona said.

"Anger transference," John announced, hosting Trotter and JJC into the *Eagle* and clambering up after them. "His passive-aggressive psychodrama is at war with his Values Alignment Interface, with suicidal impulses manifesting as homicidal terrorism."

"No, they were just wandering all over the place getting in our way," Clopt said as he climbed in. "The Tarl have always been nuisances. We can't waste a second on them." Phil scooted into the pilot seat and fired up the engines.

"Well, I admit I do feel better, Sperry," Clopt said through the *Eagle's* own set of translators. "Though I can't really say why."

"Well, that makes one of us," Phil muttered as he maneuvered through Level 23. Clopt had already paid his dues, as Phil jabbed at a control panel which overrode a computer-blocked airlock. It slid open and *The Brooding Eagle* shot into space. Phil gunned it so hard the inertial dampers had a hard time adjusting, and they were all pressed back into their seats. Trotter emitted a strangled *urk* and so did JJC with what must have felt like a two-hundred-pound puppy on his chest.

Phil took the ship two hundred thousand miles out. Then it hit him. "Oh my God! *Clopt, where is Greeney Gooney?*"

"That's right, he should be waking up today!" Hedrona said. "You sons of bitches didn't kill him just because he was in the *Kuth'rr'kq* hibernation, did you?"

"Of course not," Clopt said. "We hoped he'd wake up and lead us to victory. We felt that if he did, it would surely reverse the horrible prediction that led to this day, but, uh …"

"*And where is he now?*"

Clopt made a bizarre squeak. The translators coughed and whirred. Finally, they offered:

"*Dammit!*"

Jonathan James walked to a rear-facing port. "Greeney Gooney is back *there!*" he said, pointing at the overexposed white supernova of the *N8J'rallifh-hhu42jdnh.*

# CHAPTER FOURTEEN
## Who is Greeney Gooney?

*"You left Greeney back on the ship?"* Hedrona screamed. "Damn you!"

"I--I *forgot!*" Clopt protested, sensory tentacles waving spastically. "This has been a very hard day, you know!"

"An honest mistake, really, considering all the stress of the situation," John put in.

The glare subsided as the rear sensors traced an expanding debris cloud. Hedrona numbly watched the scanner magnifying and zeroing in on whirling chunks of twisted metal.

"Damn you, Clopt!" Phil shouted. "*You* put that into the Grid! That I *never* think about Greeney! For the last four years! Dammit, if I'd only known he was there!"

"He's *gone!* Just when we *need* him!" Hedrona moaned. "No wonder you always changed the subject whenever I asked about him. You always acted like you had no idea who I was *talking* about!"

"I needed to keep him away from Sperry," Clopt admitted. "It was obvious that, even in a deep coma, he still had latent powers. I couldn't risk him deconverting our engineer."

"You!" Phil pointed at John Root. "Did *you* know about Gooney?"

Root shrugged. "Yes, but Clopt must have done a similar thing to my programming. I knew Gooney existed, up on Warehouse Level 90, Sector 54, but I was forbidden to bring that up in your presence. Sorry sorry sorry!"

Hedrona slumped back in her seat. "God, I can't *believe* this."

"How do you think I feel?" Phil said. "He was my friend! My mentor! In politics and *everything*. I was forbidden to even *think* about him! I'm *insane!*"

"Dammit, Phil, pull yourself together! Look at the scanner!"

"Forget it, nothing could have survived that. And the rad levels are insanely high. We need to start putting some distance between us and the explosion."

"No, the *forward* scanner!"

Everyone looked to the front screen. The star patterns shimmered. Something fuzzy materialized.

Hedrona shivered. A classic Martian flying saucer, two hundred feet wide with a clear glass dome, floated before them. She looked at Phil's board to check the distance, expecting the standard couple hundred miles separation for Star Drive insertions, but was dumbfounded that the saucer was only forty feet in front of them, matching their vector. "It must be Dar! He's still here!"

"No, he was only here this morning to do the liberation," John Root pointed out. "But he immediately went back to February 2036. He did make a few other HTT journeys to different times between '36 and '53, but didn't want to set foot back in AC again until well *after* 2053. He didn't want any ACs thinking of him as their past emperor, even if he'd only been their emperor for twenty-five seconds. This must be some other Martian patrol they've just sent."

"How do you know that? You didn't even *exist* when Dar first went to 2053!"

"Oh, c'mon, Ms. Gladiator!" John snorted. "Not only would a 2043 robot know that story, but all Dar's writings about the Alpha Centaurian War, including all his mappings of battles between 2036 and 2053, became available to the Grid a long time ago. The Grid knew everything that was to happen, it knew this day was coming, but just ignored it. It couldn't handle it!"

"Damn, that Martian was *reckless*," Phil muttered, grabbing the control wheel. "He's betting our autopilot won't get disrupted by such a close Star Drive insertion."

"THAT WAS NOT A STAR DRIVE INSERTION, PHIL SPERRY," came the deafening blast from the speakers.

"Oh my God! *Greeney!*" Hedrona cried.

The saucer yawed towards them, revealing the clear forty-foot dome. Standing in its center was the small pink-finned Greeney Gooney in his silver Star General uniform.

"Oh my God! *Greeney! You're* from the *past,* then!" Phil gasped. "Somehow! Because we just *killed* you, man! I'm so sorry!"

"Cease worrying, friend!" came from the speakers at a more comfortable volume. "I'm quite all right as you can see. That was no Star Drive Insertion but a decloaking. I've been on your nose the whole way out."

"Then--you're from the *future?*"

"Why are you *arguing* with him?" Hedrona laughed. "It's *Greeney!* He's *alive!*"

"I remember Greeney!" JJC said, waddling up with the squirming Trotter in his arms. "When I was just small!"

"A puppy! How wonderful!" Greeney said. "And that must be Jonathan James!"

"Look, JJC, you can't remember something from when you were less than a year old!" Phil shouted.

"Of course I can! I am Clopt's *Garthah-/yuu!* He trained me to remember everything!"

"That's impossible!"

"Phil, what is *wrong* with you?" Hedrona said. "Who cares? This is Greeney!"

"No! It's an illusion! He's just trying to drive us crazy! He doesn't really exist!"

"I sure as hell do exist, old buddy!" Greeney laughed. "My, I see you've certainly had a time with the old brainwashing these past four years."

"Don't *say* that! God, I can't *stand* it!"

"He's--had a rough time," Hedrona put in.

"*I've* had a rough time, too!" Clopt shouted, four arms waving, tentacles writhing as he stomped to the screen. "Master! I am *insane!* Save me!"

"Hmm. May I come aboard?"

"Where'd you get that thing?" Phil said. "That saucer?"

"*Let him come aboard!*" Hedrona shouted. "Phil, I can't believe you! Greeney, we have an airlock but I don't think it'll have an interface for a Martian saucer."

"I could fashion one but I'm rather exhausted with all this Amplified Thought. I'll just come aboard."

Greeney Gooney stood in the center of the room. Clopt was

prostrate and Trotter was barking.

"You *can't* be here!" Phil stammered. "Unless you've HTT'd from the past!"

"Hi there," John Root said, extending a hand. "I don't believe we've met. I'm John Root, a 2043 recreation of John Commer, Jr."

"I've *heard* of John Commer, Jr.," Greeney replied, taking the robot's hand. "Amazing stunt he pulled on Mercury back in '34. That suicidal dive right down to the death ray! I know Jack's been quite angry with him ever since. Pleased to meet you, John Root. But excuse me, I need to assist Philip here. He's on the verge of a mental breakdown."

"Why, I--I am *not!*"

"He *is!*" Hedrona cried. "Help him!"

"Of course I will, friend Hedrona," Greeney said, his wide unblinking eyes filling her soul with peace for the first time in four years. He laid a claw on Phil's arm. "Hello, friend. Just relax, old buddy."

"*Wow* ..." Phil gasped. "How did you--what did you--"

"It's all quite simple. I could feel Dar arrive this morning and dissolve the Empire. Amazing to feel this Head stuff just *evaporate.* Of course, we have these fading remnants of it, but don't let them rile you. They'll pass in a few days."

"R-really? Because they're so *cruel.*"

Hedrona shivered at the fading wisps from the dead Grid, each loaded to the max with futility, bitter separation, lost opportunity, and the cold passage of time. Trillions of crazed Alpha Centaurians still sought to navigate these scraps, but it was like trying to step across an ocean on floating twigs. She met Phil's ragged gray eyes. So much suffering there. "Are we all getting this? This *despair?* Phil, I had no idea!"

Greeney nodded. "But it's time to let these fragments go. When they finally fade and all trace of the Grid is gone, we'll be able to send in the Martian counselors."

"Martian *counselors?*"

"*Yes!*" Clopt cried from the floor. "Counsel me! For I am *insane!* We're all *insane!*"

# CHAPTER FIFTEEN
## The Proposal

"You will be counseled, Captain Clopt, never fear," Greeney told him, and Phil could feel him relax on the floor, just as he could feel his own body smoothing in Greeney's presence.

"Look, Greeney, what's really going on?" he said. "Dar must have sent you just now? Maybe from before 2038?"

"Don't be silly, Philip. I'm from right now. We know from Dar's future history that Martian counselors will be sent here. Hundreds of them, all we can spare. They in turn will have to train *millions* of AC counselors. We have an entire empire ruined and psychologically reeling right now. We must *act.*"

"No! You were just killed on the *N8J'rallifh-hhu42jdnh!* Clopt *blew* the goddamn thing!"

"For God's sake, Phil!" Hedrona cut in. "Can't you see he knew it was coming and got out?"

Greeney crinkled into a smile. "Yes, I knew. In *Kuth'rr'kq* one does have awareness. When the Grid went down, I was fully awake and unusually well-rested, so that I could call upon more than the usual parameters of Amplified Thought. It was easy to fashion a Martian attack saucer out of my quarters. Took about twenty minutes."

"So you're really claiming you're from *now?*" Phil said. "You didn't HTT in from the thirties?"

"No, I made the saucer a few minutes ago. Then simple teleportation from there to here. One of the first exercises in Amplified Thought. I really ought to show you how to do that."

"Show *me!*" Clopt screamed, flinging himself at Greeney's feet. "Show me how to leave this *horror!* Will you counsel me *this instant,* oh Martian Star General?"

Phil stared at this unspeakable travesty. He expected Star General Gooney to pull the Martian shattergun on his belt and blast this infidel into a million tinkling pieces. Instead Phil found himself next to Clopt, wailing: "No! *I* need your counseling! Greeney! For God's sake! The Grid's *gone!* I can't function without it! Help me!"

"He--he's been *upset,*" Hedrona offered.

"No problem here," John Root said. "I've gone into Counseling Mode and begun the process myself. I must say I appreciate your prescience in determining the need for psychiatric counseling here in Alpha Centauri, General Gooney, sir. I'm ready to offer my own services!"

"I refuse!" Clopt cried. "I won't take it from this damned robot!"

"Me too! Me too!" Phil screamed, pounding the floor.

"Phil went *native* on us, Greeney," Phil heard Hedrona shouting from far away. "He got addicted to the Head, and now he's like *withdrawing.* You've got to do something!"

"Do something!" Clopt bellowed. "For me! And for the trillions of the insane of the Empire!"

"Hmm," Greeney said. "Of course we will do so. You, Clopt, are a special case. I've known for quite some time, even in the depths of *Kuth'rr'kq,* that you've always been slightly separate from the Grid."

"Yes, that's right! I've been a traitor all along! But I never knew that until now!"

"And yet this seed of individuality will carry you through the crisis, I would think."

"No! Don't abandon me like that! I need you *now!*"

"Of course, Mr. Gooney will undoubtedly be quite busy repairing all these trillions of Alpha Centaurian citizens," John Root put in. "But I can certainly download the relevant portions of Mr. Gooney's ineffable philosophy and incorporate that into my own counseling efforts."

"Robot! I refuse to deal with your *schluckbleel* counseling program!"

"Thank you, Mr. Root," Greeney said, "I think that for the good of the remnants of this sorry Empire, I will counsel Clopt here personally."

"*Thank* you, Star General," Clopt sobbed. "Thank you from the bottom of my *snatck-fagger!*"

"*What about me?*" Phil cried. "*I'm* the one who's going insane here!"

"Philip, dear friend, of course I will counsel you," Greeney said gently. "I always have, haven't I?"

"*No!* Not like what I *need!*"

"He'll … be all right," Hedrona said. "Won't he?"

"Yes, of course. He's fixable, I think. Much more resilient than he lets on."

"It's not working!" Phil leapt from the floor and lurched to the pilot's seat, thinking he ought to fly them somewhere, then abandoning that and pacing. "Hedrona's right! It's getting worse! I can't stand this!"

"*What's* not working?" Greeney said.

"Your counseling! It's not right for me! I'm going crazy!"

"Philip!" Greeney steered him back to the pilot's seat. "Concentrate on something *normal*. You'll be all right. This whole brainwashing thing has gotten to you, but it will pass."

"No! This is the *second* time I've done it! And it's *killed* me!" Phil tried to focus on the instruments. Greeney patted his shoulder. Against his will he felt himself calming.

"What about *me?*" Clopt shouted. "While you play nursemaid to Sperry, I'm *suffering!*"

"Sheesh, what a zoo," Hedrona muttered. "Jonathan James is handling all this so much better than either of you!" She pointed to JJC, who'd taken a chair with Trotter in his lap and gazed unconcernedly out the rear window at the rapidly receding glare of the debris cloud.

"So we're going to Andertwin?" Greeney said. "A good choice, I think. We must create a garden planet as our new headquarters."

"We're going to have a headquarters?" Phil muttered.

"Of course. I'm going to need all your assistance in the rebuilding of Alpha Centauri."

"That won't work. I'm totally *crazy* now. I can't rebuild anything. And if I did, it'd be the goddamn Grid! God, I hate the Grid! But I love it! I want it *back!*"

"I want it back too!" Clopt cried. "I don't know why!"

There was a long silence. Hedrona turned to JJC. "What about you, Jonathan? Do you want the Grid back?"

He shrugged. "The Grid was fun! Trotter didn't like it, though."

"Great. So Trotter didn't like the Grid," Phil mocked. "A stupid puppy that's only been here a week, and he decided he didn't like the goddamn Grid!"

"Yap! Bark snark snark!" Trotter said.

JJC shrugged. "I could tell he didn't like it. But *this* is fun, too!"

Phil met his five-year-old brown eyes. "*This* is fun? This total insanity is *fun?*"

"Yes! I'm having lots of fun now!"

"Yes, that's *it!*" Clopt said. "My *Garthah-/yuu* has nailed it! There's something *fun* about all this!" He sprang to his full seven feet. "Yes! *Fun!*"

"No, that's *insanity,*" Phil insisted. "You can't allow yourself to believe that!"

"I do! I do! And I will join with Star General Gooney and young Jonathan here to restore the Empire! Dear Gooney, you shall be our new emperor!"

"No, no empire, no emperors," Greeney said. "Clopt, calm yourself. Sit in a chair and meditate or something."

Clopt's eyes contracted. Then he bowed his head and slunk to one of the oversized Zarj-capable chairs, where he seemed to turn off.

Greeney turned to Phil. "Phil, pull yourself together and lay in a course for Andertwin. Fourth planet of Procyon A, or what the Centaurians call *Guacoazezama.* I can see this post-Grid state has your mind veering all over the place. Let's just get to work."

"I--okay." The course for Andertwin was already set, but Phil busied himself verifying it and fine-tuning the ship's performance.

"An agricultural world's ideal for our setup," Greeney went on, "because Alpha Centauri is about to transition from being an empire dedicated to war and conquest to being an agricultural entity only. I know the ACs have shunned planets as being inferior to the glories of hundred-mile-long battle cruisers, but we're going to have to ground the entire populace in what's *real* again. They've always scorned their network of agricultural worlds, but those worlds are about to become their ground of being for the next several hundred years."

"You really think that?" Hedrona said.

"I do. It all came to me in the *Kuth'rr'kq*. What Phil and Clopt are experiencing is just a taste of what trillions of Centaurians are starting to go through. It can't lead to any good. All those ships built for conquest must be converted into agricultural transports. We need to *ground* this entire empire. Agriculture will do that, as well as feed all these folks. It won't be forever. They'll have to evolve beyond that sooner or later. But for now it's what they need."

"It'll never work," Phil muttered, scanning the sensor screens. "We love the Grid too much."

"He'll snap out of it," Hedrona said. "I know he will."

"Hell with it," Phil said. "Besides, we can't go to goddamn Andertwin with you. Hedrona and I are taking the first Star Drive flight back to Sol and getting married."

During the silence that followed Phil had an eternity to scrutinize the hydrogen ion shielding matrix and adjust it five times.

"Well, *that's* certainly romantic," Hedrona said.

"*Wow,* Mr. Phil!" John Root laughed.

Another silence.

"Tell you what, Mr. Phil, I might even consider your crude proposal someday," Hedrona said. "But right now, my first priority is to help Greeney in this reconstruction project."

"You--you mean you don't *care?*"

"Believe it or not, I do care. It's just that I'm staying in AC. There's work to do here."

Another silence. "Maybe I should stay too," Phil whispered. "Maybe help or something."

But nobody seemed to hear him.

"I figure, I've fought these sons of bitches for four years," Hedrona said. "I know what makes 'em tick. That ought to be worth something."

"Yes, that is worth quite a lot," Greeney told her. "Now, everyone, sit down and relax. We've got a jump to make and a lot of work ahead of us. Philip, if you will?"

Phil nodded. "Listen, I used to fight them, too …" But again no one replied. He tried to catch Hedrona's eye but she was busy helping Greeney into the copilot seat where he peered into the forward screen, his short legs happily kicking the air.

Phil considered how he might work his '34 AC military tour into the conversation. He'd done a lot of fighting on the *Wrathspike,* after all. Then, to his shame, Phil realized he was just trying to impress Hedrona. His love, who wouldn't marry him.

There was nothing to do but prep for the Warp Transfer to Andertwin. Phil moodily rechecked the autopilot. "Do you want me to take the saucer in tow?"

"No need," Greeney replied. "I was tired of thinking about its mass and dissolved it."

"Huh." Phil looked back at Hedrona taking her seat, but she still wouldn't meet his eye.

There wasn't much else to add. Phil crossed his fingers in supplication to the buggy Centaurian excuse for Star Drive and they made the jump.

# CHAPTER SIXTEEN
## The Counseling of the Remnants
### *June 15, 2075*

Andertwin's sun was thick in the line of trees to the west as Jack Commer hovered the *Typhoon IV* to land on the concrete pad a hundred feet from the guest house.

"Hover jets off," he spoke as the jets whined to silence. "Sortie, prepare for reactor stasis."

"Reactor entering stasis," Draka Sortie reported through the intercom.

"All turrets standing down," spoke Lee Borman.

"Dammit, they were never supposed to be *up*," Jack muttered.

Copilot Robert Athens shrugged. "I thought you would've *wanted* them up, considering the situation."

Jack consulted his panel. Sure enough, all four weapon turrets were just now fading from bright red to the dull green of standdown. Why hadn't he noticed that? Of course Borman would've powered the turrets. "Well, we just wouldn't want any ACs picking up weapons signatures and thinking we were coming in loaded for bear. I mean, this is supposed to be a *vacation,* for God's sake."

Athens went through his own checklist. "Well, it's not anymore. You know that."

Jack sighed. "Yeah, you're right." He must be getting good at taking guff from his copilots. How come they were always right? "But I *needed* a vacation. Then all this nonsense got started." He gestured out the canopy at the magnificent blaze of orange light in the big leafy trees and the hulking black shape of the guest house.

"Yeah, I know. Maybe this is all nothing. You want me to stay with the ship a while, check things out while you and Amav get reacquainted with your son?"

"Naw." Jack stood up. "Everyone can come on over. Just leave the AI Shell on and it'll tell us if anything comes up." He pressed a square on the panel. "Will! Pat! Lee! Draka! You're all invited in for whatever passes for a beer on Andertwin. Amav, you ready?"

"Sure am," Amav called up from crew quarters.

She joined the six-man crew of the *Typhoon IV* on the ladder to the landing pad. Fresh wind blew away the acrid hover jet exhaust, replacing it with the smell of plants and rich soil. The air was cool, but perfect for their lightweight navy-blue uniforms and for Amav's white sundress. They found a flagstone path to the two-story guest house, its lower floor alive with yellow light and figures moving inside.

"There's Phil! And Hedrona!" Amav said. Hedrona caught sight of them, waved, then opened the huge front door and came running.

"God, you haven't changed a bit!" Amav laughed into Hedrona's hug.

"You either!" Hedrona said. "How are you? It's been ages!" She turned to Jack. "You haven't changed, either."

"Who would, with rejuvenation therapy?" Jack said. He had to remind himself that he was talking to a woman in her mid-seventies. But she looked to be no more than thirty-five. In fact, she looked younger than she did when she was kidnapped all those years ago. Of course, she'd been given those extra eleven years, as had Phil and his own son, so Jack at seventy-two had almost caught up to her. But he imagined he looked pretty young as well. He looked over at his wife, sixty-two going on twenty-five, it seemed, lovelier than ever. "You remember the old crew, don't you? Will and Pat and Lee? And my copilot, Robert?"

"Of course! How are you all? Now Bobby *has* changed. You were just a kid last time I saw you."

Athens shrugged. "Nice to see you again, Ms. Bhlon. I do remember meeting you when I volunteered for the Animal Rescue program."

"That's right! You were great with all the animals. I remember that."

"Hey, there!" Phil Sperry called, stepping outside. "Great to see you all! Come on in."

Jack shook Phil's hand. He could feel the mutual tension

after all these years. But maybe he was getting too old to worry about this sort of thing. "How are you, Phil? Thanks for your report. I read it on the way over."

"Great!" Phil grinned. "Hope it was helpful."

Who'd asked Phil Sperry to send a report on Alpha Centauri? Jack didn't care how long he'd been hanging out here. And that stuff about Gooney. Phil had sure read *him* wrong.

"Star Drives went okay?" Phil went on. "We were a little concerned you were running late."

"No, no problems, all three were fine." There were still occasional Star Drive malfunctions, though thankfully there hadn't been any fatalities in years. It galled Jack that after decades of Star Drive, they were still limited to safe fifteen-minute hops, three of which were required for the 11.5-light-year journey to Procyon A. Longer periods tended to throw the navigational systems off, and Jack was eager to get the next generation *Typhoon V*-class ships online with their new Star Drive Enhanced system. Though some *Typhoon III*-class ships were testing the Enhanced prototype, the *V*-series would fully integrate the technology. "The reason we're a little behind schedule is that we spent an hour and a half cruising here after the Drives, checking with some folks along the way, seeing how things are going." Jack sighed. "This was supposed to be a *vacation*."

"So how come Joe and the *III* aren't here too?"

"Well, I figured if we need 'em, they're only forty-five minutes away, but who knows? If there really are renegade ACs with Star Drive, and they think about hitting Sol, I want our best *Typhoon* ready to take 'em on."

"Yeah, sorry about your vacation, but maybe we can have a good time catching up."

Hedrona led them inside. Jack checked Sperry for any sign of peeping at Amav in her tight low-cut dress, but Sperry didn't take the opportunity to ogle Amav's chest or anything else. Well, he'd been shacking up with this Hedrona woman for over twenty years now. Maybe he was old and satisfied. He sure looked as if his rejuvenation treatment hadn't taken very well. The guy looked gray and worn out. He'd gotten those eleven extra years, but he had to be sixty by now. Maybe he was too old to want Amav anymore.

The last time Jack had read a report from Sperry, the son of a bitch had been brainwashed on the *Typhoon II,* spewing all that crap about lusting for Amav in total, disgusting detail. Later he'd tried to weasel out of it with some insincere apology. Then he'd gotten himself brainwashed a second time in '38, and here he was permanently living in the former Alpha Centaurian Empire. God knew what was rattling around in his brain. There was no trusting the bastard.

Why was Amav wearing such a sexy dress today anyway?

*

They moved into the huge cool space. Glass walls, high ceiling, timbers and fireplaces. It was like a ski lodge transported to Alpha Centauri. "Wow, Jonathan's really done well!" Will Connors laughed, looking up to an irregular balcony showing dozens of rooms.

"Well, this is just the guest house," Hedrona said. "Although he used to live here. He actually built this insane huge thing he calls the Castle fifty miles west in the mountains. It's ugly as hell, but what can I say? Phil and I live a mile down the road." Jack followed her gesture out the window down a road darkening in twilight. He and Amav had stayed with Hedrona and Phil there on their last visit in '67; Jonathan James hadn't wanted his parents staying with him then, either. Nothing looked to have been built on those fields of knee-high grass or in the forest to the west since. The guest house seemed to be the only structure for miles.

"We'll show everyone to their rooms, and I expect Jonathan James will be here in a bit," Phil said. "Meanwhile, I can fix some drinks."

"Well, unfortunately, there's been a slight change in plans!" came a high-pitched voice.

Jack's legs buckled at the sight of the apparition that seemed to float from behind a thirty-foot-long kitchen island to their left. *"Oh my God!"*

"Oh, that's right, he stayed away the other times you came," Phil said. "Sorry, Jack, we really weren't expecting him."

"It's okay, Jack," Amav whispered. "It's just a robot."

Jack stared.

"Hello, Admiral Jack Commer! I'm *John Root!* I bicycled *fifty miles* from the Castle just to meet you! Surely you recognize me!"

"Well, yes, but ..." Jack said, staring at the outstretched hand until he finally acquiesced and took its cool buzzing fingers in a halfhearted shake.

"How do you do! How do you do! I've wanted to meet Admiral Jack Commer for *ages* now! Very pleased to meet you! Very pleased!"

"Well ..." Jack swallowed. He forced himself to calm down. He'd known the thing was here. He'd seen John robots before, even Jim Robots. He'd even talked with a Jack Commer robot. It was all insane. Thank God no one collected them anymore.

"Anything you'd like me to do Jack, *anything*, Jack, I swear I'll do it! Anything! You just let me know and I'll be there!"

Jack stared back. This was his dead brother who died at twenty-five. He could feel Phil and Hedrona goggling as if they'd never seen the robot kick into this particular subroutine before. Was it deliberately running some crazy idea of a John and Jack program? How the two used to interact? When Jack wanted to kick him off the *Typhoon* for being so childish and incompetent, and John would come back and fawn all over him, and Dad would intervene?

He swallowed. "No, uh, we're fine. Amav and I-- everything's just fine. Don't need anything now. Uh, thank you."

"*Anything*, Jack! Anything at all!"

"We're fine, really," Amav cut in. "If we need anything, we'll let you know."

"Huh," Senator Lee Borman blurted into the ensuing

silence. "Phil, an Andertwin brewski *would* go down fine just about now."

"Everybody let me know what they'd like and the synthesizer will have it whipped out in no time," Phil said, moving behind the counter and hauling out glasses. "It'll make the bottled stuff, too." Connors and Borman and Patrick James grabbed armchairs while Hedrona and Amav spoke with copilot Athens. Ship's engineer Sortie went to assist Phil, and Jack noted how the big, balding Draka Sortie turned into a puppy next to the former *Typhoon II* physician/engineer. Sortie worshipped the concept of Phil Sperry, maintaining that Sperry was the most brilliant of all *Typhoon* engineers, and he claimed to have memorized all the technical manuals Phil had written for the obsolete *II.*

Outside, endless fields of golden grass shivered in the setting sun. Jack felt cramped and irritable in this luxurious ski lodge and wondered if he should suggest they all move out to the vast patio and enjoy the sunset and the cool rural breeze.

It really was a lovely planet. Jonathan James had chosen well. Jack might even consider retiring here if his son didn't mind his parents being fifty miles away. Maybe it was time to think about slowing down. Get far away from Sol, think about plants and crops instead of all this technological crap. All this political crap. Such a lazy place. Why did they have to hear about the Gooney idiocy just now? Couldn't it have waited a couple weeks?

And now Jack had to deal with JJC's stupid pet. *John Root.*

That was his *brother,* who threw his life away, and Jim's life, and all their friends' lives, for *nothing.*

# CHAPTER SEVENTEEN
## A Message from Our Dear Author

"Wait! To the *news!*" John laughed as Amav cringed at that voice, more for Jack's sake than her own. "I've got a message for you! From our dear author himself, Jonathan James Commer! He told me to bring it right over!"

"What's going on?" Amav said.

"Well, friends, it appears that our dear author feels he must postpone his award party until the present crisis has been resolved! To tell you the truth, he looks like *hell!* He's quite depressed by this Greeney Gooney nonsense, I would say!"

"He's canceling his own party?" Hedrona said. "But we're all set up for it."

Amav surveyed the room. Nothing looked set up. But Hedrona probably meant that the synthesizers were fully stocked with raw materials, ready to pump out vittles for an entire brigade of literary sycophants. Likewise, whatever decorations would brighten this coldly correct space and befit a bestselling author. "Are you sure? I mean, this Gooney thing could drag on for a while, and we're supposed to have what? Two hundred guests tonight?"

"All guests have been *disinvited!*" John Root sang. "You're the only ones who came!"

"Well, that's too bad," Jack said. "I guess we'll have the party another time, then."

"So he's still at his house?" Amav said.

"You mean the Castle, Madame Amav! Yes, our author is there, holed up in the Castle, depressed as hell! *Unbelievable!* I tried to talk him into coming, but he wouldn't. Just wouldn't! He *feels* for the situation, truly!"

"Well, can't you tell him we'd like to see him? Maybe tomorrow? It's been eight years!"

"No, Madame Amav, he wants to see no one! He's *that* depressed!"

"Huh? We're not having a party?" Senator Borman said, entering the circle.

"Quiet, Lee," Jack said. "I think I know what's coming next."

"Oh you do, do you?" John Root cried. "Really! I'd forgotten how prescient Jack Commer can truly *be*."

"Yes, I have a feeling it'll be just like '67, when he said he was *tired* of us. We'd only been here half a day."

"Hell with all that," Borman said, snatching a cold brown bottle from Sperry. "We'll just have our own award party."

"No, JJC's instructions are quite clear," John Root said, plucking the bottle from Borman's hands and pouring it into a potted plant. "All foreigners on Andertwin must leave immediately." He switched to Jonathan James' voice. "'*The crisis is too grave to endanger non-citizens of Andertwin. All foreigners must leave the planet at once.*'"

Amav reeled at the sound of her son's voice. *Foreigners*.

"*Dammit,*" Jack said. "Not again!"

"I'm so sorry," Hedrona said. "You know how he can be."

"No, in fact we really don't," Amav said. "We've only seen him *three times* since the Collapse. *Three times* in twenty-two years! He's a damn stranger is what he is!"

Jack looked out the window at the darkening sky. "Aw, crap, John. Tell 'im the *Typhoon* can't fly at night. Too dark. We'll have to wait until morning."

"May I remind you, Admiral Jack Commer, that I am *not* in fact your youngest brother that you can order me around like that?"

"I did *not* order you around like my youngest brother!"

"You did! You called me John! I heard you!"

"I did not call you John!"

"'*Aw, crap, John,*'" Jack's voice issued from John Root's mouth. "'*Tell 'im the* Typhoon *can't fly at night. Too dark. We'll have to wait until morning.*'"

"Dammit to hell!"

"And sarcasm is *not* permitted on Andertwin. It's considered unseemly on any planet of the Alpha Centaurian system. A word to the wise."

"Sheesh," Borman put in, grabbing another beer out of the

synthesizer behind the counter. "Screw the Alpha Centaurian system. We smashed it good in '53 and if necessary we'll smash it again." He swaggered over to John Root. "And don't try to take this one away from me," he added, gulping the beer, "or I'll smash *you*."

"Lee, it's all right, we'll leave this damn hole," Jack said. "I can't believe this! We come all the way out here to get this treatment! *Again!*"

"A journey from Sol to Procyon A only takes forty-five minutes," John Root lectured. "You can't have wasted more than a couple hours getting ready and coming here. Look on the bright side for a change, Admiral Jack Commer."

Jack turned to Amav. "I am about to ram my fist down this goddamn robot's throat!"

"I know, I know," Amav said. "But you'll just hurt your fingers. Come on, forget this nonsense, we'll just get on home."

"We *can't* just go home! We've got this *Gooney* crap to deal with!"

"That's right," Borman put in, swigging his beer. "I hereby quarantine the planet of Andertwin and declare it an occupied zone of the United System."

"*What?*" burst out of Phil and Hedrona.

"Just what I said. This Gooney thing is out of hand. We have a military emergency now. As the senator on the spot, so to speak, I'm establishing a perimeter right here. Or a beachhead. Whatever you want to call it. Bobby, fire up the *Typhoon* and make ready for orbit. It's possible we'll have to sterilize this whole stinking planet."

"Belay that!" Jack barked. "Bobby, you'll do no such thing!"

"Aye aye, sir," Athens said.

"*Dammit,* Jack!" Borman sputtered. "My sphere of control--"

"Lee, we've been through this before. Senator or no senator, you can't order my crew around."

"As a *senator* of the United System--"

"As a *crewmember* reporting to *me* aboard my flagship

*Typhoon IV*--"

"Crap on that! I clearly outrank you in a political crisis of this sort!"

"Commander Borman, you will confine yourself to Turret Control immediately!"

"*Bobby* will back me! *He* knows these ACs are slimeballs! Bobby, you'll back your senator, won't you?"

"Commander Borman," Athens said, "*Jack* is captain. Not you. As far as I'm concerned you're the weapons specialist on the *Typhoon*. Nothing else."

"I told you, Borman," Jack said, "I told everyone, back when you ran for mayor--"

"And won eighty-five goddamn percent of the vote, man! Don't you forget it!"

"--when you ran for mayor, and I said, we can't *have* this, we can't have political figures working within the USSF!"

"And now I'm a *senator,* baby! And now you're worried 'cause I have my own committee on the Council! The *USSF Oversight Committee!*"

"I *refuse* to allow my command authority to be subject to--"

"Oh, this is *marvelous!*" John Root laughed. "I'm getting the full *fascist mentality* of Jack Commer just as they programmed me to!"

"Dammit! Borman, to your turret! *Now!*"

Borman sank back into an armchair and drank his beer. "I guess I'm comfortable right here, pardner."

"*I'm* on your side, Senator Lee!" John Root said. "This is priceless! *Priceless!*"

"Dammit!" Jack sputtered, whirling to Root. "You can tell your *master* we're never coming here again! *Ever!*"

"Oh, Jack!" Amav cried. "This is silly!"

"I'm really sorry about this, Jack," Phil said. "You know how JJC can be. I think this Gooney thing has hit all of us harder than we care to admit."

"Does Gooney really think he's the *emperor?* Of the goddamn *Alpha Centaurians?*"

Phil winced. "Well, I just don't know. Believe me, all this

is as shocking to Hedrona and me, and Jonathan James, I guess, as it is to you."

Jack folded his arms. "Well, we do have a crisis. I woke up this morning thinking we were going to have a *vacation*. Then we get this *news*. We would've had to come in any case, but I guess we better face some facts. I don't know how much you've kept up with your medical training, Phil, but maybe you and Draka can work together checking out the humans on Andertwin. I'm authorized to offer them medical assistance as needed and transportation back to Sol if they want. We have evacuation ships standing by. How many are we talking about, anyway?"

Phil shrugged. "Not more than five hundred, tops. Most of the populace is Jujl. And that's only maybe ten thousand for the entire planet."

Jack nodded. "And of course this offer extends to you and Hedrona."

"We wouldn't go," Hedrona said. "Nobody really thinks Greeney's going anywhere with this. It'll blow over. There've been dozens of fads about who might be a good emperor over the last twenty years. None of it ever led anywhere."

"Hell," Phil said, "remember when they wanted to make *you* emperor, Jack."

Jack grimaced. Amav recalled the fall of 2053, when three separate AC delegations had journeyed to Sol to beg Jack to assume the emperorship. Two hadn't made it, navigating into hyperspatial nonexistence with their dysfunctional Warp Transfer. Jack had ferried the remaining AC cruiser home to make sure the former empire got his message that no emperorship was possible in Alpha Centauri in perpetuity.

"We'll blast 'em," Lee Borman muttered, sunk deep into his chair. "We'll blast the stupid mothers." Three empty beer bottles sat on the floor beside him.

"Well, this is certainly a zoo," Jack said.

Phil nodded. "But you know, Lee may have a point. Maybe you should set up a military HQ here. This planet is pretty hospitable. Needed only a little bit of terraforming."

"And this Cult of Amav thing! What *is* that, anyway?"

"Well, like Hedrona was saying, they've been trying on different emperors for years now. This just looks like another one. You know, mother of the Author of Everything, or something. I don't know." He looked over to Amav. "This entire system would freak if they knew she was here right now."

Amav stared back. "Wow, I guess I didn't think of that!"

# CHAPTER EIGHTEEN
## So You've Been in Counseling All This Time?

"Well, whatever. Looks like Greeney's claimed it now," Jack muttered.

"I know, we're all in shock," Phil said. "Believe me, this came as a complete surprise."

"I can see that." Jack pulled out his USSF Comm and called up Phil's report. "This thing you sent me. It really doesn't tell me much about Gooney, Phil. Or why he turned traitor."

"I know. I was just putting down some thoughts about what twenty-two years here without an emperor's been like. How the whole Centaurian counseling program's been going. Of course, this was before Greeney went off the deep end."

"So you're saying here that you personally have been in counseling with Gooney all this time? Ever since the Collapse? I had no idea Gooney was working with *humans*."

Phil looked away. "Sorry I kept this all from you. It was sorta private, you know."

Jack nodded. "Huh."

"I think I was ready to quit it, though. In a way we weren't getting anywhere, and then, after the last HTT on May 29th, and we knew all this time-travel stuff had ended, I thought, hell, I might as well tell you the whole story."

Jack shook his head in disgust. His instincts had been right. Phil Sperry was *damaged*. The guy had just admitted he'd spent *twenty-two years* seeing a Martian shrink.

"And to think we trusted him," Hedrona put in. "I mean, he's been my friend. Then to declare himself Emperor of Alpha Centauri! God, he's been provisional emperor of *Mars* since '60. When Dar steps down he'd have it all. What more does he want?"

"I've always distrusted his ambition," Jack said. "I guess he lulled us all to sleep with this little counseling business he's been running out here."

"He can't make this emperor thing work," Phil said. "He just can't."

"But he's got Clopt with him," Hedrona said. "And he claims he has the software for restoring the Grid. That he's been working with it all this time."

"That's impossible! There's no software that can do that."

"It's the Clopt thing that worries me," Jack said. "You say Clopt's been in counseling with Gooney all this time, too? Twenty-two years?"

"Yeah, that's right."

"If that's the case, they could've been plotting this together for twenty-two years. Maybe all this counseling has really been for gathering information. Maybe seeing how the Centaurian mindset works compared with the human mindset."

Phil met Jack's eyes, registering the subtle insult that he'd been a guinea pig in a treasonous experiment. "You know, there may be something to that. Maybe establishing a sort of psychic baseline, how an individual Centaurian, stripped of his connection to the emperor, really thinks and feels. After all, nobody's been able to study *that* for thousands and thousands of years. And then to compare that mental structure with a human who's been, well, brainwashed, and then thrown out of *that*."

Jack blinked at Phil's eerie self-assessment.

"And he also had access to a human who *wasn't* brainwashed," Hedrona said. "Me. I spent a couple years talking things out with Gooney myself."

"I thought you were helping Gooney *with* the counseling program," Jack said.

"Well, sure, but a good counselor needs counseling herself sometimes," Hedrona shot back as if this were self-evident.

"God ..." Jack muttered. How could they have let Gooney into their heads like that?

"And there was Jonathan James," Phil said. "Although he was never in counseling, he'd give Gooney another baseline. A five-year-old who was part of the Grid but somehow was never really affected by it."

"*Dammit,*" Jack muttered, seething with the daunting gulf between him and his son. Had Gooney warped JJC? Had Phil and Hedrona?

"And consider the other baseline," Hedrona went on. "A completely ruined culture. Greeney *had* to be probing into all its corners. I mean, he's had five hundred Martians reporting directly to him, and each of them trained thousands of AC counselors, and *they* trained more, and God knows how many Centaurians have actually been counseled."

"I know, I *know,* but--"

"So Greeney essentially oversaw turning Alpha Centauri back to a totally low-energy, agrarian society. Back where it was at the time the Grid first came about. A set of linked solar systems barely holding together, with revolutions, defections, sabotage of space routes, just like today. Whole planets committing suicide, like Kelstalw 3 last month."

Jack nodded. It wasn't the first AC world to blow itself up in despair. But Kelstalw 3 had been a prosperous manufacturing center, one that had never reverted to the agrarian model.

"So why are you two still here? Why is JJC still here for that matter?"

Phil shrugged. "I don't know about JJC. Maybe it's the only place he really knows."

"I don't know about us, either," Hedrona said. "I'm committed to the counseling program, but I have to admit I've fallen in love with Andertwin. It's so *slow.*"

Phil grinned. "Yeah, like some failed third-world country. It's almost impossible to get anything done here. The local Jujl authorities are *impossible.* But it's all so *beautiful* here."

Jack was tempted to take their sudden nostalgia for this backward world as more evidence of potential treason, but recalled his own yearning a few minutes ago to retire here. It *was* slow. The plant smells out there were life itself. The idea of a rural planet, almost entirely grass and trees, with just a few tiny oceans, was intoxicating.

Was he really so tired of being SCUSSF after running it since '35? Jack didn't feel old, but decades of top-level USSF responsibility did add up. Borman had been talking of retirement himself, maintaining that rejuvenation was making it impossible for youngsters like Bobby to come up any further. Bobby was around fifty now, though Jack still thought of him as a twelve-year-old. Fantastic officer, but Jack was keeping him back as a copilot on the *Typhoon*. And what about all the eager twenty-year-olds coming up? Where would they go?

Maybe it was time to pack it in. Do something different. Was Lee serious about opening a popcorn restaurant with Jack in Chicago? Said Amav could come in too, along with Lee's wife? Why couldn't Jack ever remember her name? Suzette something. Hell, he didn't don't know how to make popcorn. How could Lee talk about making six hundred kinds of popcorn?

Jack had a damn senator on his ship mouthing off about quarantining this planet. People elected him because he was a war hero, and Jack was stuck with him. And now Senator Borman wanted to go into business with the Supreme Commander of the United System Space Force.

Jack looked for a beer. None was conveniently at hand. Borman swigged his own green bottle and guffawed at Patrick James. Jack sighed.

*Aw, hell! Come on, admit it! That son of a bitch Borman makes me laugh! Face it, we have a lot of fun! The entire damn crew should retire, but we can't bring ourselves to split up! What would I do without these guys?*

# CHAPTER NINETEEN
## Why Would I Destroy This Planet?

"*What?*" Jack cried. "*What* are you saying?"

Amav tensed at the anger in Jack's voice. She turned to see him glaring at Phil.

"I was just saying that maybe the Grid might really be wobbling back online, maybe going slow, like Seed by Seed," Phil said. "We saw some Jujl today who were acting strange. Like they were plugged *into* something. It was like they were hiding something from us."

"That's impossible!"

"Well, we hope that's not the case," Hedrona said. "But knowing Clopt's programming genius, who knows?"

"Dammit, Phil, I hope to hell you're not nostalgic for the Grid yourself."

Phil shrugged. "Why would I be?"

"Because--hell, you know why. You're probably picking up these Jujl thoughts. Maybe you're getting *brainwashed* by the damn things. I mean, you were before. Twice!"

Amav was surprised to see Phil calmly nod.

"Yeah, you got that right," Phil said. "But I didn't feel anything like a connection with those Jujl. Just an odd feeling about 'em. I really have zero desire to revisit any of that insanity."

"Even that *insanity* on the *Typhoon II?* You're not nostalgic for *that?*"

"Jack!" Amav gasped.

Phil held Jack's gaze. "Yeah, even that. Hell, Jack, that was forty years ago."

Amav looked away.

"Forty years ..." Jack muttered. "Damn, it *has* been forty years!"

"And I've had all these years to move *beyond* it."

"I've made *sure* he moved beyond it," Hedrona grinned, grabbing Phil's ass.

"Ow!"

"Well … well …" Jack said, looking back and forth between the two.

"It's okay," Amav said, flustered. "Everything's fine."

Jack took a deep breath. "All right. Whatever. But with this Gooney stuff going on, it's really *not*."

"I know," Phil said. "We can hardly stand to think about it."

"But the point is, we have to deal with it. I'm going to talk to Joe first, make sure Sol isn't being probed. Then I'll call him out here with the *III*. Probably have him bring Dar."

"Well, Dar would be the best person to talk with Greeney, if that's possible."

Amav knew Dar would eagerly volunteer, especially now that newer techniques had ameliorated the formerly devastating effects of Star Drive on the Martian nervous system. Dar hadn't taken advantage of these techniques yet. His previous journeys to Alpha Centauri in '53 and a handful of other times had all been Heuristic Time Transitions, displacements in space and time as opposed to the mind-staggering space warping of Star Drive.

Well, they were finally done with all 8,178 Heuristic Time Transitions. Urside Charmouth had performed the last one on May 29th. Dar and his team had sewn up all the paradoxes they could, and they all could build again. But did this have anything to do with Gooney's grab for the emperor and the Grid? Had he just been waiting for this moment, when nobody could time-travel into his rear and undo him?

All Jack wanted was to retire, and Amav could feel him seething at having to clean up everything again. It was more than enough running Sol all by himself. Those damn senators on the Council didn't do anything. And now he was supposed to run Alpha Centauri too?

*

"Hello again, Admiral Commer!" John Root blared. "I've been having the most fascinating conversation with Senator Borman!"

Amav winced. She'd never met John Commer, but she knew what that robot was doing to Jack. She'd seen all the robots. The Jack robot had been perfect, voice, mannerisms, everything.

"Borman says you should take the *Typhoon* into orbit and *incinerate* this planet! I would like to view *that* from a porthole on your exalted ship, Admiral Commer! What a sight that would be!"

Jack stared into his younger brother's huge round blue eyes. "Are you *crazy?* Why would I destroy this planet?"

"A robot *can't* be crazy, Sir Jack! May I call you Sir Jack? Because I've always *worshipped* you, you know. Of course, it's just my programming, but worship is worship, you know! Take it where you can get it!"

"I--*no!*"

"Well, to answer your question, Sir Jack. You would destroy this planet because the first Seed of the Grid was *planted* here. Here on this beautiful agricultural world. Sterilize this planet and you may save the galaxy! That's my reasoning and Senator Borman's, sir!"

"I am *not* going to destroy this planet!"

"Aaah, the fascist mentality kicks in again, I see!"

"*What?*"

"You fascistly *deny* me and Senator Borman our wish for the destruction of this planet, knowing we crave it so much!"

"Phil!" Jack pointed to the robot. "What *is* this thing?"

"I don't know. I've never seen him like this before."

"He *wants* to put an end to my existence," John Root muttered. "I've seen *that* before! What a fascist!"

"Do you really expect me to blow up this planet just because a stupid robot tells me to?" Jack cried. "And Borman?"

"Yah!" Borman said, staggering up with a beer in either hand. "Jack, the Seed is here! We gotta blow it!"

"God, the two of you make a pair!" Jack laughed. "Borman, are you really a robot too? Did I get a Lee Borman '44 model or something here?"

"Huh," Borman said, scratching his belly with a bottle. "I

don't *think* so. Can a robot get drunk?"

"Oh, yes! Of course!" Root laughed, snatching a beer from Borman and gulping it. "We just don't feel it, of course!"

"Okay, everyone, listen up," Jack said. "All this isn't getting us anywhere. The first thing we need to do is locate Gooney. Phil, do you have any idea where he got off to?"

"Sorry, Jack. There's no technology in AC that could tell us, like it could back in Sol. We don't have the sort of network for that here."

"He *wants* me dead!" Root repeated. "Well, if he wants to blow up the planet with me on it, I'm ready! I'm just a robot! A second-class citizen! I don't care if I'm dead! I'm *programmed* not to care! To lay my life, such as it is, down for the greater good!"

"Shut up!" Jack snarled. "What is *wrong* with you?"

"This is *always* how Jack would treat John!" Root said, sniffing back a fake tear. "Patronize, and patronize, and patronize some more, then, *wham!* Out of the blue, he *explodes!*"

"Phil, tell that robot to go elsewhere! I can't think!"

"Yes, I've had *all* the history programmed right in! The whole story of Jack and Joe and Jim and John!"

"You *killed* Jim, you son of a bitch! Don't you dare mention his name! You took the *Typhoon* down and *rammed* it on Mercury! Jim was *innocent!* He didn't *deserve* that!"

"And consider Senator Jonathan Commer, Senior! What a *stew* of family insanity!"

"Damn you!" Jack cried, raising his fist.

"C'mon, Jack, easy," Phil said, getting between them. "Root could throw you clear across the hall and out the opposite window. You'd just break your hand trying to punch him out."

"That's right, Jack, this is just a piece of machinery," Amav said. "It's not John. You can't get angry at it."

"Okay, then clear this piece of machinery *out*. We need to talk, and I can't think with it around."

"Blow the planet!" Root cackled. "I dare you!"

"*Get him out!*"

"Of course, you'd blow your own son, too! Your own son,

depressed as hell, hiding out at the Castle because no one loves him! But maybe that would conveniently kill two birds with one stone, wouldn't it?"

"*What?*"

"You forget I can run my *own* counseling program!" John Root laughed. "It's so obvious that you fascistly lust for the deaths of all you claim to love!"

"How on earth can you *say* that?"

"It's in JJC's book! All through it!"

"It's in Jonathan James' *book?*"

"You haven't read it, Sir Jack?"

"Look, I've *meant* to, but there's been no time!"

"No matter, then, Sir Jack! No matter if after *two years* you can't bring yourself to read the most astonishing novel of our time! But I can help you, Admiral Jack, most glorious sir! My counseling rates are *cheap!* At least compared to Greeney Gooney's! Together we can *talk out* your most fundamental fears and insecurities!"

Jack stared back, paralyzed.

"And now that we have the beautiful Amav Frankston-Commer with us, the mother of the most famous author in Alpha Centauri, we can do group counseling at substantially reduced rates! All three of you need to probe your shattered, dysfunctional *cores!* Together! Won't that be fun?"

# CHAPTER TWENTY
## *A Fragmented Encyclopedia of Recent Self*

"Get him … out …" Jack whispered, edgily aware that he was sounding just like his father mimicking yet another heart attack to get attention, to get his way, to dominate.

What could be in that book? No wonder he hadn't wanted to read it. Did this hunk of metal really think that Jack would sit down with Amav and JJC and babble for hours about all sorts of private feelings?

"John, listen, Jack's upset. I think your presence here is upsetting him," Hedrona said. "You came to tell us JJC isn't coming, and we appreciate that. Why don't you just head back to him now?"

"No, that way Jack can plot *destruction and ruin!*" Root cried. "And outright *fascism!* Well, JJC and I won't have it! We simply won't have it!"

"*Wha-aaat?*" Jack stared back. Why was he letting this *thing from the past* whip him into incoherence?

"You think I don't know! But I do! JJC *dictated* his book to me, you know! I'm his *word processor!* I had to *memorize* the book! In a million different formats! And send it to publishers! And do all the publicity! I just blasted it *everywhere!*"

Jack stepped back, fighting for control. He'd known some of that. It made sense to dictate a book to your robot. He had to admire JJC for it, really. It took some savvy to write a whole book and use your robot to market it.

"The Mars publishers wouldn't touch it! Even though it's your own *son*. We wondered if you were the one who squashed the book in Sol!"

"No! I had no idea he was sending anything to publishers!"

"But CrimsonSwordThrust on Zorax *loved* it! Imagine that if you will, Sir Jack! A publisher on the *Zarj homeworld* loved JJC's book! Just *loved* it!"

"Look, I know. You know we're very proud of Jonathan James."

"Is it fiction, as CrimsonSwordThrust maintains? Or a

thinly-disguised memoir of a young human growing up alienated in a defeated culture stripped of its Grid and reeling out of control?"

"Well, I ..."

"He's so famous you can't *imagine!*" John Root declared, advancing with a finger pointed at Jack's chest. "I translated it into *thousands* of AC languages! Hell, we didn't have the Grid to distribute it, dear Sir Jack! And your son became a bestselling author *here* first! Only then did your miserable Sol publishers issue an English edition!"

"We know it, we're proud of him, we--"

"And he's to receive the Centaurian Hero of Literature Award tomorrow! Naturally there's no emperor to issue it like in the old days, unless we count Sir Gooney's impetuous attempt, that is. But whatever the case, the Grand See of Zorax will issue the award themselves!"

"I knew that," Jack said evenly. "That's why we're here. And now, if you'll excuse me--"

"Young Jonathan James Commer's first novel is a true literary masterpiece," John Root intoned. "Though a twenty-seven-year-old human, the author knew the Emperor's Grid in his infancy, and now manages to masterfully evoke a defeated Empire shorn of its highest masterpiece, that Glorious Grid, and left to drift into anarchy as trillions of formerly loyal Centaurian citizens reel into their private hells of unlimited insanity."

"He's into his marketing module again," Hedrona complained. "Sometimes it takes hours for him to get it out of his system."

"Disguised as fiction to avoid repercussions from the occupying jackboots of Sol, *A Fragmented Encyclopedia of Recent Self* perfectly captures the perfidious usurping of the emperor's throne and its resulting dishonor by the treasonous Martian leader Blar and his dimwitted human henchman, Hack Blommer, Supreme Salamander of the United Sneeze. As young Ronathan Rames Blommer struggles to disentangle himself from the disgusting psychological manipulations of his dysfunctional, incompetent father, a so-called soldier unfit to lick the boots of the lowliest Zoraxian toilet swabber--"

"What *is* this crap?" Jack said, whirling to Amav. "Didn't you tell me you'd read it?"

"Well, you know about first novels, and families, and all that."

"I do not!"

"Well, you know, sometimes authors use their first novel to get out all sorts of family tensions and all."

"That's crazy! I won't have it!"

"*The Review of Centaurian Books* calls it 'hypnotically engulfing down to the Fourth Genital.' Gorthl Harakcte, writing in the influential *Vessel of Profound Literary Monsters,* regards *Fragmented Encyclopedia* as 'the defining work of our age.' Citizens throughout our shattered Empire take refuge in these stunningly accurate depictions of the New Centaurian Anxiety. Ronathan Rames' stifled yearnings for transcendence must move all loyal Alpha Centaurians to tears. Not since the era of J'iiuj the Twelfth has a work of fiction so entranced this sorry Empire, and consider that *A Fragmented Encyclopedia of Recent Self* was composed and published *without* the Exalted Grid! Is there hope for our screaming souls yet?"

"Centaurians read *novels?*" Jack cried. "They have a goddamn *publishing* industry here? They let this crap get *published?*"

"C'mon, Jack, don't be so upset," Amav said. "JJC was just expressing himself."

"Stop defending him! You should have told me this was all *libelous!*"

"Oh, come on! You wouldn't bring a libel suit against your own son!"

"You should've told me!"

"Dammit, I knew you'd act like a baby about this!"

"Great, so you wait till we get here, and then tell me!" Jack whirled to Phil. "What *is* this, Phil? Alpha Centaurians read *novels?*"

Phil shrugged. "Yeah, it was a surprise to us, too. But they've been writing and publishing 'em for two thousand years.

It's just that the inspiration always came from the emperor. It's like a novel was whatever the emperor's mood was that day. One AC would just sort of take it down, like taking dictation. Any novel probably only took 'em a few minutes, I think. Then it'd immediately be part of the Grid and everyone in AC would read it at once."

Jack shuddered. More anthill insanity. This place had always given him the creeps. Why did he ever think he'd want to retire here?

"The strange thing is that they're awfully similar to human novels," Hedrona said. "They sort of reflect the whole society or something. I was able to read a few before the Grid collapsed, and somehow I didn't have to be part of the Grid to do that. Weird. Of course, all that was lost when the Grid went down."

"Yeah, it's like the emperor was the publisher *and* the computer network it was all stored on," Phil said. "When he went, *billions* of novels just went *poof!*"

"A human capable of making a novel on his own just *astounded* CrimsonSwordThrust!" John Root cried. "There were a few tries by individual ACs over the past twenty years, but they're *pitiful!* Just a bunch of wailing and flailing! Some ACs set up publishing houses, trying to find new novels, but everyone was in despair until Jonathan James came along with his tremendous *insight!*"

"*Phil, I told you to get rid of this goddamn robot!*"

"Calm *down!*" Amav snarled. "I'm so sick of this!"

"Dammit, Amav, this is my own son *slandering* me!"

"So what? Laugh it off!"

"I will not laugh it off! This is goddamn *serious!*"

"You *always* get like this when you're tired! You get so strung out you can't think straight! Then you act like a baby!"

"You're damn right I'm tired! Who wouldn't be? I've had to hold this goddamn thing together for *forty goddamn years* now! No wonder I'm tired!"

"*What* goddamn thing? What the hell are you talking about?"

"*Seventeen years of war after DamnStar!* Seventeen years

of *horrible, stupid war!* And for nothing! *Nothing!* And then *twenty-two years* of *total insanity* on top of *that!*"

"Oh, so you're feeling sorry for yourself again!" Amav yanked open the front door. "Dammit, I'm leaving!"

"Twenty-two years of *insanity! Forty* years of insanity! I haven't been able to even talk to my own son! He won't see me! It's like he's an *alien!* He's exiled himself here, in this *craziness*, with--with these--" Jack shook a finger at Phil and Hedrona.

"*You think you're the only one? You think I haven't lived through all that, too?*" Amav yelled, slamming the front door behind her.

"You--you can't do that!"

John Root whistled. "Way to go, fascist Jack!"

Abruptly Jack was aware that he was the Supreme Commander of the United System Space Force, inspecting his boots amid a shameful silence. "She's been ... sorta upset recently, I think."

More silence. Jack felt Phil and Hedrona looking away. Borman and Connors and James and Sortie fidgeted. "Maybe ... me too," Jack added.

"Are you really so exhausted, Admiral Jack?" John Root said in an inexplicably soft tone.

Jack closed his eyes. "Yeah, John, I think I am."

"I'll talk to Amav," Hedrona said, moving for the door.

# CHAPTER TWENTY-ONE
## The Cult of Amav

Amav charged down a winding slope through tall weeds. Ahead of her the sun was settling into a tree-lined ridge on the horizon. A chilly breeze rippled through the fronds all around her.

"Amav! Wait up!" she heard Hedrona calling.

Amav slowed until Hedrona caught up. "Look, I'm sorry, but I've *had* it with him."

"It's okay, I'm sure he's just upset about JJC not showing up." Hedrona wore a gold blouse and black pants. She'd kept her petite figure all these years and seemed in excellent shape for a woman of seventy-six.

"No, it's more than that. He's been antsy for *weeks* now, prepping for this trip. And now this Gooney stuff's *unhinged* him."

"Yeah, but if I remember how Jack operates, he can seem to get totally flustered about something, then--*bam!* All of sudden he makes up his mind what to do about it."

Amav smiled. She'd forgotten how Hedrona had run the Earth Animal Rescue program with unfailing energy and optimism. Whenever Amav's terraforming work brought them into contact, she and Hedrona had worked well together, even though at the time Hedrona was twenty-six years older than Amav. The kidnapping had narrowed the difference down something like fourteen.

Amav nodded. "I just need to get away a bit. Where are we, anyway?" She shivered in her thin white dress as darkness settled in.

"This is the Lower Garden. These things look like wild grass but they're really *Vultaiu Clarisft,* a sort of amazing Andertwin herb. I'll brew up some tea later. It's very invigorating."

"It smells wonderful. Everything seems so peaceful here."

"It is. Phil and I just can't believe this thing with Greeney will go anywhere. I mean, we've had nothing but the *same thing* here for twenty-two years. It's all been so slow and easy."

"But you've been working hard at the counseling stuff, right?"

"Sure, but somehow all that was just *stuff to do*. It doesn't seem as if it can end."

"But you're feeling that everything's suddenly changed."

Hedrona nodded. "Yeah."

"Well, I'm sorry we came right in the middle of all this. You must be *reeling*."

"No, it's great that you guys are here. We need you now."

They descended to a level area filled with huge rocks in the gloom. Amav looked back to see the guest house far above them. Her comm buzzed.

"Aren't you going to get that?"

"No, it's just Jack," Amav said, canceling the call. "Let him calm down a bit. I need some time to decompress."

A dry valley extended miles in either direction. The immense rocks where they stood had been aesthetically chosen and placed here like artwork. Amav leaned against one.

"I'm glad our gardeners are gone for the day," Hedrona said. "They're all Jujl. This is a Jujl planet, which is why we have the nitrogen-oxygen atmosphere. But I'm still a little leery of those guys Phil and I saw in town today. They definitely looked like they were *plugged into* something. I hope it was just our imagination, but I just don't want to look up and see, say, Ji'ourff and have to figure out if he's trying to plug himself into a new Grid or something."

"But nobody can just build a new Grid out of nothing, can they? I mean, doesn't there have to be some sort of telepathic control or whatever?"

"Nobody knows," Hedrona said, letting the wind bluster through her long dark hair. "Somehow the Grid just *got established*. It was thousands of years ago. Clopt thought there had to be some sort of trans-spatial software behind it."

"Clopt! That son of a bitch!"

"Oh, I forgot. He was the one--"

"Right. On the *Typhoon II* in '35. The one who turned us

over to the emperor. He was just *itching* to torture us all. Now I hear he's writing *poems* to me!"

Hedrona laughed. "The whole thing's silly, all right. But you have to understand this culture. Trillions of ACs have been completely cut off from their former source of well-being. Every individual has to exist on his or her own now, and they're making a hash of it, so they try to worship first one thing, then another. After they offered the emperorship to Jack, there was talk of Dar, the guy who *ended* the Empire. But none of it ever goes anywhere. I've heard of offering it to your son, because he wrote that novel, or to *me,* for being the Ultimate Gladiator of the Sled, or even to Phil, for being the one who *worked* on my sled. I guess the obsession's on *you* now."

"Great," Amav muttered. She was still shocked at how old Phil was. What she found in her mirror still looked like her normal self. She didn't think she'd aged much. Nobody around her had really seemed to. She remembered when Phil had been so hungry for her. It had been flattering in a way. She had to admit she'd expected a young, ravenous Phil looking her up and down. Well, maybe Hedrona had mellowed him somehow.

So why had she worn this teeny white sundress today? Did she really want him looking down her cleavage?

"There've also been some calls over the years for Greeney to be emperor," Hedrona went on. "This is the only time he's ever *accepted* it, if that's even possible."

Amav's comm buzzed and again she canceled it. "Can we keep walking? I'm sort of restless."

"Sure. Are you sure you're not too cold in that dress?"

"I'm fine. I need to keep moving." They walked from the rock garden and across the valley, up the far slope of ferns and into a stand of thin trees.

"Anyway, they need something to pull their society together. So far this Cult of Amav has been the only thing that's seemed to work. Apparently it's been growing for years, but it's only taken off recently. I mean, since JJC's book got published."

"I'm the center of some weird *religion?*"

Hedrona nodded, pushing low branches out of their way as

they continued their climb. "Yeah, it's all crazy. But this whole culture is crazy. Maybe we were idiots to think it could just go on and on like it has. It's been such a lazy time. We counsel the people, we train other counselors, everyone talks about how sad they are that they don't have an emperor, everyone sort of admits they're better off without an emperor or a Grid, but *nothing happens.* We all sit and stare at the *Vultaiu Clarisft* growing, and have a beer out on the patio."

Amav turned to the guest house lit in warm yellow, high on the opposite ridge. "Well, Jack's been pretty exasperated about this cult thing. He says it's demeaning and I should go on whatever passes for SolNet here and make some broadcast that I'm *abdicating.* Whatever that would mean."

Hedrona smiled. "There's nothing like SolNet here. It's funny, but in a way, Sol has more of a Grid than AC does. All the Alpha Centaurian subcultures have just been scattered to the winds. Maybe the Cult of Amav is all that's holding the thing together."

"I feel like I'm supposed to be the Virgin Mary out here. It's *nuts!*"

"Like I say, I was in that position for a little bit myself. I was the Foremost Gladiator of the Sled and all. But when I stopped Gladiation, they *turned* from me. Boy, did they turn from me! Now they think I'm some sort of cosmic *wimp.*"

"Wow, I hope you're not jealous that I've usurped you. Believe me, you can have the honor back if you want it."

"No way! But seriously, I wonder if there isn't some way to diminish it somehow. If you did make some sort of announcement that slowly got transferred all over AC, if the ACs saw you for what you really were, for instance."

"And what am I? An out-of-work planetary engineer?"

"Oh, c'mon, Amav, you could make a fortune here in AC. There are dozens of Centaurian worlds still blown from the war that could use a makeover."

"I'm just kidding. I *have* thought about working over here. Especially since we just finished with Earth."

"God, how *is* it?" Hedrona said. "I've been meaning to take a trip back."

"It's fantastic. Better than before, really. We've adjusted New Luna as well, and it looks almost like the old moon. There are some design competitions to see who can mold the surface features back exactly the way they were. But Earth itself is a paradise now. We're very happy with the result. Of course, I can't do Amplified Thought routines myself, but I could participate in some of them with the Martians. That was amazing!"

"So now you guys could relocate here. It would be wonderful to have you here."

"Assuming that Mr. Gooney isn't really about to make some sort of civil war here."

"I really can't believe that. It's got to be nonsense." They reached the crest of the hill, and were now higher than the tiny glass guest house off to the east.

Amav turned to the new plains opening to the west in faint purple post-sunset light. "Well, I don't know how to say this, but even if it does blow over, there's dealing with Jonathan James."

Hedrona nodded. "Yeah, I get that."

"Once the Earth Terraforming Project was complete, and we had all these wonderful parties for Earth Renewal Year, I thought maybe we should go see JJC and see, you know, what was there."

"What was there?"

"To see if *anything* was left." Amav pushed into the increasingly darker west. Thousands of stars were coming out. "I've only seen my son *three times* since he was kidnapped. I really don't have any relationship to him. I *pretend* I'm his mother, but you and Phil are more his parents than Jack and I will ever be."

"Wow, I'd never want you to be jealous of me or Phil. There's no way we think of ourselves as JJC's parents. He's like some bright young friend we have, that's all."

"I know, I know, but when he was kidnapped, when you all were, for two years we heard *nothing*. Of course you finally assume he's dead! After a couple months, a few months, of course you give up! Even if in your mind you say he *has* to still be alive. But there was no word from the ACs, no ransom demands, nothing! Dar wasn't able to find anything out on the next couple HTTs he did. Then in '40, he *does* get through. He makes it to AC '52 and finds out that Jonathan James was taken to 2049. And so we hope he makes it to '53, when we liberate the place."

"God, I can't imagine what that must've been like."

"We were finally relieved, but from '40 on we're waiting *another* nine years for a ransom demand! During all this time I'm concentrating on terraforming Earth, Jack's doing his USSF work, but do you think we were ever really happy? 2049 comes and *nothing!* Again no word! Dar can't find out anything new. And of course we had no idea if you or Phil or Greeney were still alive, either. We don't know *anything.* So we just wait for four *more* years."

"Wow …"

"So in '53, on May 14th, we finally know he's really alive. By this time we don't have the slightest idea how we're really feeling. We're numb to *everything.* Dar has us wait a week for the Grid to fully die down." Amav closed her eyes. "And then, when we finally get here, I'm seeing this insanely weird *five-year-old!* My God, he should've been *sixteen* by then! Dar warned me he wouldn't have aged much, but I didn't feel any connection at all!"

"I remember it was strained."

"And he felt nothing for *us!* Was it being on the Grid? Did that wreck his mind?"

"No, of course not. Phil was on the Grid, too, and he recovered just fine."

"Did he? He looks so unhappy!"

"Well … well …"

"Did you ever wonder why Jack and I didn't have any more children? We just couldn't face it! All that time we had this kidnapped baby somewhere out there. Transported to a different time! Out of synch with us! Living with Alpha Centaurian *monsters!* We came again in '59, and it was the same! And '67!

God, I couldn't stand it! I kept telling myself I loved him, that he'd come back to me, but that eleven-month-old baby was gone forever!"

"Well, maybe not. Maybe he's still in there somewhere."

"Is it my fault? Was I the one who withdrew? And Jonathan James just followed my example? Oh my God!"

"Look, we'll try to see JJC tomorrow. Maybe we can work some of this out."

"And Jack's had it worse! We don't even talk about it, but I know he's had it worse!"

"Look, there's got to be an answer somehow."

"Then he writes this book! *Stabbing* at Jack! I wanted to pretend it was all some sort of therapy! But he's *alien* to us! He's not real! I've waited all my life to find this out! I've wasted my life, that's what I've done! These monsters worship this Cult of Amav, but they have no idea who she really is!"

Amav flung all this into Hedrona's deep blue eyes in the starlight. She'd had no idea Hedrona was such a compassionate woman. "And rejuvenation just keeps *prolonging* everything! I'm old, but I'm *young!* I'm all mixed up! Nothing ever came together! I've wasted everything!"

Then light was everywhere. The stars were overwhelmed. Amav watched Hedrona cartwheeling. And she herself was *coming apart.*

*My God, they blew us up! Someone blew us up!*

# CHAPTER TWENTY-TWO
## This is Senator Lee Borman Calling the United System Council!

Hedrona slammed into the dirt, breath knocked out, eyes surging with crimson spots and bright purple afterimages. For several stunned seconds she lay there. The air was acrid with ozone. She spat out mud. Was that a lightning strike? But there were no storm clouds.

"Amav!" she yelled, staring at where they'd both been standing. "*Amav!*"

The ground was undisturbed. No plants were charred or uprooted. Hedrona got to her knees, wincing at her wrenched back. She scanned three hundred sixty degrees around the dark western ridge. Nothing. No one.

"*Amav! Amav, are you all right?*"

Amav's comm lay on the ground in front of her. It was buzzing. Hedrona picked it up.

"Hey, Amav, look, I'm really sorry," Jack began. "We need to talk."

"*Didn't you hear the explosion?*"

"Huh? No! What are you talking about? Amav?"

"No, this is *Hedrona!* Amav's *gone!*"

"*What?*"

Hedrona charged down the slope, yanking her way down through the thin trees, scrambling over roots and rocks, barely able to see the footpath in the darkness.

"*What's going on out there?*"

"She's *gone!* There was an explosion and she was *gone!*" Hedrona cried as she hit the rock garden in the middle of the dried creek.

"*Who's gone?*"

"*Amav!* We went to the top of the ridge. There was a light, and then this *force* hit us!"

"Oh my God!"

Hedrona rushed up the slope to the house. "This is crazy, but I think someone must have kidnapped her! Like when Phil

133

and I and JJC were taken!" She shot up the last concrete stairs to the patio where Jack wrenched open the sliding door. Behind him came the other *Typhoon* officers, John Root, and Phil.

"Are you all right?" Phil cried. "What happened?"

"There--there was this *light!* I think someone's kidnapped her!"

Jack pulled Amav's comm from her hands. "Draka! Analyze the sensor history off this!"

Ship's engineer Sortie took the device. "Everyone back inside!" Jack ordered. "May not do a hell of a lot of good, but at least you can't be picked off so easily out here." He pulled out his shattergun. "I'm going back to look for Amav." He pushed Hedrona inside with the others. "*So what happened?*"

"*Light*--I'm still not seeing right, but it seems like when Phil and I got kidnapped! The same *feel.* She just *disappeared!* It wasn't a real explosion, just felt like one somehow."

"Top of the hill over there?" Jack said, pointing. Hedrona nodded. Jack motioned to copilot Athens. "Okay, Bobby, you and I are going to the hill. Now."

"Yes, sir!"

"Are you sure?" Hedrona said. "What if there's radiation or something?"

"No radwaste of any sort," Sortie said, scanning Amav's comm. "Comm recorded a huge jump in Quark Matrix Flux. Lasted 1.544 seconds. The visual overloaded. Just went white. Can't figure it out."

"Let me see that," Phil said.

"Yes, sir, I'm sure you'd know a lot more about Comm History than I would!" Sortie said, handing it over.

"Hell, no. I haven't touched one of these new models, but I know they have much better holographic capability than my last USSF Comm." Phil punched in commands and then Amav in white and Hedrona in gold strode in half-size across the dining room floor.

"Leave the sound off," Hedrona said. Phil shot her a glance, then shrugged.

"Why?" Jack said

"Well, it was sorta, uh, private."

"Well, we damn well need it to get the full picture."

"No, wait," Phil said. "I've got it at one-twentieth speed. Damn, this resolution is *amazing*. And the fact that you can rearrange your perspective from any direction around the scene! I want to observe that tree as the light increases."

As he spoke, solid vertical lines of white light formed a box around Amav. Even in slow motion, the lines quickly solidified and grew overwhelming. The tree to the left of Amav, and Hedrona to Amav's right, looked as if they were being sucked towards Amav. Leaves surged, Hedrona lost her balance, and then the entire holographic cube filled with white.

"Amazing!" John Root put in. "I have a long-range scan that confirms the same thing."

"Shut up, robot," Jack snapped. "We don't need you."

Root shrugged. As the light waned, there was a jumble of images as the comm was flung wildly, coming to rest focused on Hedrona's leg.

"That's weird," Phil muttered. "You and the tree leaves were first sucked *towards* Amav, then blown the *other* way. We can clean up the scrambled part, rearrange our perspective again, but I'd say that whoever took Amav took a bunch of the air around her. So we had a vacuum which Hedrona was getting pulled *into*. You didn't hear any thunder?"

"N-no," Hedrona said. "Not that I can remember."

"Look at this air pressure reading. It's as if whoever took Amav shoved back in some *replacement* air, a hell of a lot more than was necessary. That blew Hedrona the *other* way."

"*Whoever took Amav?*" Jack cried, checking the settings on his gun. "Bobby! Let's get moving!"

Robert Athens had his own shattergun out. "Ready, Jack!"

"Hold it right there," Lee Borman said. "Jack, first things first. We need to declare martial law throughout Alpha Centauri."

"Huh? Are you crazy? I'm going to find my wife!"

"Forget it! The goddamn Centaurians have obviously HTT'd her right out of here! We have no idea where she is right now or even what year she's in."

"Well, it *has* to be contemporary," John Root said. "We're done with the Time Transition Era as of a couple weeks ago, as you're all no doubt aware."

"Hell with that," Borman said. "I'm sure these AC bastards have figured some way around that." He pulled his own shattergun out. "As United System senator, I declare--"

"*No!*" Jack shouted. "Dammit, Borman, you're under my command! You stay here and protect the civilians while Bobby and I check out the hill." Hedrona winced. She could feel Phil's dismay at being termed a *civilian*.

"Anyway," Draka Sortie pointed out, "the 8,178 HTTs between 2013 and 2075 are a *law of nature*. By definition there *can't* be any more after May 29, 2075."

"Yeah, tell that to the goddamn ACs," Borman muttered darkly, holstering his weapon.

"No, really, I know what I'm talking about. My Ph.D. is in HTT studies."

"All that namby-pamby textbook learning doesn't mean a thing. My *gut reaction* says we've gotta lock down this entire system *now*." Borman whipped out his comm.

"Dammit, Borman, put that down!" Jack cried.

"This is Senator Lee Borman calling the United System Council!"

# CHAPTER TWENTY-THREE
## The Castle

In spite of her terror Hedrona fought back a laugh. "You *can't* be calling Sol on a comm!"

"Huh," Borman said, then into the comm: "Thanks, Marcie, I'll wait for the President. Tell him it's Priority A1." He winked at Hedrona. "This ain't no ordinary USSF Comm, honey. This is a Senator Comm, with superspace radio."

Hedrona shrank from the little senator's leer. In his autobiography Borman claimed to have bedded over six hundred women. She wouldn't have believed anyone would have ever wanted this runty turret gunner until curiosity got the better of her and she'd checked Borman's SolNet site, where he'd posted video of sex with fifty of his paramours.

But the leer had given Jack the opportunity to snatch the comm out of Borman's hand.

"Dammit, give that back!" Borman cried.

Jack dialed his shattergun down to the lowest setting, dropped the Senator Comm to the floor, and fired a pencil-thin burst. Then he kicked the resulting chunks of amber glass across the tile.

"Wow!" John Root whistled. "A clear demonstration of fascist determination to dominate and destroy!"

"Shut up, robot!" Jack snarled.

"The damn thing's right, Jack," Borman said. "You're losing your head, as usual!"

"Get this through *your* head, senator. *I* am in charge of this mission from beginning to end. *Your* orders are to stay here and protect this house while Bobby and I check the perimeter."

"Dammit, Jack, those Senator Comms are *expensive*. I *insist* on using the superspace radio in the *Typhoon* to notify Sol of the threat!"

"Request denied. I am *not* going to start a new war before I know exactly what's going on. For all we know Amav is wandering around on the hill up there in a daze. Bobby and I will begin our search and report back."

"Why don't you cruise over in the *Typhoon* shuttle and use the searchlights and sensors?" Phil said. "Be a lot faster and more accurate than the comm sensors."

Jack looked to the west windows. By now the sun had set and all Hedrona could see were the reflections of the lights and people standing in the dining room, except for the open door to solid blackness. "Great idea, Phil. Okay, Bobby, let's do it."

"Dammit, Jack!" Borman said. "Are you gonna allow a United System senator his input or not?"

"Dammit, Lee! This is *insubordination!*"

"Hey, Jack," said Navigation Officer Will Connors, "you know Lee just wants to put in his dissenting opinion. You know, like he always does. If you just give him his say, then, you know, he'll follow you, just like always."

"I'm sure the senator just wants to have his input on record in case anything blows up in your face, Sir Jack!" John Root said. "As it surely will!"

Jack looked at the ceiling and sighed. "Okay, senator, let's have your input. But I remind you that I'm in command of a military situation."

"Sheesh," Borman said. "Okay, Jack, just look. Don't you see it has to be Gooney who's kidnapped her? He needs her for this Cult of Amav thing. Hell, the ACs *worship* her! Gooney did it to legitimize his claim to the emperorship."

"Huh ..."

"So this Cult of Amav is gonna be used to unify the Empire again. And since it's a religious thing, it could even be the basis for restarting the Grid."

"That's impossible!"

"In any case, her disappearance is an act of war. We have to act *now* to declare the entire Alpha Centaurian system under USSF military justice!"

"Technically, it already is!"

"You know what I mean. We have to declare Greeney Gooney a traitor. In fact, we have to kill him off, right now!"

"Oh my God," Hedrona said. "Can't we just see what he wants? I mean, he *can't* be successful at this."

"Forget it, little lady! There's no use talking to him now, or figuring how what sort of stunt he thinks he's pulling. He's one dead finback is what he is. Jack, let's declare martial law *now*, and go *after* the mother!"

"Lee!" Jack cried. "Just cut it! Let me find out where my wife is! *Then* we'll talk!" He turned to Draka Sortie. "Draka, you accompany me and Bobby to the *Typhoon* and gear her up for combat. Then monitor us as we search in the shuttle. The rest of you stay here and protect this house and the civilians. Hedrona, you contact Jonathan James and tell him the situation."

"*I* will contact Jonathan James!" John Root put in. "I am in *constant contact* with him!"

"Damn, I keep forgetting about the goddamn *robot*. Just keep him out of the way, will you?" He pointed to Root. "You tell JJC what's going on, but keep out of the way."

"Done, Sir Jack! JJC is well aware of this situation in real time! Oh yes he is!"

"Look, Jack, how can I help?" Phil said. "If you like I can go with you and Bobby in the shuttle. I know the ground around here."

"Yeah, that's a good idea, too. Okay, c'mon, then, let's--"

The house shook with thunder.

"Damn!" Hedrona groaned as the noise and vibrations built. The bones in her feet sang. Tremors built through her thighs.

"What's *that?*" Jack grabbed a chair to steady himself. Crockery shook on the kitchen island. A full drink slid off and crashed on the tile. "Are we having an earthquake?"

"We don't have earthquakes on Andertwin!" Phil said. "There's no tectonic activity!"

"Then what?" Jack pulled out his comm and aimed it all around, finally settling on due west. "It's coming from like fifty *miles* from here."

Phil wobbled over as Jack expanded his display to a three-dimensional frame five feet wide. Night vision software magnified the view, compensating for the curvature of the planet. Hedrona staggered over to see--

The Castle. Giant dark cubes stacked haphazardly, bathed

in greenish sensor light. JJC's entire three-hundred-foot-wide structure was shaking, the ground beneath heaving like liquid.

"*They're blowing up the Castle too!*" she cried.

"No!" Phil said, pointing. "It's *rising!*"

The Castle lifted itself from the churning land and swiveled, orange fire bursting from fifty rocket nozzles.

"Oh my God, the Castle is a *spaceship!*" Phil moaned as the nozzles built their thrust under the irregular dark cubes and the Castle rose further into the night.

Ozone everywhere. Air pummeled her. Hedrona turned to meet Phil's stunned eyes.

And then he was gone.

The earthquake stopped. Everyone stared at the space where Phil had been.

"Wow, no fuss this time!" John Root observed. "Looks like they got their act together with this one!"

# CHAPTER TWENTY-FOUR
## Jonathan James at Home

Phil's face was jammed into white cushions. His stomach felt ripped out. "*Dammit!* What the *hell's* going on?"

The roaring kept building beneath him. He turned his head with agonizing difficulty. There, on the couch opposite, lay Amav in her white dress, on her back, pressed into her own cushions.

And a whine. Phil saw Trotter the Beagle plastered to a third couch. Beside him, Jonathan James Commer struggled to sit erect, face dragged down by G-forces. In the center of the three white couches stood the seven-foot Clopt in his bright blue uniform, thick shaking arms splayed, tentacles slapping against his torso, legs straining against the increasing thrust.

"Sorry about--acceleration--" Jonathan James grunted. "Normally--inertial dampers would take care of it--but on the blink, I guess."

"Working--somewhat--" Clopt said, his words translated from dozens of spherical speakers that normally would be floating but were now pressed to the black carpet. "We're only feeling three G's now, but we're really taking off at twelve."

Phil gaped at the three couches in the central pit of JJC's black, fifty-foot-wide living room. "This really is a *spaceship?*" he moaned. "Why the hell didn't anyone *tell* me?"

JJC grimly studied his stomach and finally slid off the couch onto the black carpet.

"Urrrrrr!" whined Trotter. Phil could feel the dog's rattled thoughts. Twenty-two years old, but rejuvenated to about three, Trotter had picked up some of Greeney Gooney's telepathic outradiance ability the past few years.

*Insanity! Unbearable! I will bite! If I could!*

Phil hadn't pulled this many G's in years. If he could only turn over, maybe he could breathe. "You guys *kidnapped* me! And *Amav!*"

"My apologies for--rough transfer--" Clopt managed. "Emperor Greeney--has been trying to teach me--Amplified

Thought, but sadly, I am--unworthy of his teachings. Used some canned routines--downloaded into ship's computer. First one was way too much."

"Yes, Mother is still--unconscious," JJC gasped from the floor.

"What?" Phil muttered. Amav's white dress was in tatters, slit completely up her thigh, her transparent panties showing. She was shoeless. "Damn--she all right?"

"Yes--breathing--" JJC managed.

Phil stared at the slender young man who looked so eerily like his uncle Joe Commer. "You *kidnapped* us! Your house--is a *spaceship!*"

"Calm down--Sperry," Clopt said. "We need your brain-- fresh and alert for--next phase."

"Idiots! Nearly--killed us!"

"No, after Amav--I figured out--correct transfer sequence-- on Gooney's program. Yours was smooth."

"Was--not!"

"Quiet. Program recycling--pull up John Root. May take a few minutes."

"You put Amav's life at *risk!*"

At once the G-forces vanished. "Oh, Phillip, you always exaggerate," JJC said. "Is that good enough for you, Mr. Phil? We've achieved orbit."

Phil scrambled up, floating momentarily over the couch before descending.

"Oww-oooohhh!" Trotter said, also floating and coming down.

*People crazy! My pack! My people! Crazy!*

"Hmm," Clopt said. "It's only giving us one-fourth G."

"This inertial system *sucks!*" JJC spat. "Greeney claimed we'd never even *feel* liftoff. You'd at least think he could engineer *normal gravity* for orbit, couldn't you?"

"You must not insult the emperor! How many times do I have to tell you?"

"Aw, screw it, Clopt!"

"And in any case, *you* were the one who insisted on turning this ungainly pile of *scaddiz-klun* concrete into a *spaceship!* Of course it's not balanced!" Clopt turned to Phil. "You'll be able to assist us in fine-tuning the inertial system, of course."

Amav moaned and twisted on her couch. Her dress was ripped apart. Phil was startled to note she wasn't wearing a bra. Well, that was none of his business. "What are you talking about? You turned the Castle into a *spaceship?* For what?"

Clopt waved numerous tentacles in the human equivalent of a shrug. "You'll find out."

"Ooooo-rrrrrr!" Trotter said. "Yap yap yap!"

"C'mere, baby," JJC said, bounding back up to the couch and placing the dog in his lap. "It's okay, guy, you'll get used to the lower gravity in a bit. Just a bit weird, that's all."

*Not--crazy?*

"No, just a bad inertial dampening system. You'll be okay." JJC kissed Trotter's head.

*I'm okay! I'm okay! We're all okay!*

"What about Amav?" Phil demanded.

"Mother will be fine. I'm not worried about her."

"Praised be Amav!" Clopt said. "The Goddess of All! What wonderful timing, for the *actual Amav* to arrive! We *need* you now, Phil!"

"God, what's going *on?*" Phil cried. "Are you guys trying to go after Gooney? In this ship?" But even as he said this Phil knew the answer.

"Why should we go after him?"

"Well, he declared himself emperor, I mean."

Clopt snuffled out a Zarj laugh. "Philip, you amaze me. Why should we go after our new emperor? We *worship* him!"

"Huh?"

"Oh yes, we certainly worship our dear Gooney," JJC said. "But meanwhile welcome to the actual award party, Mr. Phil. You do realize I'm getting the Centaurian Hero of Literature Award?"

Phil stared at the smooth, dark, supercilious face. JJC lounged on his white couch with Trotter in his lap. He wore a sleek black outfit to match the black walls and black ceiling of the vast room. Phil turned to the only source of illumination, the twenty-foot-long window showing the blinding curved surface of Andertwin. "Yeah, I know. We were supposed to have the party at the guest house. So what's going on here, man?"

Jonathan James smirked. "Sorry for the inconvenience, Mr. Phil. But we needed to grab both you and Amav and get you into orbit with us. So we'll have the party *now*."

"How in hell could I not know the damn Castle is a *spaceship?*"

"Well, if Greeney can turn the Castle into a spaceship with Amplified Thought, he can certainly do it in a way that fools the great engineer Phil Sperry. You may wonder why I've issued so few invitations to visit over the past few months."

"This has been going on for--how long?"

"A few months. Greeney knew that the end of all time travel meant that we were ripe for a *change,* let's say. So he got everything ready for us."

"Let me get this straight. Are you saying you and Clopt are *working* with Gooney now? That you *support* him? This emperor business?"

"Yap yap!" Trotter cried. *And me too!*

Phil stared into the big brown Beagle eyes. "You?"

"The damn thing bonded into our *Garthah-/yuu,*" Clopt said, and Phil could feel his disgust even through the translator spheres which had resumed floating all around them.

"Trotter is part of your *Garthah-/yuu? A dog?*"

"Any species can form part of a *Garthah-/yuu.* Greeney commanded us to include him."

"So there are three of us now," JJC said. "Zarj brothers who will fight and die for each other. Of course Clopt takes full responsibility for his new dog brother, doesn't he?"

"*Dammit ...*" Clopt muttered.

*Big dog tribe!* Trotter beamed. *I am part! Hate this plant world! Empire should be hunting society! I will join, I will hunt! Eat!*

"Theoretically you can have up to five in a *Garthah-/yuu,*" JJC added. "Would you care to join us, Mr. Phil? Turns out

Mother is ineligible. Due to being our Goddess, of course."

"Dammit, I can't believe this!" Phil sputtered, casting a glance at the writhing, half-naked Amav on the couch. "How can you treat her this way?"

JJC leaned back. "You need to have more faith in Greeney, Mr. Phil. As you know, he can do *anything*. Now that he's our emperor, and yours, too, of course."

"Are you crazy? You really think Gooney can be emperor? That he can start up this Grid thing again?"

The Grid. Phil had forgotten all about it. But now he could feel the Grid flooding back, the lovely, all-encompassing *Grid*.

# CHAPTER TWENTY-FIVE
## When the Grid Ignites

"Yes, that's where you come in, Phil," Clopt said, pacing between the three couches. "We need to incorporate some human software techniques here."

"A *certain* human software technique," JJC said. "Phil, your task will be to restart the Grid according to Clopt's instructions."

"*No!* You can't have a Grid!" Phil cried, shuddering at what the transcendent Grid had done to him. *Twice.* He'd never forgiven himself for an instant for standing by for four years while he'd let Hedrona risk her life in the Games.

"Of course we have to have a Grid," Clopt said. "The strange thing we've found, though, is that a human being *can't* be emperor. Not without some severe human computer coding I confess I've never been able to master."

Phil stared back blankly. Clopt, who was so far ahead of Phil in programming?

"But a Martian seems to easily flow into being emperor," JJC said. "That's how Dar could do it, even if he only stayed in it a few moments. So Gooney's a natural for the job. In a way he can redeem all the crap that Dar pulled on Alpha Centauri back in '53. One Martian undoes what another Martian destroyed, and all."

"Dar destroyed our Empire! Our God! Our Grid! Then he *became* our God! Then he *abandoned* us!" Clopt cried.

Phil collapsed on his couch. "Where's Greeney? I need to talk to him! This can't work!"

JJC snickered. Phil fought the urge to scream that he'd wanted to punch that smirking puss ever since the kid had been fourteen.

"If you must know, he's out spreading the software code for the Grid," Clopt said. "Unfortunately, much of our operation has to be manual, as our computer networks are so fragmented. He'll be back soon."

"When's John Root coming?" JJC said, lazily stroking Trotter. "I want him here when the Grid ignites."

"I'm trying to coordinate that now," Clopt said, fiddling with his comm. "But this *golld-karpathugiss* AT app is *still* recharging! And you need to keep resetting its *slursing* parameters!"

"Anyway," JJC drawled, "for starters, Greeney just finished laser-blasting my novel across the surface of TwinLord."

"*What?*"

"You heard me. The entirety of *A Fragmented Encyclopedia of Recent Self!* Chiseled onto the lunar surface in letters three feet deep! Gooney'll replicate it on *hundreds* of moons and planets! You do need a telescope to read it, but an app on anyone's comm will do it."

Phil involuntarily looked for Andertwin's tidal-locked moon, but JJC's black ceiling was in the way.

"Yes, Mr. Phil, the novel's *that* important." Jonathan James leaned back on his couch like some medieval teenage prince. "How important you're shortly about to find out."

Phil had read the damn thing when it came out. *Fragmented Encyclopedia* was adolescent posturing. Not only were the insults to Jack unbearable, but the main JJC character, nobly maintaining himself "in a dream state" throughout all the contorted apocalypses in the rambling story, was a disgusting ego trip from start to finish. How the book had become so popular throughout the former AC Empire was beyond Phil's understanding.

"Oh ... *oh* ..." Amav moaned from the couch.

"The Goddess is coming around!" Clopt cried. "Emperor be praised!"

Phil looked away from the entirety of Amav's left breast protruding through a tear. Then looked back.

"Ah, yes, Mother's arrival does trigger the Grid," JJC said. "But she definitely needs to be *conscious* for it. Then you, Mr. Phil, are needed to *consummate* the programming."

Phil gaped back, pointing at that very breast. "This is your own *mother!* You can't *do* this to her!"

"Oh yes I can. She's worshipped throughout the Empire! She's *key* to the programming. And once we have your human programming *inserted,* shall we say, into the Cult of Amav--"

"That's crazy! My *human programming?* For God's sake, Jonathan, *you're* human! How can you side with this crazy *Centaurian?*"

"I am *Zarj!* Don't you ever forget that!"

"Yap yap yap yap!" Trotter added with little bared doggy teeth.

*We are Zarj! Brothers all! We die for each other! Kill for each other!*

Clopt had a hand on his sidearm. "Believe it, Phil Sperry. JJC and I, and this dog here, along with Greeney, are restarting the Empire on *Zarj principles*. I'll have you know that the *Zarj charisma* was the foundation of the Grid. In ancient times, the Brotherhood of *Garthah-/yuu* between Zarj was the Caretaker Soul of the Grid."

"I ... I knew that," Phil muttered, feeling a massive headache slam down.

*Sure, knew that, back when I was in the Grid. Everyone knew that. Forgot it until just now, that's all. God, it's all coming back! The Grid. What a beautiful thing!*

"Greeney understands that," Clopt went on. "He took my original software code for restoring the Grid and updated it for even faster transfer to all parts of the Centaurian Empire."

"Sure, sure, I guess that makes sense ..."

"God, oh God ..." Amav moaned.

"Is anyone going to help her?"

Silence.

*"Is anyone going to cover her up?"*

"The Grid requires her to be *uncovered,*" Clopt said. "No one can attend her until she rises of her own accord. The Grid has it so. Praise be to the Goddess Amav!"

"She's yours, Phil Sperry," JJC finally said. "You'll *unite* with Amav Frankston-Commer and in so doing you'll finish programming the Grid."

"*No!*" Phil stared at Amav's writhing exposed body. "Dammit, JJC, this is your *mother!* And I *don't* want her!"

"Forget it, Mr. Phil. You *do* want her. We all know the

story. It's available everywhere. Like telepathically from the Martians who rode with you on the *Typhoon II* and radiated the entire story of your *lust* for her. And from your own written account of it to Dad. The unconsummated *lust!* Now you'll have it *all,* and the Grid will be restored!"

"Dammit, all that's in the past! I have *Hedrona* now! Where's Gooney? I'm going to wring his neck!" Phil pulled out his comm. He just needed a second to send a distress call to the *Typhoon* crew below, but Clopt was on him, easily crushing the comm in his lower left claw.

"By the way, we've been broadcasting some very positive status reports from a certain Admiral Jack Commer via superspace to Sol," Clopt said, shoving Phil deep into the couch. "Especially after that idiot Borman tried to call. Of course, it's all AI programming. Greeney set up an interface that lets our onboard computer converse naturally with anyone."

"So the *Typhoon III* is already neutralized," JJC added. "My Uncle Joe won't be coming, unfortunately. Amplified Thought is marvelous, don't you agree?"

"Your stupid book has gone to your head!" Phil snarled. "It's infantile *crap!* You're a *nothing!*"

"I'm the greatest writer in Alpha Centauri! And Sol too!" JJC shrieked, standing up. "And you will address me as Sire! Sire!"

"Why the hell would I do that?"

"Because--damn you, Sperry! Convert to the Grid or die!"

"There *is* no Grid!"

"You're wrong!" Clopt cried. "She wakes! Amav wakes! The Grid is back!"

"Yap yap yap!" *The Grid is here! Hunters love the Grid!*

Amav sat up. Her deep brown eyes were unnaturally clear. They locked onto Phil's and would not let go. Slowly she stood and yanked at her ripped dress. Huge swaths came free in her fingers and flowed slowly to the carpet in one-fourth gravity.

"*No!*" Phil gasped.

Amav slipped out of her panties and flung them at Phil with a luscious smile. He caught them in astonishment, turning them over and over. Finally looked up.

Amav stood nude before him. In the blinding light of Andertwin, everything came back. Everything from the past.

*Oh my God! She knows she's perfection! Like the Grid is perfection!*

*Is this it? Am I really doomed? Again?*

# CHAPTER TWENTY-SIX
## It Floods Through Amav

"Phil," Amav called, reveling in the deep sensuousness of her voice. "Don't look away. Never look away from me."

It was like pulling on his jaw with a fishing line. Dragging his gray eyes to meet hers. Phil gulped in dismay. Amav laughed to see it.

"I'm on *fire!* This is the *real me!* At last! I'm One with everything! The true Amav flows into the Grid! And life flows back! Back and forth forever! Why have I never known this *bliss* before?" She cupped her breasts. "Yes, look, dear Phil," she murmured. "Look at *everything!* Not bad for a sixty-two-year-old woman, eh?"

*I'm twenty-five! I look twenty-five and we both know it!*

Phil swallowed. "You … you look *amazing.* Always have, I mean."

She watched his gaze travel down her chest, past her navel. "Soon you'll be kissing *all* of this. *Worshipping* it. Because all this is *yours.* You've always wanted *this.*"

"God, yes, but *they're* here!"

She shrugged, shaking her long hair across her bare shoulders, aware how this set her breasts bouncing. "Mmmm … they're just puppets. Pay them no mind." She glided to his couch. "I've always wanted you! I just never realized it until now!"

"What about *Jack?*"

"Puppets!" she smiled, widening her thighs. "Come here."

"You--*you're* the puppet! Amav! For God's sake! There's a Grid again! I can *feel* it!"

"Oh yes, can't you feel Greeney right *now?* Our emperor? Can't you feel him *extending* this Grid beyond this solar system and on to the next? The emperor *wills our union,* Phil!"

"This can't *be!*"

"This is the real *us,* Phil! At last! We have the Grid now! Dammit, *do* me! Now!"

"Oh my God!" Phil groaned. Amav was pleased to see him

buffeted in the expanding Grid hurricane. Pleased to see his eyes wide with shock and lust. "Amav, that's your *son* there! *Watching* everything!"

"Don't mind me, folks!" JJC laughed. "Now Clopt's recording the entire *human* interaction for software purposes, of course."

"*Puppets,*" she purred. "We're *all* puppets! All of us, in the Grid! But for me and you, Phil, Greeney wills us to *unite!*" She tugged at his shirt. "Get this *off.*"

"Excuse me, excuse me, I feel *sick,* I think!" came a wheezing burbling.

"*What?*" Phil cried, turning.

"Something happened to the *house,* master!" came a voice. "I was just mopping the tile in the bathroom when all of a sudden the house *shakes!* And I'm pinned to the floor! It *scared* me and made me *sick!* I'm gonna *barf,* I'm warning you, I'm gonna *barf!*"

"How the *scuck* did *she* get in here?" Clopt snapped.

"C'mon, she's just the scrubwoman, don't get all riled," JJC said.

"I *know* that! Dammit, we were supposed to dump all the staff!"

A short, squat, four-legged, four-armed creature scurried to Jonathan James. Six eyes circled the pumpkin-shaped head under a short brown mop of hair tentacles. The mouth was a long squirming black line. Amav knew through the Grid that this was K'ufunb, of the Fkuuh species, who'd been on her son's staff for years. Like all Fkuuh, she was not intelligent but possessed a cunning well-suited to survival on barbaric Fkuu.

"Well, we need a servant to keep the place clean!" JJC said.

"Not on this mission!" Clopt cried.

"Yap yap yap!" Trotter put in. *She doesn't know to hunt! She not Zarj brother!*

"Well, it's too damn late now!" her son shot back. "Drop it, both of you!"

*Her son.* What an interesting concept. What did that mean to the Grid? Apparently not much.

"Is the young lady spreading herself for the *Jkucll-Atkat-Hfucl?*" K'ufunb said, pointing to Amav's crotch.

"Yes, dammit, if you'll just get the *gnassid pleewagger* out of here!" Clopt screeched.

"Don't insult my scrubwoman!" JJC said.

"Mmmm, *puppets,*" Amav smiled, snapping a button off Phil's shirt.

"I won't have *Fkuuh* in the Grid!" Clopt shouted. "They're unclean!"

"That--that's *racist!*" JJC shouted.

"She belongs on some stinking *ag world* with the rest of her kind! Some cesspool like *Andertwin!*" Clopt roared, pointing out the window. "God, I hate that place!"

"We make no distinction between the formerly High Head and the Low Head! That's written right into the Grid!"

"Well, then, I'll *rewrite* that section! Nobody knows the programming better than me!"

"Urrrrrrrppp!" came the awful sounds from a far corner. "Urrrrrrrppp!"

"*Ruddzza-scuck,* the Fkuuh have *no* self-control! Three G's of acceleration is *nothing!*"

"C'mon, Clopt, we've *talked* about this issue before!" JJC said. "I know you're anxious to have the Grid up and running, but *everyone's* been anxious for twenty-two years now! But if everyone's patient, everything will *integrate* under the New Grid! *All* the Centaurian races!"

"Now you're sounding like that fool robot Root, with his condescending psychological clichés!"

Amav smiled. "What are they talking about, Phil?" She knew that Alpha Centauri had suffered through one shaky provisional government after another since the Collapse. Former leaders made feeble attempts to govern, straining to remember how it felt to be high in the Grid hierarchy, struggling to translate that emotion into daily political strategies, but they were so nervous, so lacking in confidence, that they rarely functioned longer than a few months.

It was so easy to know all this with the Grid. Once it

surrounded you, you just knew the answer to anything. Now life could go on, and she and Phil could do it all. Amav pulled Phil's shirt apart and fastened her teeth onto each of his nipples in turn.

He pushed her back. "Dammit, Amav, I can't do this! You know I have my own *Jkucll-Atkat-Hfucl* with Hedrona!"

"Who cares? Phil, I'm so *horny* for you! I'm *gushing* for you!"

"I thought you were *immune* to this Grid stuff! You *resisted* it back on the *Typhoon!* I was the one who got brainwashed! You and Jack *resisted* it! You were my heroes! And now--"

"Now you'll have *me,* Phil!" She slid back on the couch and spread her legs wide. "*This* is for *you!* Get those pants off!"

"But I haven't converted! The goddamn Grid's up again, but I haven't converted! How can that *be?*"

"Get on with it, Mr. Phil," JJC said dryly from above the couch. "We haven't got time to waste on all this coy build-up. Yank it out and cram it in. We'll measure your brainwave activity and convert that into the code we need."

Amav felt Phil tear himself off the couch. "What's going on?" she said woozily.

"Forget it!" Phil yelled. "I'm not doing this!"

Amav laughed. "Oh, yes you are! Get back here! You wonderful *puppet!*"

"No, I'm *outa* here!"

Clopt guffawed. "Be my guest, Phil Sperry! The main foyer is our airlock! Where do you think you'll wind up? You're certainly not qualified for *Garr/thahg!*"

*Grid reference,* came something like an encyclopedia entry unfolding within Amav. *Clopt still believes, as did most Alpha Centaurians of the Zarj species during the Era of the Grid, that all Centaurian troopers killed in battle go to an alternate universe called* Garr/thahg, *where they've built an alternate Zarj-based Empire and worship an Alternate Emperor. This belief accounts for the fact that Alpha Centaurians were able to shrug off a fifty percent Warp Transfer accident rate. But as the years following the collapse of the Empire have seen the increasing utilization of more reliable Warp Transfer technologies, based on human Star Drive systems as modified by Engineer Phil Sperry, the belief in the alternate universe of* Garr/thahg *has correspondingly eroded.*

"Oh, what a charming myth!" Amav laughed.

"It's *not* a myth!" Clopt roared, sharing the same Grid reference. "Goddess Amav, forgive my outburst! But we believe in *Garr/thahg!* I have friends and comrades in *Garr/thahg!*"

Amav felt waves of grief pouring out of Clopt, the Grid supplying thousands of names of his comrades killed in Warp Transfer accidents, as well as Clopt's obvious survivor guilt at having undertaken 233 Warp Transfers himself and coming through unscathed. She also boggled at the idea that his 2038 kidnapping mission, which combined an HTT event with Warp Transfer, had had a fifty percent chance of sending Hedrona, Phil, JJC, and Greeney Gooney straight to *Garr/thahg.*

"I'm sorry, Comrade Clopt! But I can *soothe* you, and all of Alpha Centauri! *By banging Phil!*" She turned back to Phil. "Get your sexy damn pants off and *screw* me, honey!"

Phil blanched. Amav rushed him and knocked him to the floor. She floated down onto him in one-fourth gravity, straddling him, tugging at his belt.

"Stop it! Stop it! Dammit, Amav, you're delirious! Brainwashed!"

"And your *zipper's* stuck!" Amav moaned. "God, I can't *stand* this! I'm coming *apart!*"

"If it helps the programming, Mr. Phil," JJC said from above them, "you should know that Greeney is really just our temporary emperor. He's just sort of a regent, holding the Empire together until we get the *human* programming in place!"

"You mean, *you'll* be emperor?" Phil cried as Amav abandoned the stuck zipper to smother his mouth with kisses, shoving her tongue deep into him, pressing her naked breasts to his open shirt, reaching down further to fondle and squeeze him.

"You haven't figured that out? Who wrote *A Fragmented Encyclopedia of Recent Self* anyway?"

"Puppets!" Amav laughed, wrestling with Phil's pants. "*Help* me with this, Phil! God, it's the only way for all of us!"

"It's the only way, gentle sir!" echoed K'ufunb of the Fkuuh. "I feel much better after barfing, I really do! Please comply and all shall be well, sir! All shall be well!"

# CHAPTER TWENTY-SEVEN
## Port Wing Hover Failure

"No!" Hedrona screamed at the space where Phil had been. "That was just like with Amav! She and Phil must both *be* somewhere!"

"There was no explosion! He's got to be all right!" shouted Draka Sortie, rushing up with his comm blinking. "And it's not any sort of Time Transition. The quantum signatures aren't right for that."

"Sortie! What the hell's going on?" Jack cried. "Did they take Phil too?"

"Looks like a simple Amplified Thought teleportation routine, but one that's been saved on a computer. It doesn't need a Martian brain running it. I may have a vector on it."

Jack whirled to the robot. "You! What did you mean by *getting their act together?*"

"Oh, nothing, Captain Jack! Strike my comments from the record! They mean nothing!"

"Damn you, you're in *cahoots* with whoever's doing this!"

"Not me, Captain Sir Jack! Most honorable and glorious sir! If I meant anything at all, it was a relief to see that Phil wasn't blown into a million pieces! Which probably happened to Amav, considering the forces brought to bear on her! What a way to go, Sir Jack!"

"Dammit!" Jack waved his shattergun at John Root's impassive face. "When I find out who did this--"

"Sir!" Sortie called. "The vector leads to the *spaceship.* That Castle thing. It must be pulling ten or twelve G's. It's hitting orbit now, looks like a stable circular orbit four hundred miles up."

"The Castle? Jonathan James? Dammit to hell!"

"C'mon, Jack, let's go *after* the mothers!" Lee Borman shouted.

Jack straightened, holstered his shattergun, and belted his comm. "Okay, everyone, battle stations. I'm betting they have both Amav and Phil up there. Let's intercept 'em now, before

157

they try to leave the system."

Patrick James, Bobby Athens and Will Connors scrambled out the front door towards the *Typhoon IV* looming silver in the dark field across the road.

"May I make a suggestion, dear Captain?" John Root said, blocking Jack's way.

"No," Jack said, pushing past him.

"Wouldn't it be more honorable to first mount a search for *Amav's shredded body* on top of the hill, sir?" John Root said. "After all, you *are* the husband of the deceased."

Jack paused, then hustled out the door with Borman, Sortie, and Hedrona.

"Dammit, John, watch your mouth!" Hedrona hissed. "I can't *believe* you! Is there something wrong with your programming?"

"Not at all, fair maiden. I was just pointing out the opportunities for dear Jack to achieve total closure on his wife's unfortunate gut-spewing *death!*"

"Damn you, she didn't die! She was taken to that damn Castle with Phil! And we're going to get them right this second! Are you coming with us or not?"

Jack turned from thirty feet ahead. "Leave that damn thing here! I don't want him on the *Typhoon.*"

"He's afraid I'll fly it!" John laughed. "Maybe I'll suicide it right into the Castle! Is that what you're so scared of, Captain Jack?"

"Dammit, Hedrona, this is *worse* than whatever crap John used to give me! I've never heard anything like this! This robot's wasting my time! Come on! Let's get going!"

Draka hoisted himself up into the ship through the ventral hatch. Jack scrambled up and extended a hand down to Hedrona. "Sorry we don't have time to get the stairs down."

"Oh, please!" Hedrona said, grabbing the hatch opening two feet above her head and swinging her torso into the *Typhoon* fuselage. "I need to show you some video of my days as Gladiator of the Sled, mister! I don't want to hear any ageist crap about losing my edge, either!"

"Okay, then," Jack said, swinging the latch up as the *Typhoon* engine howled to life.

With the opening just two feet wide something like a rocket hurtled inside, shoving Jack and Hedrona against the far wall. John Root stood in the ship, then snapped the latch shut. "All aboard, Captain Jack! I'm ready for action!"

"Hatch secure. Cabin pressurized," came Bobby's voice from the Control Room. "Ready for takeoff, Captain. If everyone's not secured I can set inertial dampers to 1."

"Tracking the Castle," Patrick James called down.

"Got it," Will Connors said. "Intercept course laid in, Bobby."

"I'll hover off from the guest house," Athens said. "Then kick in the intercept."

Jack's face was straining purple as he faced the robot. Hedrona felt the *Typhoon* wheels lift from the ground. "Look, we don't have time for this crap," Jack finally said, setting his shattergun to Electron Oblivion Sequencing and handing it to Hedrona. "Strap this robot in that seat and *vaporize* him if he tries anything. I need to get to the Control Room." He pressed his comm. "Continue hover takeoff to two thousand feet, then intercept course ASAP. Inertial Level 1 until we get everyone strapped down." His boots clomped down the fuselage past the six-man shuttlecraft.

"I can take the ventral turret," Hedrona said. "I've kept up my gunnery skills here on Andertwin, believe it or not."

"Thanks, we may need 'em," Jack said from the ladder to the Control Room.

"Hell with *that*," Borman called from the dorsal turret. "I got all four turrets remote-controlled from up here. All PlanetBlasters set to Maximum Sterilization."

Hedrona motioned John into the seat to her left as Sortie studied his console on her right. "Just strap yourself down like Jack said. I'll be here next to you."

"Oh great! So you can *obliterate my electrons!* I can't believe you'd do that to me after all we've been through!"

"Listen, I've killed hundreds of very worthy gladiators in

combat, and I'll do whatever's necessary. We're on Jack's ship, and we'll obey his orders to the letter."

"But that's precisely what I'm doing!" John whined, tugging the straps across his chest. "I'm following his orders precisely! I'm here to *help!*"

"It's like being near Jack has *unhinged* you. You're never like this!"

"I'm *always* like this! Always in service to the concept of Jack Commer, Supreme Commander! I *love* Jack! I'd do *anything* for him! Anything at all!"

"Then just sit there quietly while we do this mission," Hedrona said, exchanging an exasperated look with Sortie. "God, Phil's got to be all right, doesn't he?"

"I'll know for sure when JJC springs me out of this filthy militarist *weapons platform!*" John cried.

"*What?*"

"Oh, yes, they're going to teleport me right out of this pile of crap! Any second now! I can *feel* it! Then you'll be sorry!"

"Dammit, John, a second ago you were saying how much you wanted to *help* Jack!"

"I *am* helping him! By just being here! For however long this experience lasts! Why can't he see that? He's like a *god* to me! Why can't he see that I'm like a god to *him?*"

"I can't believe a robot would go *crazy,*" Sortie muttered from his console.

"Don't you see, Jonathan James has it all planned out! I've helped in the entire thing, of course! I've *got* to get back to JJC! Please transport me *now,* Jonathan James! I know the vectors and the velocities will be more of a challenge, but *release* me! Now!"

Hedrona stared at the floor. Had the robot cracked? What if it blocked them from getting to Phil and Amav? Should she go ahead and EOS it now?

The craft jerked hard left.

"Port wing hover failure!" Bobby called. "Compensating!"

"Starboard and tail down to forty-eight percent!" Jack cried as the nose of the ship swung up at a forty-five-degree angle.

"*Wow!*" John laughed. "Greeney *knew* this would happen!"

"*What?*" Hedrona said. "What's Greeney got to do with this?"

"Our emperor can do anything! In this case, a simple little computer virus!"

"No! He wouldn't!"

"Straightening!" Jack called. "Thruster balance matrix *now!* Draka, what's going on with the hover thrusters?"

"Don't know, some sort of *drain!* I'm checking!"

"We're falling! Altitude two hundred fifty feet!" James called. "Two forty! Two thirty! Jack, we need main engine *now!*"

"Hedrona!" Jack shouted. "Anybody still in that house?"

"Not that I know of!"

"Main engine!"

"Main engine offline!" Sortie shouted. "Jack, we are ninety-eight percent drained! Ninety-nine!"

"Switch to battery power! All power to hover thrusters! Wheels out! Prepare for hard landing!"

"Let me have twenty percent for inertial dampers, Jack!" Bobby yelled.

"Do it!"

Hedrona could feel the hover thrusters kicking in hard and the ship shakily leveling, then the thrusters trailing off, the wings waggling.

The *Typhoon IV* dropped in silence.

The entire ship rang with the impact and the dismayed grunts of all crewmembers. Hedrona felt the wheels blow as the PlanetBlaster turret below her crumpled into shattering plastiglass.

# CHAPTER TWENTY-EIGHT
## The Mad Plan

The *Typhoon IV* lay twenty degrees to port off its axis. Thin pungent gas floated everywhere. All illumination was gone except for a line of tiny yellow lights running the length of the ship. Hedrona was struck by how the line of lights continued even past the huge jagged gap in the fuselage above her.

"Ah, God ..." someone groaned above her.

"I'm all right!" John Root cried. "Don't worry! Wow! What a *trip!*"

"*Dammit!*" came Jack's voice from the Control Room. "Who's hurt?" After everyone slowly reported themselves more or less intact, Jack called down: "Hedrona, how'd the shuttlecraft come through?"

"Well, its landing gear collapsed. And the canopy's shattered."

"Crap! Yeah, we have some cracks in the canopy up here, too. And I can see the left wing has snapped. This ship is *toast.* Bobby, you saved us by ramping up the dampers. This much force probably would've killed us all otherwise."

"John Root here seems to think Greeney planted a computer virus onboard," Hedrona said.

"*What?*" The Control Room door creaked open and Jack scrambled down the ladder, shaking his head at the smashed shuttlecraft and the huge gash in the *Typhoon* fuselage.

Draka Sortie pulled himself from under his uprooted chair. "She's right, Jack. It was an attack on our computer systems. We're wiped clean. We don't even have superspace radio."

"You okay?"

"Yeah. Just twisted my back a bit."

Jack turned to Root. "Okay, robot, you seem to know a lot about all this. So Gooney planted a virus on my ship, huh? Why the hell didn't he just vaporize us with AT?"

"He didn't want to harm you! He just wanted you not to take off! That's all!"

"He cripples my ship and nearly kills us all, and you say he doesn't want to *harm* us?"

"And anyway he's not here right now. He's off spreading the Grid throughout Alpha Centauri. A virus was the easiest way to deal with the *Typhoon,* really."

"Sortie, why didn't our computers flag that virus?" Jack said.

Sortie looked away. "It's another one of those canned Amplified Thought routines, Jack. I'm sorry, I've never seen anything like 'em before."

"Hell with it. What's done is done." By this time the crew had assembled in the space behind the smashed shuttlecraft, under the meager yellow lights on the ceiling. "There's got to be superspace radio somewhere on Andertwin, correct?" Jack asked Hedrona.

She nodded. "There's a media center in town. Maybe fifteen miles from here."

"Okay, we walk over there."

"We have bicycles. At least ten of them around the house."

"Sheesh," Jack said, evidently dismayed at the idea of setting out with his space force on bicycles. "Okay, we send a message to Sol, and Joe's here with the *III* in forty-five minutes."

"Along with the biggest goddamn battleship fleet you ever saw," Borman said.

"Cut it, Lee. Joe will round up extra help but we have to leave Sol defended."

"*Crap* on it, Captain. We need to sterilize this damn place! If you hadn't shattered my goddamn Senator Comm we'd be able to call in everything we need right now!"

Jack sighed. "Everyone take out your comms. Anything up? Mine's blank right now."

The crew checked their comms and shook their heads.

"Are we okay now, senator?" Jack said.

"Hell, my Senator Comm would've come through. It had its own network."

"Forget it, Lee. In any case I'm leaving Sol defended. Now that the ACs have access to our Star Drive technology, Greeney can mount any sort of invasion he wants."

"You really think Greeney wants to do that?" Hedrona said.

Jack shrugged. "Have no idea. But if he does restart this Grid thing, he has an entire anthill Empire ready to swarm us if he decides to."

"Why should we want your filthy Sol anyway?" John Root demanded.

"*We?* So you *are* one of them!"

"*All* of us are! Greeney Gooney and Clopt and me! And Jonathan James! Yes, that's right! Your own son!"

"I can't believe it! So he's *there?*" Jack said, pointing up. "In the Castle? He and Clopt and Gooney?"

"Well, Gooney's moving through solar system after solar system right now, activating the Grid software. Boy, are you ever in a fix, Mr. Space Captain!"

"And Phil!" Hedrona said. "He's up there, right? With Amav?"

"If they didn't accidentally blow her up!" John Root laughed.

"Hedrona, give me back my shattergun!" Jack said. "I'm going to *execute* this pile of junk!"

"You can't do that!" Hedrona cried.

Jack snatched the gun from her. "I can! He's aiding and abetting the enemy. Probably recording this whole damn mess for them." He checked the weapon. "Dammit, *it's* offline too! Damn those bastards for coming up with *networked* blasters! The damn virus got 'em too!"

"We have standalone blasters in the gun racks," Sortie said, pointing.

"Yeah, break 'em out," Jack said. "Robot, that saved your ass for now. Let me tell you though that I'm *sick* of your crap! If I have to reverse-engineer you to extract every bit of information you have on this violation of the Sol/Centauri Treaty, I will!"

"Damn right!" Borman said. He nudged Hedrona. "First damn time he's mentioned the Treaty in all this. That's my boy, finally thinkin' like a real pol!"

"But you don't have to threaten me," John Root said. "I

*worship* you, Jack Commer!"

"Hell, I thought you worshipped Greeney Gooney now," Jack shot back.

"Well, yes! But I'm programmed to love and honor *Jack Commer!* Jack Commer is *central* to my programming! Just as *you* were central to John Commer!"

"John was--hell, I don't know what he was! God, I can't believe I'm discussing this with a *robot!* Get to the point, damn you!"

Hedrona stepped up. "John, just tell us what we need to know. Everything that's going on." She met John's wide blue eyes.

"Well, well …" Root shot a frightened glance at Jack. "Should I?"

"Tell it!" Jack cried. "God, John, the fate of Sol is at stake here!"

"Well, it's not really *my* fault! It was *Clopt* who wrote the Grid code."

"*Clopt* wrote the code to restart the Grid?"

"He's a marvelous programmer! He knew exactly what was needed to ramp up a Telepathic Kernel. That's what he called it! He said it was an ancient ritual on Zarj, and the Grid evolved from there to include the entire Alpha Centaurian Federation."

"Wow, so it *is* software after all!" Sortie whistled.

"Dar indicated it could be," Jack said. "We could just never be sure, though. There was never any trace of it."

"All I did was write the book!" John Root said. "Was that so very bad?"

"*What* book?"

"*Fragmented Encyclopedia!* I wrote it! That was my contribution!"

"C'mon, John," Hedrona said, "I know JC dictated it to you, but--"

"You don't think I can write a work of major literary genius?"

Hedrona shook her head. "You're a robot, John, you can *store* a novel, but--"

"*Chapter 1! We Are All One! When the Boche bullet bit into my brain at First Battle of Ypres, blasting my blighted soul to blobby bits, I knew I was called to a new and higher reincarnation. I just never suspected it would be fourteenth-century Cambodia. As I--*"

"C'mon, John, we get the point! But you're just a computer!"

"No! I *wrote* it! Don't you see a computer was *necessary* to write it? I had to take Jonathan James' silly four-page outline, and Clopt's software code, and mash them into something that would *work!*"

"*What?*"

"I must've downloaded characters from a *million* novels, and changed them around, and brought in all these *plots* I found, and changed them around, but all the while I was inserting Clopt's code too! Takes a real computer to do all that!"

"You can't be serious! JJC--"

"JJC couldn't write his way out of a paper bag! But I made everything *reverberate!* It's like I got the collective unconscious of both Sol *and* Alpha Centauri, with this Grid code perfectly mixed in! No wonder *The Tarl Imperial Guardian of Fascinating Literary Gems* called it 'a novel to soothe the freaking masses of Centauri.' And as influential critic Arg'uuy Hyyr, writing in the prestigious *Daily Centaurian Post,* says--"

"Dammit, are you saying you wrote that entire book?" Jack said. "And infiltrated some sort of *software code* into it?"

"No wonder it's entrancing all of Alpha Centauri! And now, even *Sol* is being seduced by my book!"

"I can't believe this!"

"It's the raw code for an exponentially growing Seed of the Grid! JJC's fame made it easy to distribute this novel everywhere! *Everyone* wants to read it! We've hit critical mass now! A *trillion* readers! All Greeney has to do now is visit each star system and activate the Code! It's so simple! Everyone's half-hooked now, but in an hour or two they'll be *One* with the emperor! Greeney Gooney!"

"We'll have to kill Gooney," Jack said quietly. "It's ugly,

but it's the only way. Let's get to that media center, Hedrona. We've got to get Joe here fast, and we'll need Dar and as many Martians as we can get to make the trip. Looks like we'll have to play AT against AT."

"Forget it, wondrous concept of Jack Commer!" John Root laughed. "Your power is *ruined!* Greeney Gooney is *light-years* beyond anything your pathetic Dar can think of!"

Will Connors pressed a fresh standalone heat blaster into Jack's hand.

"Don't kill me, Jack! I'm your *brother!*" John screamed, rushing Jack, arms wide.

"I'm not gonna take--ooof!" Jack grunted.

Hedrona reeled with the bright blue eruption. A monstrous thud turned out to be her head slamming against the fuselage wall. She went black. Then came voices, shouting, and an acrid smell.

"Ow!" She raised her head and opened her eyes to chaos. Her hands were bloody. Her ears buzzed and she couldn't sort out who was screaming. The floor was littered with wires and circuitry, servo-mechanisms, and AI wafers. There was a flopping John Root hand, fingers clenching spastically, dozens of multicolored wires splayed from the sundered wrist.

Stench. Bad coppery stench.

"They got *Jack!*" someone was yelling.

"The robot *exploded!*" someone else cried.

Hedrona saw the rest of the crew blown back against the fuselage but apparently unharmed. There were scorch marks on the curved metal surfaces. "They--they took Jack?" Wires and circuit boards trailed from a basketball-sized hole in John Root's headless torso. His shredded tan pants showed melted metal and the charred artificial skin of his mangled legs.

She stared at the pool of blood beneath her fingers. Shreds of navy-blue USSF uniform. Jack's blaster. His comm. A black USSF dress boot. A severed lower left leg protruding from the boot, blood oozing from the flesh. It smelled like a ripped-open cow.

"They--they got *Jack,*" someone repeated. "I can't believe

it!"

"Oh, God, John was a *bomb* all this time ..." Hedrona whispered as she lost consciousness.

# CHAPTER TWENTY-NINE
## Puppets!

Jack crashed into a pair of writhing bodies. "*Uhhh!*"

"Idiot!" came a woman's return snarl.

"Jack! Oh my God!" a man shouted.

"Stupid *puppets!* Nobody can stop us! Get those pants off and *ram it into me!*"

Jack stared in shock. The woman was naked, wrestling some man on the floor. She was spurting streams of gore. It was Amav. She was *dying*.

"Amav--" he croaked, scrambling to his knees, then blundering into the bodies again. "*Uhhh!*"

The problem was that there wasn't much remaining of Jack's left knee. The leg was gone. The blood was spewing out of his own *ripped-off leg*.

"Clopt!" cried the crimson Amav. "Help me with this goddamn zipper!"

"With pleasure, my Goddess!" Captain Clopt bellowed, the vertical folds of his face wrenching into a Zarj grin as he whipped out a blaster and stepped into the central pit.

"Dammit, Amav, that's *Jack!* He's *hurt!*" the man below Amav groaned as Clopt's boots clomped around his head. Phil Sperry.

"Puppets!" Amav laughed, drenched in Jack's blood. "*Do me, Phil! Oooh, do me hard!*"

"Oh my God!" Phil gasped.

A vicious spang echoed through the room. Something bright and hard glanced off Clopt's forehead and bounced on the soaked carpet.

"Ow! *Plellsukkcj!*" Clopt shouted, rubbing his right whirlpool eye.

"Hi, everyone!" sang John Root's dented, severed head. "Sorry I'm late! I was trapped on that son of a bitch Commer's spaceship!"

"*Puppets!*" Amav laughed again. "Puppets, puppets, puppets!"

The next sound was a thunderous slap. Amav fell back with a hand to her cheek. "*Ow!* Okay, Phil darling, if you want it rough--"

"Shut the hell up! I'm done with you, Amav! Done with you forever! You ignore your *husband,* who's *dying!*"

"I'm--dying?" Jack said woozily. He checked his leg again. Yep, that was definitely a lot of blood. It seemed Phil might be right. "Hey, why're you slapping my wife? And how come I'm not feeling anything if my leg's been--*yaaaaaa! Yaaaaaa! Dammit!*"

"Take it easy, Jack!" Phil said, stripping off his open shirt. "I can tie this off! JJC, do you have any meds onboard? Alpha SynMorph, or even Gamma?"

"God, Clopt!" Jonathan James cried. "What are we gonna do? That's *Dad!* He wasn't supposed to be taken!"

"Hey, Phil, forgot you're a doctor, too, man," Jack muttered as Phil tightened his shirt around Jack's thigh. "*Oh my God! Damn!*"

"That's nothing compared to *me,*" John Root said, jaws working, head vibrating on the carpet, trailing yellow and blue wires spattered with Jack's blood. "I've lost *my entire body!* Jack just lost a stupid leg!"

By way of answer Phil kicked the head into Amav's lap.

"Damn, Phil, why's *Amav* here?" Jack moaned. "And with no *clothes?*"

"Long story, man," Phil said. "Take it easy."

"Yaaaaaa! *Oh God!*"

"Why'd John *explode?*" JJC hissed at Clopt. "We need him for the final subroutines!"

"I don't know!" Clopt muttered.

"You don't know how to run the AT apps, fool, admit it!"

"Dammit, I had that last one set perfectly! Maybe the AT couldn't lock onto the right personality matrix. Root's been damn flaky ever since Commer set foot on Andertwin. Maybe his programming got too messed up for a transport."

"Crap! Maybe that's why we got Dad too. Dammit, what're we gonna *do?*"

"Phil, I think this is it. Not gonna make it--" Jack muttered.

Phil finished the tourniquet. "You've lost a lot of blood, man. But we've got most of it stopped now. Just stay cool. There's a hospital in Andertwin City that's set up to do human medicine. If we can get you there. Dammit, JJC, where's that SynMorph?"

"Don't have any!" JJC shouted. "Zarj warriors don't need sedatives!"

"Yark yark yark!" came from that demented Beagle Jack had seen on their previous visits. Now it was sniffing Jack's blood.

Phil pushed it back. But he was blindsided by naked Amav tackling him from behind.

"*Bang* me, Phil! Bang me bang me bang me!"

"Well, aren't *you* the life of the party!" Jack gasped.

Amav widened her eyes. "Jack! It's *you!* Look, I'm the Goddess Amav now! Isn't it *great?*"

"Yeah, but look, I'm having--little problem here. Can't hardly talk."

"*I* can talk! I can talk with only a *head!*" John Root cried. "I'm *better!*"

Amav peered at Jack's leg. "Wow! Looks nasty! Better have Doctor Phil take a look at it! In a few minutes, of course! C'mere, Doctor Phil!"

"Amav ... what's going on here?" Jack whispered.

"Jack, I have to do Phil here! In order to--hell, I don't know! I'm the Goddess Amav!"

"Believe me, Jack, I don't want any part of this!" Phil cried, fending off Amav's fresh kisses to his naked torso. "They converted her! They've started a new Grid!"

Jack regarded his wife's blood-soaked fingers tearing wildly at Phil's belt. Then came darkness.

# CHAPTER THIRTY
## Pack Leader Changes!

Bright purple flooded through Jack's closed eyelids.

*There, is that better?* came high-pitched singing.

"Muhhh …" Jack muttered, entranced. Waves of well-being flowed through him.

"Thank God you showed up, man," someone said. Phil. "He was slipping away."

More music through Jack's brain. Outradiance from a Martian. Images of the *Typhoon* crew staring horrified at Jack's mangled leg amid the ruins of the robot's body, then the leg disappearing in a burst of purple. Jack had a quantum microscope view of atoms in flux, electrons whirling to new atoms, fresh molecular bonds forming, leg and thigh interweaving.

"Wow, man, those knees are complex thingies, aren't they?" he burbled as he felt functionality coming back online down there.

*Yes, they are*, Greeney Gooney beamed. Jack opened his eyes. Gooney sat beside him. *You should see a Martian knee sometime. A hundred times more complicated.*

Jack stared into Gooney's huge unlidded violet eyes.

*You'll be fine. We'll talk more later.*

"*Emperor!*" Clopt shouted. "Thank the Source you've arrived! Was healing the Commer vermin really necessary?"

"Yes, idiot!" Gooney shot back. "Jack certainly wasn't supposed to lose a leg! Nor was the *Typhoon* supposed to get wrecked! Can't you follow simple instructions on the canned AT?"

"Well, it's been busy! And I've been stressed! Where the hell have you been, anyway?"

"I've been stressed *Sire!* Where the hell have you been anyway *Sire!*"

"Uh, Sire! I'm sorry, Sire! I'm just not used to calling you that!"

"Sire!" Jonathan James said. "He didn't mean it! He'll call

you Sire, I mean, as long as *necessary!*"

"Enough," Gooney said. "K'ufunb, get Amav cleaned up and get something on her. We all need to sit and talk about our next move."

K'ufunb glued her forehead to the wet black carpet. "It shall be done, Sire!"

"Sire! What about the Holy Lay with Phil Sperry?" cried the bloody nude Amav.

"Canceled," Gooney said. "Phil, mop up the floor with something. I find the sight of human blood distasteful."

"Screw it," Phil said. "I'm not converting. Find someone else."

"Hmm. JJC, clean up the blood."

"Dammit, Greeney!" JJC said. "I'm not gonna--"

"Dammit Greeney *Sire!* And clean up the goddamned blood!"

"Crap!" JJC muttered, stomping down a hallway.

Jack stood up shakily. His leg held in his polished left boot. Greeney had mended his navy-blue uniform as well.

JJC returned with a mop and a bucket but just stood there, looking over his shoulder for K'ufunb to take them up. But they all listened to a shower running down the hall and K'ufunb cooing: "There, there, Miss Goddess, we'll have you all nice and sparkling in a jiffy, we will! And we have *dozens* of sheer nightgowns to choose from! Oh, yes, they're from Jonathan James' collection of fully functioning sexbots, they are! No, I don't think those girls will get cold now, Goddess Amav! They'd *want* you to look your best! Here, let me wash under here ... and here."

"Mmmmm ..." came Amav's purr.

"*Dammit,*" JJC said, mop in hand, moving down the stairs to the central pit.

"Oh, can't you take a joke from your emperor?" Greeney said, nodding at the mess in the pit. Instantly the blood was gone and Jack smelled a forest meadow. He had the odd feeling that Gooney had sucked all his blood off the floor, cleaned it up, and beamed it right back into his veins. He felt much stronger.

"Sheesh," JJC muttered, shaking his head at the clean carpet.

Greeney cocked an eye.

"Sire," JJC finished. "Look, Greeney, I understand the need for protocol, like for the masses and all, but between us--"

"Enough. You and Clopt have both been highly irresponsible today. You must learn how to properly address your emperor. And my instructions for the use of three canned AT transport subroutines, and the canned virus subroutine, were so simple a child could have followed them. Yet all four were executed amateurishly. Look what you did to Jack on that last one!"

"Sire!" Clopt came to attention. "I've determined that the robot was suffering a mental breakdown at the time of transfer, thus causing him to inadvertently explode!"

"Excuses, excuses! You screw up because you're so impatient! You Zarj lost the war for the ACs because you're so *impatient!*"

Clopt swallowed. "Then I'll go to *Garr/thahg* immediately! I'll use the escape shuttle, on Warp Overload! And I shall be free at last! With the Alternate Emperor!"

"Oh, calm down!" Jonathan James sneered. "Both your Zarj brothers forbid that!"

"Yap!" Trotter echoed.

"Oh, *kartuthuck* to the damn dog!"

"No one seems to care that I'm *disembodied!*" John Root complained, jaw working, battered head rolling on the carpet. "I've suffered the most, and no one cares!"

Jack stared. Was this how John looked at the moment of impact? What was he feeling when he took the *Typhoon I* down to Mercury? What was everyone feeling? Jim and the others? At 4.9 million miles an hour they didn't have time to know what was coming, did they?

"Aaah, that's no big deal," JJC said, finally dropping the mop and sliding a door open in the black wall. "Your head's a little dinged, but it's probably functioning okay. We'll just slap it onto a spare robot." Lights snapped on in a storeroom crammed with frozen figures.

"Oh my God!" Jack gasped. There was Jim. His dead brother Jim. And Mickey Michaels. And Harri McNarri. General Scott. There was Joe. All from 2034.

The robots stood silent in the harsh yellow light. "Almost a complete collection," JJC said. "Been working on it for years. I just couldn't bear to get a Dad robot, though. We do have a Mom robot, but she's on indefinite loan to the Utilitarian Church of Goddess Amav."

To Jack's consternation there were also numerous well-endowed female robots in bikinis and camisoles that had nothing to do with *Heroes and Villains of the Thirties.*

"Let's see, who'd be the closest fit to Mr. John here?" JJC mused, wandering among the statues. "Yeah, here!" He clicked something and marched a figure from the back. The short but massive body wore an obnoxious green and orange plaid sport coat over a hairy bare chest. His long equally hirsute wrists hung far out of the short coat sleeves.

"Huh? What da goddamn *hell,* man?" came the rough slurred voice of Samuel Jay Hergs, traitor to humanity and briefly Emperor of the Martians. "Is that *Jack Commer* there?"

Jack instinctively reached for his blaster at the same time he realized it was somewhere back on the *Typhoon.*

"Urrrk!" Hergs grunted as JJC twisted his neck and lifted off the head. Jonathan James strode into the pit, tossing the Hergs head onto a couch, scooped up the John Root head, climbed back out and mounted John on the Hergs body.

"*Wow!*" John Root said, flexing the Hergs fingers. "*This* is a strange piece of work! Bet I could punch Jack Commer right the hell out!"

"That's *my* job, ya BLEEP BLEEP!" yelled the stubble-bearded Hergs head from the couch. "Ya hear that, Commer? I'll BLEEP ya! I'll BLEEP ya through the BLEEP BLEEP!" His mouth worked so violently that the head quivered off the couch onto the floor.

"Hey, where's that Amav chick? Last time I saw her she was aiming a *shattergun* at me! And I was just about to BLEEP her BLEEP! She was gonna be the emperor's wife, but then she *shatters* me! Aw, BLEEP it!"

"Would you like Censor Mode off so you can get the full effect?" JJC smirked.

"BLEEP yeah!"

"I wasn't asking *you!*"

"Sure I forgive her! She's so BLEEP *hot!* Guess she thought she had to protect her BLEEP Jacko! But it's okay! The BLEEP mothers who programmed me even included the last seconds of my BLEEP life! What a way to go, huh? Aw, BLEEP it! You know I loved every second of my death! I replay it every BLEEP day!"

"Jonathan James, what on earth is going *on?*" Jack moaned.

"I'll *ream* ya, Commer, I'll BLEEP my BLEEP up your BLEEP BLEEP! Ya goddamn BLEEP BLEEEEEeeeeee--"

Hergs' head burst into a sphere of orange energy.

"*Dammit,* Greeney!" JJC complained. "I spent *five years* hunting down a Hergs!"

"We Martians find former Emperor Hergs ... *yucky,*" Greeney said.

"Hi, I'm back! The Goddess Amav is back!" said Amav, emerging from the hall in an icy blue nightgown. A virtually nonexistent nightgown, Jack noted. She sat to his left on the couch. "Hi, baby! Glad you got the leg back together! I knew Greeney wouldn't let you expire!"

"Well, *you* sure look nice," Jack said. "Are you coming out of it now?"

"Coming out of what?"

"This Goddess thing!"

Amav leaned back. "Oh, no, I just *love* it! I'm sorry about the trip with Phil. The Grid says it's all over now. Apparently we got *just enough* programming from him into the Cult of Amav! It's fun to be a Goddess of the Empire!"

"Sorry, Admiral Commer," Greeney said. "The command was to *play the part,* not to really *do* it. I didn't think she'd actually get swallowed by the Grid. After all, she resisted it fine back in '35."

"Oh, what's he *talking* about, Jack?"

"Then again, you had a rough teleportation up here. All this has probably been too much. Not only all the strain of the war, and the Time Transitions, and the Earth Renewal Project, but coming here and finding our dazzling new literary sensation freezing you both out again. I could definitely see how that could throw you off balance and make you susceptible to conversion."

"You just can't stop counseling, can you, Greeney?" JJC sneered.

Greeney inclined his head to JJC. "And now, unfortunately, you have to deal with the fact of this same cold-hearted son becoming emperor."

"Yap yap yap!" Trotter cried.

*Pack leader changes!* the Beagle radiated to all. *Let the hunt begin!*

"There you go, Sire!" Gooney said. "I leave it all in your not very capable hands: *Emperor Jonathan James Commer of Alpha Centauri!*"

# CHAPTER THIRTY-ONE
## Oh, Most Holy Head

"*What?*" Amav cried along with Jack.

"That's right, Mom and Dad," Jonathan James said, scooping Trotter up and standing in front of Jack and Amav in his sleek black getup. "It's *me* now!"

"Sorry, guys, I just found out myself a little while ago," Phil said.

Amav wrapped her arms around her chest. What on earth was she wearing? What was she doing here? Why was she so excited?

*Oh my God! Phil! Jack!*

She fought for some way to delete everything that had just happened, but knew she'd never forget a second of it. "God, Jack, your *leg!* Is it all right?"

"I'm fine, Amav, just fine. Just trying to figure out what the hell's going on here."

"*I* can tell you!" John Root shouted from atop his tight plaid sport coat. "Now that the Final Grid's in place!"

"Quiet, robot," JJC said. "I'm in charge now. The Transfer is complete."

"Aw, c'mon, JJC!"

"*Sire!* Aw c'mon JJC *Sire!*"

"Sire, I'm just a robot, Sire, I don't really have to call you Sire."

JJC turned his back on Root. "In any case, once we had the Human Programming Module in place, we were able to drop our temporary emperor and activate the permanent, *human* emperor. The masses of Alpha Centauri are now waking up to the fact that their restored Grid is connecting them no longer to the Martian regent, but to me, the author of their beloved *Fragmented Encyclopedia of Recent Self.*"

"Believe me, Jack, I didn't want to do it!" Phil said. "That software stuff! They brainwashed Amav! But I didn't get brainwashed again this time. I must have *resisted* it somehow."

Amav stared at Phil Sperry. What had she been feeling for

him just a minute ago? Was that really her? Ripping his shirt off? "*I'm sorry too!*" she wailed.

"It--it's *okay!*" Jack said. "I just need to *think!*"

"I really don't *want* Amav, Jack! Can't you see that? It's *Hedrona* I love!"

"Jack knows that! *I* know that!" Amav said. "And it's a beautiful thing! Oh my God, what is *wrong* with me?" She stared at her breasts so clearly visible through the thin blue fabric. She would've ripped it all off in disgust except that it would've made the problem worse.

*This beam for you only! When I abdicated in favor of JJC, I pulled you out of the Grid.*

"Wha--"

*Don't look at me. It's Greeney. Look, we needed some human male-female appreciation for the software, but not that much! You were magnificent, though. What a performance!*

"I can't *stand* this! Jack, can I have your coat?"

"Sure! Of course!" Jack said, draping his navy-blue coat around her.

*Just keep up the act for now, dear!*

"Oh--okay," she whispered, putting her arms through the sleeves of Jack's uniform and holding it close around her.

"I was only needed as the Martian catalyst," Greeney said aloud. "But the plan all along was for our dear bestselling author to become emperor."

"Sire! You will address me as Sire!" JJC shouted.

"I wasn't addressing you directly, Sire, so in that case I don't need to use Sire," Greeney explained. "I'm sure all the protocol will come to you momentarily. In fact, the full Grid Transfer does take a minute or two. I'm just now feeling the initial transfer of your subjects to you, dear Sire."

JJC staggered back. "Wow! Oh my God, *wow!*"

"This--this is *horrible!*" Jack cried.

"*What's going on?*" Amav said.

"God, it's *amazing!*" JJC muttered, shakily finding his way down to the pit and collapsing on the white sofa next to Trotter, who snuggled up to him. Meanwhile Clopt and K'ufunb knelt in front of him, foreheads to the carpet.

"*Oh, most Holy Head ...*" they sang.

"I don't need to hear the whole damn song right now! I *am* the Head! I can feel it all! God, I can't even stand up! No wonder the Crab Emperor stayed cut up into little pieces in his box! It was the only way he could survive the full plug into the Grid!"

"It's pretty damn powerful, all right," Greeney observed.

"I feel *all* your plugs! Except Dad's! And that Phil bastard! *Convert!* Both of you! *Now!*"

Jack got to his feet and stood above Amav.

"No, I don't think we're intending to convert," Phil said quietly.

"I can't have any Nonconverted!" JJC shrieked. "The Head demands *all!*"

"Wait--" Amav broke in.

*Quiet!* came Greeney's tight beam outradiance. *I've got a simulation running on both you and me. They just think we're in the Grid. Jack and Phil I can't touch right now.*

"God! *Damn!*" JJC cried. "More and more are *coming in!*"

"Yes, Sire, I was able to visit all seventeen Centaurian solar systems and activate the Grid," Gooney said. "I must say, it's almost *intolerable* pleasure when those first few billion souls start joining up!"

"My *God!*" JJC sank further into the couch. "I can't *believe* this! I know it *all!* I know what everyone's *thinking!* And *feeling!*"

"But even then, it takes time for all *twenty trillion AC subjects* to finally sign on the dotted line!" Greeney laughed. "You must be feeling that about now, Sire!"

"Oh my God! Oh my God! *I can't stand it!*" JJC wrenched at the top of his head. "There's so much *suffering!* Oh my God! *Trillions* of them! *Calling* to me! With their *pain!* There's so much *pain!*"

"Well, too late to back out now!" Clopt laughed. "Uh, Sire."

"Jonathan James!" Amav leapt to her feet but Jack held her back. "He's having a bad time! Jack, what do we *do?*"

"I don't know! Amav, I really don't know!"

"All because I wrote a stupid book?" JJC screamed. "*All because I wrote a stupid book?*"

"*You* didn't write it, *I* did!" John Root said, waving his hairy, bony Sam Hergs wrists. "I know every word! And all the hidden code!"

"I can feel everyone's *pain!* Dammit, John Root, I can even feel the pain beneath your *programming!*"

"You can? Under my *programming?*"

"I can feel *everyone's* pain! My brother Clopt's! K'ufunb's! Even Trotter's!"

"Yap!" Trotter cried. "Yap!"

*I am one with pack leader! Love pack leader!*

"Even *Jack Commer's!* Even if he's not converted! I feel you *all the way through,* Dad!"

"Oh my God!" Jack gasped.

"I can't get a thing out of Mother, because she's hiding behind some Greeney Gooney *programming!* They're both *faking* the Grid with *programming!* God, I hate *programming!*"

*Whoops!* Greeney beamed at Amav. *Stay the course, dear, matters are coming to a cusp.*

"We couldn't leave all these Centaurians so anxious and *alone!* You have no idea of the *suffering* of this Empire! After we lost our emperor, everyone was so *apart!* I wrote my book to *relieve* the suffering!"

"Or John Root, word-processor robot and raconteur, did!" John Root laughed.

"But it didn't do a damn thing! There's still too much *pain!*" JJC threw himself to his feet. "Clopt! I need *knives!* Thousands of *knives!* Cut me up and put my guts in a box! That's the only way I can handle the Grid!"

"No! *That* I forbid!" Jack said, moving to JJC as Amav joined him.

Clopt blocked them both. "The emperor has expressed a Divine Wish, and I will assist him in carrying it out. He is in fact emulating the Crab Emperor. He too requested that his body be cut up and placed in a box. That was the only way he could handle the voltage of the Grid."

"Dammit, JJC, just *abdicate,* then!" Phil shouted. "You can't do this to yourself!"

"No, my *Garthah-/yuu* has commanded me to do his will. And I just happen to have a Zarj Gutter right here suitable for the occasion." Clopt pulled a twenty-inch-long, three-inch-thick blade from a scabbard on his belt.

Phil leapt between Clopt and JJC. "*No,* dammit! Jack, I never told you this, but Jonathan James and Clopt *bonded* somehow when JJC was five! They're Zarj brothers now! They *have* to support each other! Clopt would carry this out even if JJC weren't the emperor!"

"*What?*" Jack said. "Jonathan James *united* with Clopt?"

"Oh my God, my son's a *monster!*" Amav said.

Clopt held the quivering blade high. Phil backed away. "All along, Jonathan James has been trained to be a Zarj *killer!* I just thought he'd found what he needed to do with *literature!* Hedrona and I wanted to believe that!"

"*Cut me to pieces!*" JJC screamed. "God, I never thought the Grid would be so *cruel!*"

"Praised be the emperor! And all his body parts!" K'ufunb cried.

"*Ooof!*" Clopt grunted as a whirl of navy-blue and white came away with the Gutter. "Commer! You *golld-karpathugiss!* You dare take my weapon? *Snurggit* you to *snafliss!*"

Jack held the Gutter before him. "All right, everyone calm down. We can all see JJC's suffering some sort of breakdown. Greeney, if you have any conception of honor left, you'll help him abdicate or whatever he needs to do. Amav and I will take him back to Sol and get some help for him. Not this stupid Grid crap everyone's talking here."

"Oh my, Admiral Commer," Clopt said calmly, encircling JJC with three arms as his fourth positioned his heat blaster at JJC's temple. "Don't you think an easier alternative would be for me to dispatch JJC here with a simple *vaporization?*"

# CHAPTER THIRTY-TWO
## John Root Rewrites the Program

"Dammit, what *is* this?" JJC cried. "Damn you, Clopt! I can't *breathe!* What's gotten into you? I need to be cut up and put in a *box,* so I can serve--uhhh!--the Alpha Centaurian *people!* I don't need to be put out of my misery like--like some common *scaddiz-klun!*"

"Hmm," Clopt said. "You flaked a lot faster than I thought you would, brother. I think we'll just have to move the succession up a bit. We haven't had a Zarj emperor in hundreds of years. Why I don't know, because everyone knows that only a Zarj can handle the pressures of the emperorship!"

JJC's eyes widened. "You? My brother? Are doing this? But I *am* a Zarj!"

"Apparently not a good enough one," Clopt said, twisting the blaster barrel hard into JJC's temple. "Your human weakness is disgusting. You can't handle the voltage, just like our disgusting Scihk Crab Emperor. How we all secretly despised him!"

"No! Not my son!" Amav screamed. She felt Gooney radiating, this time to everyone in the room:

*By way of background to this rather sordid murder in progress, I have to remind all present that it was Clopt who developed the Grid software code and then had John Root write up JJC's novel idea and add the code to it. The original code would have made Clopt emperor on the spot, no half-hour Martian Interregnum being necessary.*

"*Cuckj* and *clus* your damn telepathy," Clopt said calmly. "I now give JJC the opportunity as emperor to declare that his death is divinely fated and that the succession to me as his *Garthah-/yuu* shall be smooth."

"Why--why should I?" JJC gasped.

"You can't do this!" Amav cried, noting Clopt's obvious reluctance to execute his own Zarj brother. She saw that Clopt was concerned with his honor. He needed Jonathan James to say this was all great somehow.

And Greeney went on broadcasting:

*But unfortunately for dear Captain Clopt, I saw what he was up to six months ago. When I praised the marvelous code he'd come up with, and then told him what we could do with JJC as emperor, he had no choice but to go along. Especially when I convinced both of them that a Martian was needed to undo the damage Dar had caused back in '53.*

"Get out of my head, Martian!" Clopt snarled. "JJC, do you accept my terms for your death? Yes or no?"

*The code was too far advanced, the Grid was too far along, for me to stop it, even with Amplified Thought. JJC's book was already a bestseller throughout the former Empire. I just thought to divert the Grid to something more manageable, i.e., myself!*

"Damn you! What would we want a Martian emperor for?" Clopt shouted.

"Well, it couldn't have lasted," Greeney said. "Even Dar didn't realize that he couldn't have held onto an alien emperorship for more than an hour. It's exhausting for our nervous systems as well. I knew I had to pass it to JJC and try to figure out a sane way to dismantle it from *there*."

Jack sidled towards Clopt with the Gutter, but Amav knew there was no way he could rescue JJC, whose soft brown eyes were staring shellshocked into the limitless sufferings of the battered Alpha Centaurian Empire.

"All right, then, damn you!" Clopt screeched, squeezing the trigger.

Something brown and white flew sideways and fastened to his wrist.

The room filled with blaster light. "*Shif!*" Clopt screamed as jaws clamped down and tore his claw off his forearm. "*Claz* it to *slif-cuck!* You damned *dog thing!*"

"You *bastard!*" JJC shouted, hair on fire, as Clopt tightened two other claws around JJC's throat. "Clopt, you *traitor!*"

"Yark! Yark yark yark!" cried Trotter, seeming to hover as his merciless fangs tore flesh up and down Clopt's torso. Amav stared as one arm came completely off at the shoulder. The seven-foot-tall, five-hundred-pound Clopt released JJC and stumbled backward onto a couch, soaking it with streaming blue-purple blood.

"Yark! Yark yark yark!" Trotter screamed as he went for Clopt's throat.

*Betrayal of the pack! Zarj brother dishonors us all! Outcast now! Fit for death eat!*

"A--a *Beagle*--can do *that?*" Amav gasped.

*I programmed Trotter in as a failsafe when I found out about Clopt. A third Zarj brother who'd protect JJC. I engineered some massive Amplified Thought resources for him if he felt them necessary. Come on, now Trotter, enough's enough.*

*Leave enemy traitor monster alive? Don't think so!*

Greeney gently picked Trotter off Clopt's shuddering body. "Not now, little one."

*Dammit! Okay, but I will stand guard! No danger permitted to emperor!*

"Damn …" Clopt moaned. "*Kashpisz … slotterblaggen …*"

"It's more the emperor's *mind* I'm worried about," Greeney said. "I thought his ego looked big enough for the job, but apparently not!"

"No, I can't *stand* it!" JJC groaned, rocking on his knees behind a couch as K'ufunb poured a vase of water over his flaming head, leaving the room stinking of burned hair.

"Come on, Greeney, this isn't funny!" Amav said, yet finding herself unwilling to get near her son.

"Greeney, can you do something about Clopt?" Phil finally said, bending over the writhing Zarj.

Greeney walked over and pointed. "Hmm. Okay. I've healed these lesions on his throat. Now I've sealed off the lower right forearm stump, sealed off the top right shoulder stump. The upper left arm is shredded to hell as you can see, with major bones broken. I've canceled out his pain receptors there and stopped the bleeding. That leaves him one usable arm. I could revive the others, but why take a chance?" To support his case Greeney materialized three metal straps around the couch to hold Clopt down. "We'll figure some suitable judicial process later."

"Dammit, Greeney, we have to help my son first!" Jack said, pointing to Jonathan James curled in a catatonic ball under K'ufunb's four soothing hands.

"And then we have to deactivate this damn Grid somehow," Phil added.

"Doesn't anyone care about *me?*" John Root cried. "Trapped in this pathetic Sam Hergs body? Nobody's asked *me* about anything!"

"Hell, who cares?" Jack snapped.

"When I wrote the novel? When I bonded so well with JJC and know his every foible? And transferred all that to the book? With the code and everything? I can see as well as anyone that JJC's circuits can't handle the emperorship! The question is, who can? Trotter here, the third Zarj brother?"

"Rark rark rark!" *No! Absolutely not!*

"No, I don't think the ACs would accept a Beagle as their emperor!" John Root said. "But who *could* handle it? I say, there's only one person who can do it now! The concept we all love and worship so dearly!"

"No!" Amav said. "Are you crazy? I won't do it!"

"I wasn't thinking of you, Goddess Amav! I was thinking of the immortal Jack Commer, Supreme Commander! *He'll* be our next emperor, whether he wants it or not!"

"Idiot!" Jack cried. "There's no way I'd do that!"

"You *have* to accept! Because I'm rewriting JJC's novel on the spot! Updating *all* the characters! And revising all the secret code to make *the one person who can handle the Grid* the Emperor of Alpha Centauri! I *worship* you, Jack Commer!"

"Idiot! A revision doesn't change a thing!" Greeney shouted. "I've engraved the original on *hundreds* of moons and planets! That's an ancient Centaurian ritual! Only *they* can change the lawful succession!"

"Forget it, Mr. Gooney! I picked up enough of your canned AT concepts to *redo* those moons! *And* the desert planets! The Grid is spreading my revisions now! *All* electronic copies of my book, *all* physical copies, *all* those engraved moons and planets, are being rewritten *now!* I hereby declare the emperorship transferred to *the one person who can handle it!* There, *done!*"

"Forget it!" Jack shouted. "I don't feel a damn thing!"

"And to keep anyone from ever rewriting it *back,* I hereby *short-circuit* myself forever! There, Jack! Is that good enough for you? Am I loyal enough to you? To the glorious concept of *Jack Commer?* To *off* myself in your cause? So goodbye forever, Jack!"

"Dammit, John, *don't!*" Jack cried. "Not--not *again!*"

Amav stared at John Root's head sizzling atop Sam Hergs' jerking body. The room filled with the smell of burned wiring. A cloud of gas spewed from the rear of John Root's head. The eyes went dead and the robot tumbled face down on the carpet.

"Oh my God ..." JJC moaned. "It's *gone.* Thank God it's *over.*"

"Well, I'm still not feeling anything," Jack said.

There was a long silence in the room.

"Well, *I'm* feeling it," Phil finally said. "I've got the whole damn thing now."

## CHAPTER THIRTY-THREE
### The Only One Who Can Handle the Full Plug

"*Break out of orbit!*" Clopt ordered. "We have our new emperor! He has our full allegiance! We shall spread him to the entire Galaxy!"

Phil turned to the crippled Clopt who'd just snapped all three metal bands with his stomach and now stood with his one good arm raised in what Phil recognized as a Zarj Bond Salute to the True Emperor.

"Castle computer," Clopt spoke crisply. "Prepare maximum thrust dependent on condition of inertial dampers. We want to stand on our feet in celebration of our new emperor!"

"INERTIAL DAMPERS HAVE BEEN REPAIRED, CAPTAIN," the translation spheres crackled. "ALL ENGINEERING SYSTEMS ARE GO FOR MAXIMUM THRUST."

"We have *engineering systems?*" JJC moaned as a vast whine built beneath their feet.

"Of course!" Clopt shot back. "This is a damn *spaceship!* Not just your stupid Castle! You think I wouldn't have computerized *everything?*"

"Stop him! Stop this!" Jack cried, pointing to Gooney. "We are *not* leaving orbit!"

"I--I'm *sorry, Jack!*" Gooney said, staggering back to a couch. "I'm trying to concentrate, but all this emperor stuff *does* take a lot out of you."

"Dammit, Sperry, Gooney's *offline* or something!" Jack spat.

"He's just exhausted," Phil said, gulping for air. "He's right. You can barely stand all these *people* in your head!"

"What? You really have it now?" Jack said as the rocket engines opened up in a deep reverberating hum that shook throughout the Castle.

And then shut down.

"LASER STRIKE ON MAIN ENGINE ELECTRONICS!" the spheres blared.

188

"*Ruddzza-scuck!*" Clopt snarled. "Who the *snuz* is firing at us? At the True Emperor?"

"Phil," Jack warned, pointing to Clopt, "does he acknowledge *you?*"

"Of course!" Clopt said. "I'm fully One with Phil now! Sensors! Determine origin of that shot!"

"SENSORS ARE OFFLINE, CAPTAIN."

"Dammit! Listen, everyone! I know I would've made a bad emperor! I never wanted it! I just wanted the Grid back, and I thought I was the only one who could run it! But I was wrong! Everyone! See the truth through the Grid for yourself! That I now worship Phil Sperry, the One True Emperor we have sought! *The only one who can handle the full plug of the Grid!*"

*I can?* Phil wondered. Endless thundering waterfalls poured through him from thousands of miles up, from below, from every direction. He stood frozen. What were all these *voices?* The Centaurians were *here*. What were they saying?

"It's *true,*" Greeney Gooney said in wonder. "Phil really *is* handling it! Unbelievable!"

*Very confused! Which is the real pack?*

"*This* is the real pack, Trotter!" Clopt yelled. "My wonderful dog Zarj brother! Don't worry about my arms! They'll grow back!"

"Yap yap yap!"

Phil considered the Beagle at his feet. JJC prostrated there as well, his mind nearly burned out. But he'd regenerate over time, Phil saw.

"Emperor!" Clopt called. "I remind you that your flagship's engines have been disabled! We are still in orbit around the despised planet! Suggest you convert the infidel Gooney immediately and force him to repair our Drive!"

Greeney waved this off. "Sorry--can't *concentrate* right now."

"There's no need," Phil grunted, forcing himself to stay on his feet amid the tumultuous flooding of every possible reservoir deep in his brain with voices, and souls, and desires, and problems, and delusions, and conflict and pain. It was impossible there should be so much pain. Phil knew that if he sank on a couch as JJC and Greeney had done, he'd break in despair. He too would cry to be cut into a hundred chunks of gore and shoved into a glass box full of electromagnetic flux.

"Greeney's probably shot for a while," Phil said. "And I won't convert anyone. We'll just stay in orbit."

"Sire!" Clopt protested. "We don't know who's firing at us!"

"Oh, we do," Phil said, pointing to a dazzling play of sparks across the twenty-foot-long picture window of JJC's living room. "Those are coming from Andertwin. From a PlanetBlaster on the night side, as a matter of fact. At the finest resolution, extreme low power, if anyone's interested."

Shards of plastiglass billowed off the viewport in gushing yellow fog. Particles twirled in the outside vacuum, catching the sun rising over the eastern limb of the planet. Phil stared at the loveliness. More minds pumped into his own, trillions of Alpha Centaurians, each finding a place deep within him as they all pitched their tents and threw down their sleeping bags or their rags or the AC equivalent of torn plastic grocery bags filled with old socks and underwear. They brought their heat blasters and their pulsar tubes and their meson bombs and their knives and swords, they brought laughter and shrieks of terror and fantasies and desire upon desire upon desire. And somehow it was all *beautiful,* as beautiful as these laser strikes on the window. The silver-white blasts, the floating shards in the sun, seemed to sum up everything Phil had ever lived for, every beauty he'd ever wanted.

The Others of the Grid followed Phil's gaze. All Alpha Centauri knew this moment. "If that plastiglass is breached …" Jack muttered. "Dammit, Clopt, are there EnviroFields on this thing?"

"Enviro-whats?" Clopt says. "Oh, those force field things that hold in air. Huh. No, I didn't think we'd need 'em."

Spangles danced on the glass. "Greeney, you *will* save our air if the window breaches, won't you?"

Greeney shrugged. "Maybe … sorry so out of it … let's see

how it goes."

Phil had never seen Greeney Gooney at a loss. Had the Grid burned him out? Everyone stared at the continuing strikes on the viewport. Would it hold? All Alpha Centauri wondered what sort of Unconverted sadist on the planet below would blow the air their new emperor so badly needed to survive. Phil pointed to the letters taking shape on the window. "Let's read the message."

OKAY, DUDES, THIS IS SENATOR LEE BORMAN OF SOL DEMANDING YOUR UNCONDITIONAL SURRENDER. AM WRITING THIS WITH DORSAL PLANETBLASTER CONFIGURED TO PENCIL POINT DIAMETER AND SET TO POWER .00000005. DON'T MAKE ME GO TO 10,000.

Greeney stared. "Borman? That can't be! My virus shut *down* the *Typhoon* network!"

"Lee's grounded," Phil said. "I can feel the blaster firing from the *Typhoon* on the ground. He can't move, so he had to wait for us to come up over the horizon again."

"Martian! Repair our Drive! Now!" Clopt yelled.

"Belay that," Phil says. "Lee's still writing. I want to see what he has to say. Keep in mind he's writing this message *mirror-backward,* on an object moving over 17,000 miles an hour, at low enough power to just etch into the glass."

CASE YOU'RE WONDERING HOW THIS POSSIBLE. USSF OVERSIGHT COMMITTEE OF WHICH I AM CHAIRMAN HAS RECOMMENDED INDEPENDENT BACKUP NETWORKS FOR YEARS. APRIL 2074 I AUTHORIZED EXPERIMENTS INTO USE OF INDEPENDENTLY NETWORKED PLANETBLASTERS WHICH COULD EMPLOY GRAVITATIONAL FIELDS OF NEARBY STARS, PLANETS, OR ASTEROIDS AS THEIR POWER SOURCE.

Greeney managed a laugh. "By Dar, this is worthy of an AT adept! Who'd have thought Borman had it in him? I may have to teach him some real AT someday. When I clear my mind, that is. Phil, how can you *stand* this?"

"I--I really don't know. Somehow it's all *beautiful.* If I concentrate on the *beauty,* everything's all right somehow."

"Oh, God!" Jack cried. "Borman sneaked *secret weapons* onto the *Typhoon?*"

MAY I HAVE PLEASURE OF REPLY BEFORE YOU DIP BELOW HORIZON?

Phil had no doubt Borman had just thumbed the PlanetBlaster up to 2,000, more than enough to fry an Imperial Battle Cruiser.

"Forget it! We'll never surrender!" Clopt screamed, staring into Phil's eyes. "Sire! You *are* considering surrendering! Why don't you just order this Gooney character to *save* us? It would be ignoble to fail now!"

"Clopt," Phil said calmly. "I can't connect with Borman through the Grid, obviously. And I see he's managed to completely fry our ship-to-ground communications."

"Then we must fight! Ram this Castle down his throat if need be! The honor of the Empire demands it!"

"We can't maneuver until Greeney gets back *online.*"

"Are you saying the Empire is *doomed?*"

Phil laughed. "Are you saying the Empire is doomed *Sire!*"

"Sire! Of course I worship you, emperor! But, Sire! This Empire is *new!* We have it back at last! All Alpha Centauri rejoices! We must preserve our new Empire!"

"Don't worry," Phil said, feeling his way into the lovely cool night of Andertwin below, the smell of the fields, the wind over the plants and the dirt. "That's the very message I'm giving to our Jujl gardener Ji'ourff. He's been standing by in the Grid, waiting to take my message to Hedrona."

# CHAPTER THIRTY-FOUR
## Marry the Scrubwoman? Or Engineer a Warp Transfer Accident to the Alternate Universe?

The first Gladiator Sleds rose from the side of the mountain into the harsh blue sky and at first they were all manned by Phil's friends. Twenty or thirty sleds floated next to him with warriors behind their big guns, but at his slightest thought they shifted until Phil finally got them in a line of four sleds abreast and moving in a wide left curve away from the mountain, topping its heights and aiming for the thin cirrus spread all over the sky.

Hedrona flew beside him in her glossy black skintight suit, her long brown hair flying, a small EnviroField glowing soft blue around her face as the sleds rose higher.

Hundreds more sleds rose from the big green squares below, from the lakes and the hills. They joined the procession, widening it to fifty across. Thousands more sleds rose, or flew in from the horizon, or swooped from above, until Phil looked back to see a wave of sleds a thousand across and ten thousand deep sweeping higher and higher until they were out of the atmosphere.

"Isn't it beautiful?" Hedrona cried at the panorama of the blue-white planet below. "And that we can all fly together, to *there!*" She pointed to the billions of stars arrayed around them. "All of us! Forever!"

Phil loved the feel of the sled, the engine pounding through the steel at his feet, the pleasant magnetic pull of his boots in the stirrups, the thick gun handles in his gloved fingers. Everyone felt this same delight.

"Why do we have guns?" he laughed. "Why do we all have *guns?*"

"Well, we have to have something to hold onto!" Hedrona laughed back.

She was so beautiful. So desirable. Phil looked back at billions of sleds coming up from the clouds of their planet to join the procession. Soon they would meet trillions more from all corners of this marvelous universe. They were all beautiful. All these souls.

Phil was shocked that Hedrona, riding to his right, wasn't part of the Grid. She was independent. No one commanded her. Yet no one minded this.

Even more astonishing, Phil himself wasn't part of the Grid. He was just Head of it. The emperor had never really been part of the Grid. He'd always known the loneliness, and the Disconnect. It was simply his job to accept the plug and regulate everything. But the ecstasy of the Grid was foreign to him.

"Wow ..." Phil muttered, gazing transfixed at the beauty of his mate as the trillions joined. Hedrona smiled back. She'd known all this for eons.

*

Gooney shook him. "Phil! We thought you were dead! You weren't breathing!"

"I ... I don't know, Greeney. Think I'm okay."

"Listen, Phil, if you can't handle this, *abdicate!* We'll find some other way to dismantle this thing!"

"You sound ... a lot better, man."

"I'm recovering some, I think. But look, Phil, you need to get out! Now!"

"Sire, don't listen to this Nonconverted traitor!" Clopt said.

"It's--it's okay," Phil murmured, lapsing back into the *vision.* Trillions of *them,* of *us,* plugged into the *all.* To his dismay Phil saw that his slightest thought was magnified by countless orders of magnitude. Some tribal schism had erupted on Zorax, the Zarj homeworld, in the wake of the endlessly increasing pressure of New Grid flooding the system. The Nonconverted in this room felt the pressure as insanity, but Phil felt it as trillions of sleds flowing together, proud gunners at each, ready to blast away ... at what? What were those guns *for?* Phil diverted a billion gunners to Zarj to quell the schism. No shots were fired, but the show of force brought a hundred billion Zarj to their knees in new comity with each other and the Grid.

Then there was the Culstati scheme to blow up twenty-one

planets in a tribute to the emperorship of Phil Sperry. They were mining these planets even now: seven were to be blown for Greeney Gooney, seven for JJC, the temporary rulers, and the last seven for Phil. Oh, those mystical Culstati priests with their love of the number seven. Phil countermanded their order. Whoops, a little too strong: 777 Culstati killed themselves instantly, "calling home" to the emperor in a flash of somber violet spirit fire. Phil soothed the disturbance, provided for widows and children, assured Culstati Prime of his undying respect, then tried to quiet his mind lest he start shoving entire solar systems into chaos.

"Phil, wake *up!* You can't keep doing this!" Greeney shouted. "And I don't have the strength to take it back!"

"He *can* keep doing it! He must!" Clopt said. "He's the one True Emperor!"

Phil opened his eyes. "Jack, did Borman get the message to stand down?"

"Yeah, he just carved 'message received' on the plastiglass," Jack said.

"Good." Phil settled back, staring at the black ceiling and feeling the trillions of sleds in armed procession behind him. One signaled him.

*Hello, love!* Hedrona beamed. *Ji'ourff got your message! Listen, I will fly the sleds with you any day! The* Seven of Cups *stands ready! I just now figured out what you're going to do and it's great! Go for it! All my love!*

Phil smiled. "Say, look, Greeney, I hate to say this about your own emperor, Monsieur Dar, but he really screwed up when he liberated AC back in '53, you know."

"Well, there *were* complications," Greeney admitted. "We had no idea the ACs were that deep into addiction to the Grid."

"And he just expected Martian counseling to take care of the problem. Well, all the talk in the world couldn't dig deep enough into the Centaurian anxiety about losing the Grid."

"Well, maybe. But we did our best. Look, I've been thinking about even better counseling. I've wondered if we could use some simple Amplified Thought techniques in conjunction with our current therapeutic programs."

"Naw, that'll never work. Look, Greeney, you know where I am right now. You felt all this a few minutes ago. And I think you know what has to happen."

Greeney's eyes widened. "No! We *can't* keep the Grid intact!"

"It's their *way,* Greeney. I think Dar must have known that. Must have considered this option, too."

"No!"

"But I won't make the same mistake Dar did. He freed everyone in AC without really *freeing* them. I'm really going to *free* them."

*

"*Kartuthuck, no!*" Clopt screamed, his one good arm seizing his forehead. "Damn you, Sperry, what have you *done?*"

"Damn you, Sperry, what have you done *Sire?*" Phil laughed.

"Sire, damn you then! But you will also address *me* as Sire!"

"And me!" K'ufunb yelled. "Sire, what have you done to my little *mind?*"

"*Wow!*" Greeney muttered. "I can't believe you really pulled that off!"

"Pulled *what* off?" Jack demanded.

"Can it! Don't say a word!" Clopt said. "It's too blasphemous! We are all *dishonored!*"

"Phil just commanded every single AC citizen, including all future generations, to *become* the emperor," Greeney explained. "*Unbelievable!*"

"Each one of them now has all the emperor's power, and now they'll know the Grid from *his* standpoint," Phil said. "Wow, that's a load off *my* mind!"

"We really have to share *everything?* The *whole load?* With *everyone?*" Clopt said. He looked at the floor. "Yes! We do! Damn it all, Sperry!"

"But you're still *connected,* Clopt Sire. We all are. We have the Grid. It's just not what you all thought it was."

"No, dammit, Sperry, it's not! And--oh, *flucgk, no!*"

Phil followed his gaze to K'ufunb. "What?"

"Dammit, Sperry, don't you know that the first woman the emperor sees after crowning he must *marry?*" he cried, shaking his remaining claw. "And you have married me to a *Fkuuh scrubwoman!* More dishonor! *Ruddzza-scuck!*"

"Sire, you may rest assured that as empress I will ignore that stupid edict and rebuff every advance you care to make!" K'ufunb shot back.

"You? A scrubwoman? A Fkuuh? You dare resist me?"

"Yes! You have always disgusted me! Sire!"

Clopt turned to Phil. "She can't say that! Can she? A Fkuuh says that to a Zarj? My future wife? And does not commit suicide on the spot?"

Phil laughed. "She's *not* your future wife!"

"There's only one level of the hierarchy now!" K'ufunb laughed. "And that's the *top!* We'll all make, and *enforce,* our own rules now!"

"God, Phil, what have you *done?*" Jack cried. "If everyone in Alpha Centauri is like this, dammit, they'll overwhelm Sol in weeks! Days maybe!"

"No, it's brilliant!" Greeney laughed. "I see it now! A race of emperors doesn't *need* to do that sort of thing!"

"Listen, Clopt," Phil said, "it's going to take some time, but--hey, where'd he go?"

From down the hall they heard clunking. "I refuse! I will *not* marry that scrubwoman!" A heavy metal hatch banged shut.

"What?" Jack said, moving down the hall.

Phil held him back as fresh whirring opened up below them. "Look, I have no idea if there's a proper airlock here. Let's move back."

More clanging. A heavy scraping. Thruster noises. Out the viewport, Phil watched one of the cubes of the Castle maneuvering against the morning terminator line of Andertwin.

"It's our *lifeboat,*" JJC muttered. "I think Clopt needs some time by himself or something."

"Goodbye, fools!" came a transmission over the translation speakers. "I don't *want* to be an emperor! I want to serve the *True* Emperor!"

"Crap!" Phil said. "JJC, does that cube have Warp Transfer?"

"Yes, but--"

The cube disappeared. Seconds later, and perhaps a million miles away, came the sharp blue explosion symptomatic of a failed Warp Transfer insertion.

Trotter was barking out of control.

"*God!*" JJC moaned. "*Our Zarj brother! He's gone!*"

"So he did go to *Garr/thahg* after all," Phil said. "At least, I *hope* he made it."

"What ... are your orders, emperor?" JJC quavered.

"I don't know. What are *your* orders, emperor?" Phil said.

"I ... I don't know, I guess."

"Well, that's as good a start as any. Greeney, are you feeling more yourself now?"

"Yes, I am, friend," Greeney said. "I can do some simple AT now and land us if you like."

"Sounds good. Rest up and we'll make sure everyone's ready."

"Phil, are you still feeling this Grid thing?" Jack said.

"Yeah, sure am."

"And you're not giving it up?"

Phil shrugged. "The emperor can duck in and out of it anytime he chooses. So that applies to *everyone* now. It's not a fascist empire anymore. We all need a little privacy now and then, after all. Get this too, Jack: *anyone* can join without a problem. Just like SolNet. Log on, log off anytime you want. You and Amav are welcome anytime."

"Well, thanks, but what about Jonathan James?" Jack whispered as Amav came up beside him in the blue USSF coat topping her nightgown. "Is he going to be all right?"

JJC sat stunned with Trotter on the couch still smeared with blue and purple gore. "He'll be okay after a while," Phil said. "No physical damage. I think he should stay in AC awhile and recuperate. The Grid will help him, I think. Then he can decide where he wants to go."

"I can see that, maybe. Look, what about you? You're still the emperor of Alpha Centauri?"

"*An* emperor of Alpha Centauri." Phil turned to Greeney. "Hey, Greeney, can you bring up Hedrona? I need to talk to my empress."

"She's already here," Greeney said, motioning her into Phil's arms.

## About the Author

Michael D. Smith was raised in the Northeast and the Chicago area, then moved to Texas to attend Rice University, where he began developing as a writer and visual artist. His Jack Commer, Supreme Commander science fiction series is published by Sortmind Press. In addition, Sortmind Press has published Smith's literary novels *Sortmind, The Soul Institute, CommWealth, Akard Drearstone,* and *Jump Grenade.* All titles are available from Amazon.

Smith's web site, https://sortmind.com, contains further examples of his novels and visual art, and he muses about writing and art processes at https://blog.sortmind.com/.

Amazon author page
https://www.amazon.com/author/smithmi/

## The Jack Commer, Supreme Commander Series

The Martian Marauders
Jack Commer, Supreme Commander
Nonprofit Chronowar
Collapse and Delusion
The Wounded Frontier
The SolGrid Rebellion
Balloon Ship Armageddon

www.ingramcontent.com/pod-product-compliance
Lightning Source LLC
Chambersburg PA
CBHW060931180626
46817CB00004B/1495